Revelation

The Wasteland Chronicles, Volume 4

Kyle West

Published by Kyle West, 2013.

This is a work of fiction. Similarities to real people, places, or events are entirely coincidental.

REVELATION

First edition. October 8, 2013.

Copyright © 2013 Kyle West.

Written by Kyle West.

10 9 8 7 6 5 4 3 2 1

Also by Kyle West

The Wasteland Chronicles
Apocalypse
Origins
Evolution
Revelation
Darkness

Watch for more at kylewestwriter.wordpress.com.

Prologue

It's been three months since the fall of Bunker 108. In that time, I've survived raiders, gangs, empires, cold, hunger, and monsters. By all rights, I should be dead. We all should be. It seems impossible that we aren't. Impossible that we are still fighting this.

I just wonder how much longer we can last.

The odds are stacked against us. At every turn, the xenovirus gets more deadly. The number of Blights in the Wasteland has tripled. The monsters it creates are more dangerous. Crawlers roam the dark, cold nights in packs, killing any they find. Anyone without a wall, without a home, is as good as dead.

The Great Blight has expanded one hundred miles further west over the past two months alone – a rate which will see the entire Wasteland covered by this time next year.

And, somehow, we are expected to stop all this. The four of us are expected to be the world's saviors. We are all too young for this job. I'm sixteen. Makara is nineteen, Samuel twenty-three, and Anna is seventeen. That's too much weight to rest on our shoulders – hell, too much weight for *anyone's* shoulders. Maybe, we aren't kids anymore. Responsibility is enough to make an adult of anyone.

As leader of the New Angels, Makara is now in charge of the group. Samuel still leads the mission against the Great Blight, but as far as building the group, Makara calls the shots. First on her agenda is finding the Exiles, Marcus's gang, somewhere in the Boundless. After we find them, they can lead us to the Raiders. Or at least, that's what we hope.

With the fall of Raider Bluff to the xenoswarm, we could only hope that'd been Char's thought process. Overrun by crawlers and Howlers and worse besides, we could only *hope* he had laid down his pride to seek the help of the brother he'd exiled over a decade before.

This is no longer a time for enmity and blood. The power of the Great Blight grows by the day, and the Great Dragon of Raider Bluff has yet to make his next move.

Yes – two months after we had left it, the Wasteland is a far more dangerous place. And the Wasteland is only the beginning. If we do not find some way to stop the Great Blight, the entire world will be swallowed by it.

With Raider Bluff gone, it makes sense for Vegas to be next on the Great Blight's list. That city is the closest to the Great Blight, and that's where all our roads lead – whether we are Angel, Exile, or Raider. With the alliance between Augustus of the Empire and Carin Black of Los Angeles, it's up to us to grab whoever is left and take the fight to Los Angeles – taking out Carin Black before Augustus can arrive with his legions – before the worst of winter is upon us.

But before we can do that, we have to find the Exiles. We have to find the Raiders.

It is our newest challenge. It is hard to tell whether this will be easier, or harder, than what we did in the Empire. Now back in the cold, bare reality of the Wasteland, I have a feeling it will be harder. Our mission is getting a bunch of people who don't like each other to work together. We have to convince them to leave the safety of their walls, strike out across the Wasteland in the dead of winter, and take out Black and the Reapers before Augustus arrives.

We have about two months to do it. Augustus's army is far – but it could be here in as soon as two months. Winter might help us, but we are planning for the worst. Our success as a group depends on being prepared for the worst. Augustus said he was going to be here in two months. We will take him at his word.

Even if such preparation seems impossible, we have to try. The entire world, literally, depends on it.

I would say it is a lot of pressure, but we are used to that by now. We are a well-honed team. We each know our strengths and weaknesses. We have two spaceships at our disposal, meaning we can jump between points quickly.

Even though we have new capabilities, so does the xenoswarm. The dragons are a game-changer that none of us could have predicted, and I'm sure they're not the last thing the Great Blight will throw at us.

First, we have to deal with the human opposition. Until everyone is standing together and on the same page, we can't make our attack on the Great Blight. We can't even protect ourselves from Augustus and Carin Black. If we do not unite, and unite soon, everything will fall.

And that's exactly what the Voice in Ragnarok Crater wants.

Chapter 1

Makara was still flying. It was night, and *Odin* hummed all round us, sailing through the air at three hundred miles an hour. She stared ahead as if her willpower alone could pierce the veil of darkness cloaking the Boundless below. Everyone else was sleeping. Anna dozed in the copilot's chair, her head tilted to the side. Makara did nothing to wake her, taking the burden of both piloting and copiloting upon herself. It was very Makara-like.

Behind his sister, Samuel also slept. I was fighting my own battle with weariness, a battle I was sure to lose. It was two in the morning, and Makara had yet to cease her search for Marcus and the Exiles. This had been the story of the last three days, and still her reddened eyes scanned the desert floor with *Odin's* two floodlights, revealing nothing but dune, hill, mesa, and the sudden pink of a patch of xenofungus. Periodically, Makara glanced at the LCD, which displayed topography, speed, and *Odin's* location. We were somewhere in central Arizona.

I felt it was all useless. This time-consuming search was eating away at us all, and we could only take so much before it was time to examine other options. Samuel had told Anna and me as much in private earlier today. He dared not tell Makara; not yet. And with each day that passed with no results, no clues, she became edgier.

She still believed the Wanderer had wanted her to search here, when all seemed lost. And certainly, everything *did* seem lost. It was the four of us, and Ashton, expecting to stop an entire army that would soon be thundering its way north. And not only *that* army, but the army of xenolife readying itself to strike from the east. Everything depended on swelling our ranks, and all of us could feel the clock ticking.

With a curse, Makara leaned back in her chair. She sighed, shutting her eyes. It was the first time she had broken her concentration for hours. *Odin* flew on in a straight line, due east, about a thousand feet above the surface.

I closed my own eyes. My conscious mind faded under the weight of drowsiness. Makara's voice snapped me to attention.

"Let's call it a night."

She slammed the controls, the sudden sound doing nothing to wake either Samuel or Anna. Out in the Wastes, both of them would have been up in a heartbeat at the disturbance. But *Odin* was a safe place, and there were allowances here that didn't exist on the surface. Makara returned to the controls, angling the ship toward the surface. Again, the change in trajectory did nothing to shake either Samuel or Anna from their slumber. How I was still awake, I didn't know. Even a week out of Nova Roma, I was exhausted from the entire ordeal. Makara's side, which had been injured in the *Coleseo*, was still tender, but healing. But our time in the Empire had taken it out of all of us.

I would have thought sitting all day in a ship would be relaxing, but it wasn't. We had to stay alert, for either the Exiles, the Raiders, or the ever-present threat of the xenodragons. None of those had ambushed us – at least, not yet – but that didn't mean they wouldn't at some point.

Makara guided *Odin* down, toward the top of a mesa that rose above the desert floor, its massive shape shadowy in the darkness. The dunes below were discernable around the mesa, but just barely. Now that we were back in the Wasteland, the atmospheric dust from Ragnarok had returned. I was already missing the feel of the sun on my skin. The sunburns I had received while in Nova Roma were still peeling.

Odin hovered, giving a tiny lift as it alighted atop the mesa. Powering off the ship, Makara unstrapped herself from her seat and immediately left the cockpit. Anna and Samuel slept on, oblivious to the fact that we had stopped. Samuel snored lightly, his head leaning back against the headrest. Anna's head was still cocked to the side, a dribble of drool dripping from the corner of her mouth.

I touched her shoulder. "Hey. We've stopped."

Her eyes fluttered open. She gave a nod, wiped her mouth, and unstrapped herself from the seat. She stood, and we left Samuel where he was, walking down the corridor toward the bunks in the back. I knew Anna would prefer sleeping in her own bunk, and would have been upset if I had left her in the copilot's seat like that. Samuel, however, could probably sleep on a pile of rocks and not notice the difference.

When we got to the crew cabins, we were alone. Makara had appropriated the captain's quarters off the galley to herself.

"Sleep tight," I said, leaning in for a kiss.

She kissed me – not too enthusiastically, I must admit. She turned for her bunk, and I watched her lie down. Before she even covered herself with her blanket, her breathing became even with sleep. I'd always envied people with the ability to do that – fall asleep as if there *weren't* a million things wrong with the world.

I sighed, turning for my own cabin, which I shared with Samuel. I lay down on my bunk, closing my eyes. The hum of the ship, on low power, lulled me to sleep, a sleep none too fitful.

***

The next day I awoke early, stepped out of bed, and got dressed. I ducked out the doorway, went through the galley, and headed to the kitchen. The air was cool in *Odin's* metallic hull, automatic lights flashing on as I passed under them. I found the coffee pot and filled it with water, placing coffee grounds inside. Now back in civilization, I had the means to nurse my caffeine addiction with Skyhome's own brew.

As the water heated and filtered through the grounds, I went to the fridge, grabbed some fresh grapefruit, and then opened the cabinet to get some granola, the latter sealed in a reusable, airtight bag. By the time I'd prepared my breakfast, the coffee was done. I'd made a whole pot, in case someone else wanted some later. The resources provided by Skyhome were almost as good as what I'd had back in Bunker 108.

I grabbed both my food and coffee, and walked to the table in the galley. I sat, the first steaming sip of coffee warming me up. The stuff was like an elixir. Though Makara and Anna liked to sleep until the last possible moment before we left (in fact, Makara usually just rolled out of bed and headed straight to the pilot seat), I liked to be up an hour earlier than everyone else to have some alone time. It was great to have the entire ship to myself, to be alone with my thoughts, my food, my coffee.

After downing the last of my coffee and finishing off my grapefruit and granola, I got up and headed for the blast door. I pressed the button. The door slid open, letting in a rush of frigid, dry wind. I stepped outside, ignoring the extreme cold. It was winter now, and it showed in every way imaginable. The darkness was near absolute, and though I could not see it, I knew the cliff's edge was just a few feet away from the edge of the boarding ramp. Nevertheless, I stood on the ramp, weathering the harsh wind as it buffeted against me. I peered into the sky, trying to discern where the moon was. On the western sky, there was a milky glow of cloud. Such was the effect of the meteor fallout – we all might as well have been in a cave deep in the heart of the Earth.

I took out my digital watch, and lighted it up. I went to the temperature tab. It was minus nineteen Celsius. Two below zero Fahrenheit.

"Yeah," I said. "Time to go back inside."

I entered *Odin*, the door shutting behind me. The ship's interior, once cool, now felt warm by comparison, tingling my skin. To my surprise, Samuel sat at the table, a cup of coffee in hand. His handgun was partially disassembled, its parts lying neatly at the table's center. He was brushing the action of the handgun. I noticed several other guns sitting on the table corner.

"Put yours in line, if you like," Samuel said.

After two months of heavy use, my Beretta was probably much in need of a cleaning. I set the gun down, removed the magazine, and checked the barrel to make sure it was empty.

"You can use an AR, right?" Samuel asked.

I nodded. "It's been a while since I've used one, but yeah. Chan, the CSO of Bunker 108, had everyone trained on a variety of things."

"Good. I'm thinking of having everyone diversify a bit. We're seeing a lot of action, and there are points where it would be useful to have a rifle. We have an entire armory on *Odin* that is hardly getting any use, except when we need to restock on ammo."

"If you give me some time to practice, I'm sure it'll come back quickly."

"You'll have to show me a few things too, then," Samuel said. "I've always wanted to fire one of those things."

"Will do."

Samuel moved on to Makara's handgun. His movements were deft, methodical. Within moments he had the essential parts disassembled and was already brushing the interior with the cleaning solvent.

"What's our next move?" I asked.

"We keep going, until we find the Exiles."

"I mean, if we *can't* find them. It's been three days, after all." I hesitated a moment. "You said it yourself, yesterday. If we can't find them..."

"We're all here because Makara believes the Wanderer told her to find the Exiles," he said. "And until we do, I don't think she's going to want to move on."

"I want to know what that guy's *exact* wording was. Maybe she's just interpreting it wrong."

"I've interpreted *nothing* wrong."

Makara glared at me from the doorway to the captain's quarters. I hadn't heard her come in.

"I know that's what you believe," I said. "But..."

"Alex..." Samuel said, low. "Careful."

Makara was still staring daggers at me. She walked up to the table and placed a hand on its edge. She looked at me, her green eyes blazing.

"We *will* find them. And what the Wanderer said...it's between me and him. Got it?"

"Yeah. Sure."

Makara walked off to the kitchen. I heard the sounds of her digging in the fridge, then filling a cup with coffee.

"What's up with her?"

"She's just stressed," Samuel said. "Don't take it personally."

From the kitchen came the sound of Makara cursing about something. Apparently, she had burned herself.

"You're up early," Samuel called.

"A lot to do," she called back. "Today's the big day. We're going to find them. I feel it."

"I hope so," I said, low enough so that Makara wouldn't hear.

Makara returned to the table with two slices of cantaloupe, toast, and coffee. She sat down, her eyes red, dark underlines set deeper than ever.

Makara dug into her cantaloupe, as if her mission were to get it down as quickly as possible rather than enjoy it. While she ate, Samuel finished cleaning the last handgun, which happened to be Makara's. Anna's saw so little use that it probably didn't even need a tune-up. After putting the brush and solvent away in the kit on the table, Samuel closed the kit, then slid the gun over to Makara.

While Makara finished her food, Anna walked in. Dreary-eyed, she looked at all of us before heading for the kitchen.

"Well," Makara said, standing up, "I'm going to fire up the engine. Figured we'd make a sweep a little closer to the Great Blight today."

"Not until we've exhausted every other option," Samuel said.

Makara frowned. "It's the biggest chunk of land we haven't surveyed yet. Trust me, if any of those *things* come flying at us, I can handle it."

"I don't see how anyone could survive being that close to the Great Blight," I said. "Even the Exiles. It would make sense for them to be further away."

"Well, no one asked you. I just have a gut feeling about this that I want to follow." She stood, leaving her dirty plate on the table for me to clean. "We'll be in the air in five minutes."

Makara headed for the cockpit, just as Anna sat down next to me with her breakfast.

"Hey," I said.

"What's up?" She started to eat.

"Try to be up in the cockpit in five," Samuel said, rising to go.

He left Anna and me at the table.

"I had this random thought this morning," Anna said.

"What?"

"You know that toothpaste we use, the minty one?"

I paused. "Yes?"

"Well, where the hell does it come from?"

I frowned. "Skyhome?"

"Yeah, I know *that*. Back when I lived on the surface, you were lucky to find anything salvaging, and most of the time it would be so old that it was like brushing your teeth with caulk. Mom and I would always use ashes from our fires mixed with water."

"Ash and water? I would have never thought of that."

"It's because you're from a Bunker. What did *you* guys do for toothpaste?"

"I don't know. We just always seemed to have it. How it's made is probably in the archive, somewhere. Or maybe they stocked up enough to last for a long time."

She shrugged. "I guess it will always be a mystery, then, huh?"

She went back to her food. Like Makara, Anna favored cantaloupe.

"I'll have to remember the ash and water thing. Might come in handy."

The ship began to hum as the fusion drive warmed up. Within minutes, we would be in the air.

Anna finished the last of her food. I touched her shoulder, causing her to pause mid-bite.

"Come on, let's go up front."

After she swallowed the rest of her food, we left the table and the dirty dishes behind.

Chapter 2

It was midmorning, and we had been searching three hours. The long, pink border of the Great Blight crawled north to south on the ship's right side. Just seeing that field of blaring pink, orange, and purple was unsettling. The xenofungus coated the desert floor, climbed over rocks, stretched over plains, slithered up mountains. The eastern sun cast a red, fiery light on the alien growth, setting its colors aflame. Swarms of creatures – probably birds – flew in tornado-like clouds, for the time being ignoring our presence.

It was like staring at the surface of an alien planet. And I guessed, for all intents and purposes, it *was* an alien planet. *This* was what we were fighting. Seeing all that alien growth was depressing.

We followed the line of the Great Blight until it started veering northwest. As the minutes passed and we continued our search, the Great Blight's border turned even *more* toward the west. The Great Blight stretched not only to the east, but also endlessly to the north.

"Was all this here before?" Makara asked.

We stood in silence seeing the fields touch the far horizon. We had never been this far north before, so maybe it had always been like this. Or maybe it had only recently expanded in this direction. It gave me a sense that time was definitely running out.

"I don't know," Samuel said. "Keep following the border, toward the west. That'll put us closer to Vegas in a couple of hours."

We followed the ground at a low altitude of about a thousand feet – high enough to be safe, yet low enough to easily see anything, or anyone, below. The Great Blight persisted in its westward crawl, sliding past our field of view. A purple lake glimmered far to the north, making me think that it was filled with purple goo rather than water. The xenoviral flora stood thick along its alien shoreline in a tangle of webbed growth.

The comm on the ship's dash began to beep, lighting red.

"Did anyone check in with Ashton last night?" Makara asked.

We all looked at each other. We were supposed to update Ashton once a day on how things were going.

"I forgot," Samuel said. "Put it on speaker."

Makara answered the call. "Yeah?"

"Give me your update from yesterday," Ashton said.

"Nothing to report, really," Makara said, angling the ship as the Great Blight's border started heading due west. "Did some more recon on the coordinates I sent you. We found nothing but dust."

"Makara, if you can't find anything soon, then..."

"We will," Makara said, interrupting. "I feel it in my bones."

"Feeling has nothing to do with it," Ashton said. "We are on a limited timetable, and I can't have you guys wasting time searching for a needle in a haystack."

"I understand that," Makara said. "But I know Char. If he went anywhere, it would have been to his brother."

"Even though he *hates* him?" Anna asked from the copilot's seat.

"I need you on my side, Anna," Makara said.

"I'm allowed my own opinion," Anna said. "Maybe Ashton is right."

"Alright," Makara said, annoyed, "if not the Exiles, then who do we go to?"

No one said anything.

"Well, there's Vegas," I said. "There are the northern Bunkers, 76 and 88..."

"Have you tried calling those Bunkers, Ashton?" Samuel asked.

"Repeatedly. I'm getting nothing. On 76, the line is going through, only...no one is answering."

"That's not a good sign," Makara said.

"What about Bunker 88?" I asked.

"Nothing," Ashton said. "It's safe to assume they are both offline, though at some point, you guys will still have to check it out yourselves. That is, if we have time. With what we're facing from Augustus and the xenovirus, we need every ally we can get."

"So, what about Vegas?" Samuel asked. "Why not just go there first?"

"Did you not learn from the Empire?" Makara asked. "If Char and Marcus back us up, we'll be bargaining from a position of power. We'll have hundreds at our back from the get-go. The Vegas Gangs will be more willing to listen to us."

"Good luck getting those two to work together," Anna said.

"They *will* work together," Makara said.

"I hope you're right, Makara," Ashton said. "Because this is your last day. I *cannot* allow you to waste any more time on this exercise."

"It's *not* an exercise," she said. "It's a necessity. I'm not allowing us to walk into Vegas with our pants down. From what I've heard, it's just as bad as L.A."

"That remains to be seen," Ashton said.

"How's your project coming, Ashton?" Samuel asked.

"I've finished one of the two wavelength monitors. The one Makara and I dropped earlier is still functioning, so getting these two done will help us triangulate the Voice's exact point of origin. Although I'm missing a few parts that I will have to find down on the surface."

"Where are they?" Samuel asked.

There was a pause. "Bunker Six."

Bunker Six. It was just a hop from Bunker One, toward the north. Like Bunker One, it had fallen in the xenoswarm's first major attack on humanity. That place was going to be thick with crawlers, if our time at Bunker One was any indication.

"Ashton, it's too dangerous," Makara said.

"I can handle myself," Ashton said. "I've gotten in and out of Bunker One half a dozen times over the years. What makes you think it will be different with Bunker Six? If the dock doors are still functional, then getting in is easy. My preliminary scans show that the Bunker's empty. No waves coming from that area, so the Voice is focused on something else. In fact..."

Ashton paused a moment.

"What is it?" I asked.

"Just give me a second." Once again, Ashton was quiet. I could hear the clacking of keys from his computer. "The Voice seems to be focused on where you guys are right now. Lots of waves coming in your direction."

That didn't sound good.

"Well, we have visual on the Great Blight right now," Samuel said. "It looks clear."

"Still, be on the lookout," Ashton said. "Something fishy is going on. Like Makara said...don't get caught with your pants down."

"So, you're *really* going into Bunker Six?" I asked.

"I have to, kid. In fact, I'm going as soon as this call is over. With the Voice focused elsewhere, it might be my best time to get in. The parts I need aren't too far from the hangar." Ashton cleared his throat. "Sorry. Anyway, another thing we might add to our to-do list is liberating *Perseus* and *Orion*."

"The other two ships?" Anna asked.

"That's right. That's further in the future, but if we have four ships at our disposal, and more trained pilots, it will give the New Angels flexibility. It will also give us an edge in any upcoming battles we have to fight."

Battles. Yes, there would be those, soon. But those battles were months away. Augustus was coming for us, and would have troops in the Wasteland as soon as he possibly could. That could be two months – that is, if the Wasteland winter didn't stop him first. Ashton had mentioned that fact on one of his radio calls a couple days ago. For now, it looked as though his legions were still coming. When they got here, we had to be ready to pull out all the stops.

"Wait," Makara said. "I think I'm seeing something."

At the top of the ridge to the west was a swarming movement. It took me a moment to discern the distant shapes.

"Crawlers," I said. "I wonder what they're after."

As Makara sped up and we drew closer, we could see more clearly. Crawlers surrounded a large group of people whose discarded bikes formed a perimeter around them.

"Ashton, we have contact," Makara said. "The Exiles need our help."

"Go get 'em, kid."

Ashton cut out, as we zoomed in close.

***

"Turret engaged," Anna said. "Fire?"

"Fire."

The turret opened up, rattling *Odin* as its rain of lead fell upon the crawlers slithering up the hill. Chunks of pink alien flesh and fountains of gooey purple blood shot into the air, splattering onto the hillside. Several of the creatures tumbled down the hill, lifeless. The men faced outward, continuing to fire into the teeming mass. As *Odin* circled around to the hill's other side, opening fire again, the creatures moved as one, fleeing their position. They scuttled toward the border of the Great Blight.

"They're retreating," Samuel said. "Make sure they're good and gone."

Makara nodded, following the line of fleeing crawlers at a low hover, keeping *Odin's* nose pointed at them. Anna continued using the computer to aim and shoot, leaving a trail of dead and dying that lay twitching on the desert floor. Finally, at enormous speed, the last few remaining crawlers slithered into the xenofungal border of the Great Blight, burrowing themselves into the fungus. How quickly that fungus sucked in their bodies made my skin crawl. They were lost to view.

"Alright," Samuel said. "Put *Odin* down on the hill."

Makara veered *Odin* around, so that now the hill faced us. The Exiles still stood in the center of their ring of bikes, staring up into the sky. I could only imagine what their reaction to *Odin* would be. On the fourth day of searching, we had finally found them – and right in the nick of time. A few minutes later, and they would have been the ones lying dead in the dust, not the crawlers.

Makara set *Odin* down lightly about a hundred feet away from the Exiles, who had not changed position. Makara powered the fusion drive out of flight mode, and unstrapped herself from her seat.

"Alright," she said. "Let's do this."

We followed the New Angels' leader from the cockpit and into the bitterly cold air.

***

I followed Makara, doing my best to suppress my shivering. My standing outside in the morning was my way getting used to the cold, bleak lands of the north once again.

The Exiles were grim as they turned to face us. Many had blood, both red and purple, on their clothing and bodies. They had thick beards, sunglasses, and thick, leather jackets. At their head stood the man we were looking for: Marcus. It had been awhile, but I recognized his short, solid frame, light red hair, and matching red beard. The hair fell to his shoulders, and his beard came down to the base of his neck.

"Makara," he said. "Samuel." He broke into a small, grim smile. "I thought you all dead."

Makara came to a stop a few feet in front of Marcus. Samuel, Anna, and I stood in a line just a few feet behind her.

"We thought the same of you," Makara said. She hesitated a moment before continuing. "We need your help."

Marcus chuckled. "Straight to the point, then."

Marcus had a slow, slightly arrogant way of speaking that made him seem like he was in control – that no matter what Makara told him, he was going to be his own man.

"Truly, thank you," Marcus said. "Without you, we'd be dead." He gazed at *Odin*, over Makara's shoulder. I'd thought he would have been a little more surprised to see it. "Looks like you've found a new toy."

"A little something we picked up," Makara said.

"So, what do you require of me?"

Samuel stepped forward and stood beside his sister. "We found the Black Files, but it wasn't easy. It's an alien virus causing all of this, and it's only going to get worse." He made a fist. "We mean to stop it."

Marcus looked down at his shoulder, flicking off a gooey chunk of crawler flesh that he had missed. "Clearly. You don't need any Black Files to tell this stuff is from another planet. The crawlers used to stay in their Blights, for the most part. Now, they swarm the Wasteland in packs, hunting and killing whomever they find. Sometimes, we come across corpses." Marcus shook his head. "No one can survive outside walls these days. The settlements are overrun with refugees – that is, what cities that allow them in. That is where we're headed, now."

"Headed where?" I asked.

Marcus pointed backward, over his left shoulder. "Vegas. I hope to offer the Exiles' service to one of the gang lords. We are experienced fighters, so we should get in. And if not..." Marcus paused. "Well, we'll figure something out. We might return to the Empire, where it will be safer."

"Nowhere is safe," Makara said. "Not even the Empire."

The two dozen or so men looked at each other. This was clearly unexpected news.

"You know this, how?" Marcus asked.

"We just returned from there," Samuel said. "The dragons attacked Nova Roma, unleashing dozens of crawlers within the city walls. Despite this, Augustus is on his way here. He wants to conquer the Wasteland, and a few crawlers and dragons running amok in his Empire won't stop him."

Marcus nodded. "That's no surprise to me, actually. Augustus wants to find and salvage the Bunkers, mostly for weaponry. The networks also contain a lot of information that he is interested in. He understands that these two things will help him hold his Empire in the long run."

"We expect the first of his forces to be here in two months," Samuel said.

Marcus's eyes widened. "Two months?"

"He is working with Carin Black," Makara said. "I don't know what their plan is, come winter, but we are preparing for the worst. We need to unite anyone we can to stand against him."

Marcus looked from Makara to Samuel, saying nothing. "There is nothing we can do."

Makara took a step forward. "We still have time to mount a resistance. If we take down Carin before Augustus gets here..."

Marcus looked at Makara, trying to see if she was serious. Then he began to laugh. Makara's face reddened.

"That's cute, kid," Marcus said. "And where do you plan on getting an army big enough to stand against the Empire?"

"Well, I hoped you would be my first recruits," Makara said. "With you and Char both, we might be able to convince the Vegas gangs to help out."

Marcus frowned at the mention of his brother. "Have you spoken with him?"

"No," Makara said. "We were hoping that you had. We've been searching for you for the past four days. And now, with so much on the line, I'm not leaving until you are with me." She paused a moment. "The Lost Angels have reformed. I am their leader."

Marcus looked Makara up and down, recalculating her strength. The men behind Marcus grumbled at each other, and after a moment turned their attention back to Makara.

"How many men do you have?"

"After this conversation, I'm hoping a little over two dozen."

Marcus gave a bark of a laugh, then shook his head. "You got gumption, kid. That isn't a bad thing, though." He eyed Makara, hard. "What makes you think *I* will follow *you?*"

Makara shrugged, a slight smile playing on her lips. "This isn't about me leading. It's about stopping Augustus. Besides, if you say no, you'll be hunted by crawlers. You need us just to get as far as Vegas. You can't run forever. Not from crawlers, not from dragons, not from the Blights. And, on the other hand, we need you. We need the New Angels to be strong enough to take on the Reapers in L.A. If the Angels can make it to Vegas already thirty strong, the gang lords there will be forced to take us seriously. With Char and the Raiders, we will number in the hundreds."

Marcus nodded, thinking. "What about you, Samuel?"

"Makara heads up the Angels. I head up the mission against the xenovirus. We can't do anything against the Great Blight until we stop Augustus and Black. We need to take those two down before they ruin every chance we've got."

Marcus said nothing, merely looking at all of us, weighing Makara's and Samuel's words. The Exiles behind Marcus listened, waiting for the decision of their leader.

"This is a group decision," Marcus said. "I lead, but only by the consent of my men. We will need to confer."

"Please do," Makara said. "Just don't take long. Because when it comes to them..." Makara pointed ahead, toward the Great Blight, "there's no time to waste."

Marcus nodded. "Come back in an hour and we will have an answer for you, Makara of the Angels."

As Marcus and the Exiles walked back to their ring of bikes, Makara turned toward us.

"Let's go."

Chapter 3

"They will follow us."

Makara sat in the pilot's seat, staring out the window at the circle of conferring Exiles.

"You seem so sure," Anna said.

"It can't go any other way. If they don't come with us, they die."

"All the same," I said, "we want them with us because they're *with* us. We don't want them having their own agenda."

"When Marcus accepts, I will let him know about everything that has happened," Samuel said. "If that still doesn't sway him, he needs to get his head checked."

"You see what I'm saying, though," I said. "They could just use us to get as far as Vegas."

"Maybe," Makara said. "But we really don't have much choice, do we?" She sighed. "Besides, I have a few more tricks up my sleeve."

I wanted to believe Makara. I really did. But I knew she was improvising. It was a lucky thing she happened to be good at that.

"When we finally find Char," Anna said, "those two are going to be a mess to deal with."

"It's time they reconciled," Makara said.

"How do you know if Char is even alive?" I asked.

"He is. I *know* he is. If Marcus doesn't know where his brother is, then that tells me Char is probably in Vegas. He would not go to L.A. – the Reapers and the Raiders have always been on bad terms." She turned back toward the windshield, staring at her potential recruits. "Process of elimination."

Samuel said nothing. Makara was in control, now – of where we went, who we talked to, and what we did. It was a different, yet not unnatural change. I remembered what Samuel had told me back in Skyhome – if he died, he expected me to lead the crew. How was I supposed to do that if Makara was in charge now?

The potential of *me* being in charge seemed so unnatural. I felt far more comfortable in a support role, and I wondered if Makara, or even Samuel, were the same way. Maybe leaders were made more out of necessity than necessarily being born that way.

At last the Exiles turned, heading as one toward the ship.

"They're coming," Anna said.

It was time to hear their decision.

***

"We will ride with you," Marcus said.

Makara nodded. "Good."

"On one condition."

Makara arched an eyebrow.

"We are our own men. At any time we may leave, and never return, if we so choose. At no time am I, or any of the Exiles, to be under your direct authority." Marcus stared hard at Makara through his sunglasses.

"I understand your reservation," Makara said. "But I will *always* be willing to listen to your opinions. In the end, however, *I'm* the one in charge, and I make the final decision. If you join the New Angels, it's as a New Angel." She waved a hand backward, toward us. "It's the same for them."

Marcus did not say anything for a long while.

"Your brother as well?" Marcus asked.

Samuel nodded. "Yes."

"Then we will join you."

Makara held out her hand. Marcus took it.

"We leave now," Makara said. "We'll stay behind at a hover, and if anything enters our sights, we'll flash our lights."

"I suppose our bikes will be too heavy for the ship?"

Makara nodded. "Maybe if it was just you guys, but the bikes cannot go on board. I guess we could ferry people back and forth, but I don't want the group split up for any reason – not with the threat from crawlers."

"In that case, Vegas is a two days' journey from here. The land is rough, but it should be passable."

Makara nodded. "If you have any wounded, we have a clinic aboard *Odin*."

"My thanks," Marcus said, "but as you can see, our wounded died long ago."

Behind the Exiles, the bodies of three men were laid out, side by side.

"Do you need time to bury them?"

Marcus shook his head. "No. We burn our dead – it is our way."

"Do what you need to do." Makara turned aside. "When you leave, we will follow."

"I'll go over everything we've learned about the xenovirus when we camp tonight," Samuel said.

Marcus nodded, then turned back to the Exiles. As he began giving orders on what should be done with the dead, we returned to *Odin*.

***

As the bodies caught flame, sending thick plumes of acrid smoke into the air, the Exiles circled the fire and rode west. It was only when we picked up their trail that I realized how amazingly fast *Odin* went. Going at the Exiles' pace made the surrounding terrain pass at a crawl. Where we could have made Vegas in an hour, it would take the Exiles two days to make the same journey.

However, it did afford us the opportunity to study the landscape, making sure nothing else jumped out at our newfound allies.

"I have to admit it, Makara," I said. "You were right."

Makara smiled. "Have a little faith, Alex. I'm the Chosen One."

"I'm starting to believe it."

"This is only the beginning," Samuel said. "I don't think you'll find the Vegas Gangs as accommodating."

"No," Makara said. "Probably not."

The Great Blight spread northward with ethereal beauty. The sunlight had even somewhat broken through the layer of meteor fallout, casting the unearthly colors in a light golden glow.

"I wonder what they're planning," I asked, staring at the Great Blight.

Everyone knew what I was talking about. After the xenovirus had revealed the dragons, all of us just had to wonder what was next.

"That giant one, guarding Raider Bluff – I wonder who *he* is," Makara said.

"Or she," Anna said.

I laughed. "Yeah. I could see that thing being a girl."

Anna raised an eyebrow, while Makara gave me a dangerous look. I shut my mouth.

"I thought at first the xenovirus had access only to genes of Earth origin," Samuel said. "I'm beginning to think they have genes from other places, too – perhaps from their home world. There's nothing on Earth that looks like those dragons, or even the crawlers, for that matter." He sighed. "We're always running behind. This thing is always one step ahead of us."

Makara reached for the transceiver. "I'm going to update Ashton."

The light on the dash blinked while we waited for the doctor to pick up. In the meantime, we continued staring out the windshield, making sure nothing was creeping up on the Exiles.

Ashton's voice came through. "What's the update?"

"We found the Exiles," Makara said. I could hear an "I told you so" tone in her voice that she didn't bother to mask.

"And?"

"They've joined up with us," Makara said. "We're all heading north and will reach Vegas in two days."

"Good work, Makara," Ashton said. "That's one group down. Any news of Char?"

"No. I hope to find out more when we reach the city. There's nothing else to do until then."

"They were ambushed on a hill," I said. "We barely got there in time."

"Casualties?"

"Three Exiles," Samuel said. "They still number two dozen or so."

"It's a good start," Ashton said. "I don't suppose you've let Marcus know about the xenovirus yet?"

"He knows we've found the Black Files, and that we have a plan to stop the xenovirus," Samuel said. "Other than that, no. He knows nothing. I'm going to catch him up when we camp tonight."

"See that you do."

"I guess you haven't left for Bunker Six yet?" I asked.

"No, not yet. Something was holding me up here in Skyhome. We discovered a leak in Delta Quadrant. Probably a holdover from the impact we had a couple weeks ago. It's taken care of, so I'll be out of touch for the next couple days until I find those parts."

"Ashton..." Anna said. "You don't have to do this. Just send us instead."

"That's a negative, Anna. I need all of you focused on recruiting for the Angels. The old man can be relegated to the less important tasks."

"Getting those wavelength monitors set up is hardly unimportant," I said.

"Right you are, Alex. This Voice won't find itself. Luckily, Makara and I have already dropped one off, so I only need the parts for two more. And it's not even the whole thing, just a homing chip that will help with the tracking and..."

"Ashton," Anna said.

He chuckled. "Right. Well, you kids be safe. If anything changes, don't hesitate to call me on *Gilgamesh*, though I may be out of touch most of that time."

"Copy that," Makara said. "Anything else?"

"Yeah, I've got something." I looked at Anna, and smiled. "How do you guys make toothpaste up there?"

There was a long, awkward silence as everyone in the cockpit looked at me blankly, except Anna, who smiled.

"Um...you know, Alex, I'm not rightly sure of that. I'll make it my top priority to find out, though."

Ashton cut out.

"What the heck was that about?" Makara asked.

"Nothing," I said. "It's a question that's really, really been bugging me for the past two days. Toothpaste: where does it come from?"

"Well, if you want a serious answer..." Samuel said. "Baking soda, mint, some other things, maybe..."

"Seriously," Makara said. "Let's just focus on following the Exiles and not letting them die."

I laughed. "A bit wound up, are we?"

"Humph. Maybe so. This leading thing is a little harder than I'd thought."

Samuel gave a rare smile. "Trust me, it's only going to get worse."

"Thanks, Sam," Makara said.

The day wore on with no further incident. We passed over gnarled desert hills and into a long, low flatland – at the end of which was a giant, jagged chasm. Its interior and sides were coated with xenofungus, and swarms of birds flew in and out of the great rent in the Earth.

"The Grand Canyon," Anna said. "Never thought I'd get to see it."

"It's completely taken over," Makara said.

"That can't be good for Vegas," I said. "Isn't the Colorado their water supply?"

No one answered. That was a question that had to wait until we actually got there.

The Great Blight had spread further in two months than I would have ever thought possible. The power of the xenovirus was terrifying. It was evolving in ways we could have never predicted. Who could have guessed that *dragons* were coming? There was so much more going on below the surface, answers that likely could only be found in the Great Blight itself and its alien heart – Ragnarok Crater. Those answers were not going to come anytime soon. We had barely survived our harrowing one-and-only trip into that heart of darkness. That we had lived this long to tell the tale seemed like sheer luck.

The Grand Canyon to the north passed slowly, jagging its way through the bleak landscape. Finally, as the sun ebbed in the sky and as the shadows lengthened, the dust cloud below pulled to a stop between two dunes.

Makara piloted *Odin* downward, setting the ship down a hundred feet or so from the Exiles.

After unstrapping themselves, both Samuel and Makara left the cockpit. Anna and I followed them outside.

Chapter 4

A few minutes later, we were all basking in the warm glow of a bonfire. I held Anna's hand, sitting on the ground, as both Makara and Samuel spoke to Marcus.

"It's going to take them a while to go through everything," I said.

Anna said nothing, merely watching the fire.

A stout, muscled man sat next to me. He had a scraggly black beard that went down to his chest. His weathered face was pockmarked with scars, and the skin of his hands seemed more like leather than flesh.

Even though the man was a little intimidating, I decided to initiate a conversation.

"What's your name?"

"Harold," he said, in a deep, raspy voice.

"How long have you been an Exile?"

"None of us are here because we chose to be. It's Char that keeps us here."

Around the fire, other heads nodded.

"So, you all hate Char?"

"He was in the wrong," another Exile said from across the fire. "He kept us from passing Raider Bluff. Any who tried, he killed."

"Can you remind me what happened again?" Anna asked. "You said there was a disagreement a long time ago. What was it about?"

The Exile who had just spoken stared at Anna balefully. The fire gave his dark eyes a devilish gleam. All the same, Anna did not look away.

"You're about to see it, girl. You might not know this, but there was another city, on the opposite shore of the Colorado. Rivertown, they called it. It was a peaceful city. In the old days, Bluff and Rivertown would help each other. Then, the Raiders took over. Bluff became Raider Bluff. The old ones remember those times."

The man stopped speaking. Everyone was listening now – Makara, Samuel, and Marcus included.

"Nathan was there from the beginning," Harold said.

Nathan, the man who had been telling the story, nodded. "Aye, I was there. My wife lived in Rivertown. She died, that day, twelve years ago."

"When the dam broke?"

Nathan scowled. "It didn't break on its own, kid. Your friend Char broke it. Marcus was the only one with the guts to stand up to him." Nathan shook his head. "Even when we backed up Marcus, Char wouldn't listen. He was hungry for power, and he did not care who died in order to get it."

"That's not the Char I know," Anna said.

Nathan stared hard at Anna. "You are still a child. You are too young to know anything."

Anna's face burned. She was about to speak again, but I held her arm. She kept her mouth shut.

"Maybe Char is different, now," Nathan said. "But at the time, he was not. One night, in the Bounty, Marcus and Char fought. The entire bar was cleared to the edges of the room. They did not hold back – any weapon they found, they used. Then, Marcus won the upper hand, throwing his brother in the fire. Char landed face-first, earning the wounds that will mark him for the rest of his life as a sign of his sin."

I watched the fire in front of me, probably not too different from the one that had burned twelve years ago. I wondered what Char's side of the story was. I wondered, with twelve years of resentment burning, how it would be possible for everyone to work together.

"What happened after the fight?" I asked.

Nathan shrugged. "So began our exile. There was fighting in the streets, between Char and Marcus, and those who supported Marcus. But we could not win. I fought for my wife, who had lived in Rivertown before it was flooded. Violence was the new code, those days – and it all changed when the first Alpha took over – a man by the name of Victor." Nathan paused. "I hear he is dead, now."

"This Victor," Anna said. "You are saying he changed Raider Bluff from a place of peace to a place of violence?"

Nathan nodded. "This was in 2048. Food was scarce, and some tough decisions had to be made. Victor decided that violence was the best means by which to attain food – from other settlements, mostly. This included Rivertown. This was before the farms, before the slaves."

"Now, all of that is gone," I said.

"Aye," Nathan said. "It is. Raider Bluff was an evil place. It only became more corrupt as the years passed. It infects anyone who lives there long enough. You either become a violent barbarian, or you are crushed, subjugated into slavery, or worse." Nathan sighed, long and tired. "When the dam finally did break, no one in Rivertown was safe. Those who survived had nowhere to go when the waters rose – nowhere to go but Raider Bluff. There, they became slaves, forced to work the farms outside the city."

Nathan said nothing about his wife, having already said it earlier. She had died. I didn't doubt his story. I didn't like it, though, only because it complicated things. Char was supposed to be our main ally. And yet, he had done something horrible. He had killed innocent people for his own personal gain.

Somehow, we had to get these two disparate groups working together – Exile and Raider. Only, the Exiles were right. *They* had been the ones forced to wander for twelve years, eking out an existence in the most desolate part of the Wasteland. The Boundless would have long killed off other men, and it had probably killed off many Exiles over the years. I remember Marcus mentioning working for the Empire, when we had met them on our way to Bunker One. Maybe that was how they got by.

Though the Exiles were right, the Raiders were more numerous. We needed their help. More than anything, we needed Char and Marcus to reconcile. But when there was so much hatred, was it even possible?

I looked at Makara, who now spoke to Marcus in a low voice. It all now rested on the shoulders of this nineteen-year-old girl. It amazed me, what circumstances could do to a person. Makara had stepped into a leadership role seamlessly. If there was anyone who could get the Raiders and the Exiles to start thinking of themselves as New Angels, it was her.

But first, we had to find Char and the Raiders.

"Hopefully, the Raiders are in Vegas," I said.

From beside me, Harold spoke.

"If they are, there will be blood."

"Why do you say that?" I asked.

"Did you not hear the story? You are either for us, or for them." He turned to me. "Who are you with?"

"We still need to hear Char's side of things."

Harold shook his head, standing up to walk away from the fire. Yeah, I had offended him. But I couldn't tie my loyalty down to one group over the other. Not until I had heard everything.

Marcus stood, along with Makara and Samuel. I focused my attention on their conversation.

"I will speak with Char, but no more than that," Marcus said. "He did something unforgivable. I will never let him go free from his crimes."

"Even if it means the survival of the Wasteland?" Makara asked.

"Kid, there is something you must learn about being a leader," Marcus said. "You can't just do whatever you want. You have to have a moral compass. If you compromise with my brother – if you let him off the hook for what he has done – you place yourself in the same category he is in."

Makara said nothing, merely staring hard into Marcus's eyes. It was rare to see Makara rendered speechless, but it was clear that Marcus's words had affected her.

"Char is like a father to me," she said. "To think he would have done something like that is almost unthinkable, even if it was twelve years ago. Of course, I have heard of Rivertown before. Every Raider has. I just didn't know all the details. I will have to talk to him about it."

Marcus nodded. "See that you do. You must be unyielding. Don't give him any slack because you think of him as a father. In fact, demand even more of him. If he is worthy of the name of father, then he might think twice about what he has done."

"It could be that he has regretted it all these years," Makara said.

"I think not," Marcus said. "Wouldn't he have found us, if that was true?"

"Char has a lot of pride," Makara said, looking at Marcus. "Kind of like someone else I know."

"Humph." Marcus folded his arms, turning to stare at the crackling fire. The orange light reflected off his blue eyes. I couldn't help but think of the rage that burned within him.

"We will see. But mark my words about leading, Makara. You must remain true to yourself and to your conscience. Otherwise, the only way you can possibly rule is by fear. And by doing that, you make yourself no better than Char, or Augustus, or Ohlan, for that matter. You say you want the New Angels to be like they were in the days of Raine." Marcus turned back from the fire, and looked at Makara. "Ask yourself what Raine would do, and let that be your guide."

"I have asked myself that question every day for the past three years," Makara said.

"It is well, then." Something in his tone signaled that the conversation was over. He looked at the ship. "Hard to believe, that such an artifact of the Old World still remains. I hope it will be enough to stop it."

By "stop it," I knew Marcus meant the xenovirus. Now, he knew everything we did. But would that knowledge be enough to get him to work with us, when it meant Char was going to work with us, too?

"We have a long day tomorrow," Marcus said. "We will be passing a site of great sorrow for all of us."

The men around the fire nodded, and it took me a moment to realize what they were talking about. To get to Vegas, we would have to pass through where Hoover Dam had once stood. It was all river, now, but apparently there was still some way to cross over.

I felt afraid, for a moment. With the Exiles and the Raiders enemies, we had to get our own house in order before approaching the Lords of Vegas. Yet there was no time for that. We just had to hope for the best.

And hope, in this world, was rarely enough.

***

We arrived at the crossing around mid-afternoon. The sight took my breath away. We had parked *Odin*, and now all stood on the edge of the canyon, looking down into the great chasm. Hundreds of feet below, the Colorado River churned angry and cold. Intermixed with the rock and water were the ruins of the massive explosion of twelve years past – large chunks of concrete, turbines, and metal, that were piled so thick so as to form a dam of their own. But the water flowed through, white, frothy, violent. The dam had long been conquered, and it was likely that the force of the water being released twelve years ago had pushed most of it downriver.

At points along the cliff edge, the sides had collapsed. This would have happened because the enormous force of water would have blasted away the canyon's lower walls, leaving nothing to support the canyon's upper reaches. This had another effect – the giant bridge that had once spanned the canyon now lay at the bottom of the gorge –broken, twisted, and useless. It was amazing what the people of the Old World had been able to construct. It was even more amazing how fast these intricately designed feats of engineering could be destroyed.

To the north, where Lake Mead once spread, was a great, empty basin, dry, cracked, and lifeless. It wasn't only the cities downriver that the emptying of Lake Mead and the destruction of Hoover Dam had affected. Surely, that large lake had also been Vegas's main source of water, even Post-Ragnarok – and without it, I couldn't see how they survived, twelve years after the destruction of the dam.

"There's the path down to the rapids," Marcus said, pointing. "It leads to the bridge."

At first, I couldn't see what Marcus was talking about. Then, I saw it – a thin, crude bridge made from rope and planks that stretched across the river precariously. Below, the water of the mighty Colorado churned between rocks and ruins. If anyone were to slip and fall through one of the many gaps of that swinging bridge, it was sure death. At the far end stood two shapes, bearing rifles. Guards, most likely.

"Our bikes can't cross," Marcus said. "We'll have to use *Odin*. Take a few at a time, so as not to overburden it."

"Why can't we do that now?" I asked.

"We have to talk to them, first," Marcus said, pointing to the guards. "They need to know who we are and why we're here. Otherwise, there'll be trouble."

"Marcus, Alex, and I will go down there," Makara said, turning around to face the others. The rest of you, see to loading a few of the bikes into *Odin's* galley. We'll do six at a time."

Makara turned back to me, her hair caught in the wind. I didn't know why she had asked me to accompany her. I put a hand on my Beretta, ready to help keep both her and Marcus secure, should the need arise.

"Let's go," Marcus said.

We marched down a trail that snaked down the cliff's side. It was clear from the many rocks covering the trail that not too many people came from this side of the desert, which made sense, because no one really lived on this side. The guards would surely be surprised once they saw us, if they hadn't spotted us already.

As we neared the gorge bottom, its either side lined with red rock, the ferocity of the river became even more apparent. For so many years, all this water had been locked behind Hoover Dam. Just seeing the ruin of the dam, both up and downriver, made me wonder just what *kind* of force could have done this.

"Was the bomb nuclear?" I asked.

"I don't know," Marcus said. "It was powerful, so that could have been the case. They also could have used *a lot* of high-grade explosives. The U.S. developed some very dangerous toys during the Dark Decade. There are several military bases nearby. By now, I'm sure they are stripped clean, but at the time, maybe my brother had managed to find something there."

Makara said nothing, setting a quick pace down the trail. At last, we stood before the beginning of the bridge. On this side, the bridge was anchored to a piece of rock with a set of thick metal stakes. One of the guards held a rifle in one hand, and raised the other to indicate that we should remain where we were. Then the guard holstered the weapon on his back and began his long, torturous journey across the bridge to meet us. The bridge looked so fragile that it might snap at any moment.

When the man reached the middle, the very bottom of the bridge sagged so low that it was only a few feet above the raging river. A metallic turbine jutted from the water, reaching for the man's leg. The man passed on, unworried. He had probably made this trip many times before. Finally, his speed increased as he came to the tauter section of the bridge. The shabby wooden planks now bore his weight rather than giving in to his step.

He exited the bridge, and now stood on the edge of the cliff. Up until now, I had not paid attention to his face. The man had a thick, black beard, coppery skin, and thick muscles. But I'd recognize that face anywhere, and when I saw who it was, it knocked the very wind out of me. It was a man I had believed dead three months, and it took me a moment to feel like I wasn't staring at a ghost.

The man smiled as he looked at me. Unbelieving, he broke into a wide smile.

"Holy...!" The man shouted. "Alex! Alex *Keener!*"

I shook my head, walking forward to greet the man. We clasped arms; he drew me into a bear hug, nearly crushing me with its ferocity.

It was Michael Sanchez. He had survived Bunker 108.

Chapter 5

"I can't believe it," I said. "Michael. You're *alive!*"

The boom of my voice echoed off the canyon walls, unmasked by the sound of rushing water. Makara and Marcus stared at us, confused. Michael did not heed them. His eyes shone brightly and his face had split into a mile-wide grin.

"What the hell happened?" he asked. "Who else is with you? Did your dad make it?"

I shook my head. "No. Just me. My dad...he died. Khloe was with me, and her parents. All of them died."

"Damn. I'm sorry. That's..."

I looked at Officer Michael – or the man who *used* to be Officer Michael – still unbelieving. He was still the same, if only a bit thinner. He was all muscle before, but the three months between then and now had made him a good twenty pounds lighter.

"Alex, I hardly recognize you," he said. "You've changed."

I was about to say the same to him, when Makara stepped up. "Who is this?"

"This is Officer Michael Sanchez. He lived with me at Bunker 108."

"Just Michael now," he said, holding out a hand to Makara.

Makara didn't take the hand. "I know you."

Michael looked at me, then back at Makara.

"You were the one with Alex on his recon."

Michael, at first, did not react. Then, it looked as if he had been punched in the gut.

"You were the one who killed that man," Michael said, with realization. "The one we let in. The guy who infected the rest of them with the Blight Fever."

Makara just stared, not saying anything. "It's complicated, Michael. For now, I can say no more than that."

"We can catch you up on everything later," I said. "Give her a chance. I gave her hell at first, but it was all a mistake."

Michael nodded, resigning himself to that. "I guess I have a lot to be caught up on. I've been here for the last two months. I'm working for the Dragons now."

"The Dragons?" I asked, looking up.

"Not those," he said. "They're a gang, in Vegas. They control this crossing."

"Guard duty, huh?"

He shrugged. "I have to start somewhere. I consider myself lucky to even be alive. More so because my wife and kid made it."

"That's great news, Michael."

"When it all went to hell, we took one of the Recons and..."

"...Michael, right?" Marcus asked. "I hate to interrupt the reunion, but daylight is failing, and we need to get thirty men across the river. Are we clear to do that?"

Michael looked at Marcus. "Right." He reached for a radio on his side, raised it to his mouth. "Franco, you have a copy?"

"Go ahead."

"I've got thirty men here that need to cross. They're friends. I'm sending them over."

"Has this been cleared with Boss Dragon?"

"No, but I'm staking my integrity on it. They can camp outside the Sunset Wall tonight. Trust me – they are friends, and we can use the help."

Silence from the other end.

"Mike, I can't just let thirty men pass without being cleared by the Boss. That's just not done."

"Trust me," Michael said. "Besides, we don't have time for clearance. With the Blighters about, I don't think they'd be safe out here. They need to be behind walls."

The man Franco sighed from the other end of the line. "No one goes behind the walls that's not already cleared by one of the gangs. You know that as well as I do. Anyone who is not a citizen can camp outside, no more."

"I'll talk to the Boss about it later." Michael paused. "I'm letting them cross."

"Fine," Franco said. "It's your ass, though. If I get asked about this, I'm pointing your way."

"That's fine."

Michael put the radio back, breaking into a smile again. "I still can't believe it."

I smiled back. "You don't even know the half. Wait until you see *how* we're going to cross."

Michael frowned in confusion.

"Come on," I said. "We'll show you."

***

We led Michael up the snaking trail, a man whom I had thought dead. I had not seen him once in my escape from Bunker 108, but somehow he had managed to save his wife and kid and find himself here. Suddenly, I felt a lot less alone. I was not the only one to have survived Bunker 108. Even if it wasn't my father, even if it wasn't Khloe, it was someone who shared my story, someone who knew my past.

"Did anyone else make it that you know of?" I asked, halfway up the cliff.

Michael shook his head. "No. I thought me and my family were all that was left."

"Well, there's a few more of us, at least." I pointed to Makara. "Makara is from Bunker One."

"Really?" Michael asked.

"It was long ago," Makara said, cutting the conversation short.

I shrugged. A minute later, we crested the rise. We were greeted by expansive red desert and dune, and a crumbling highway curving to the southeast. About five hundred feet ahead was the *Odin*.

"Whoa!" Michael said. "What is *that* thing?"

"Meet the *Odin*," I said, proudly. "It's one of four spaceships that survived Ragnarok. It's the property of the New Angels now."

He shook his head, his smile never breaking. He turned to me, squinting one eye. "The New Angels?"

"I'll have to tell you about that, too."

Samuel, Anna, and the Exiles walked forward to greet us, awaiting news. Then they noticed Michael.

"This is Michael Sanchez," Makara said. "He is a representative of the Dragon gang out of Vegas. He has cleared us all to pass."

Several whoops came from the crowd of men. Michael frowned slightly.

"Didn't expect there to be a spaceship," he said. "That might complicate things."

"You're in trouble now, huh?"

Michael nodded. "Yep. At best, I'm going to get the chewing-out of my life. At worst...well, let's not think of that."

"You're one of us, now," I said. "We've got your back."

Makara spun around. "Not so fast. I'm in charge of the Angels, and *I* decide who joins us."

"Why wouldn't you accept Michael?" I asked. "He's a good fighter."

Before Makara could answer, Michael held up his hands. "Alright. I wasn't going to accept, anyway."

"Why not?" I asked.

He pulled back the sleeve of his gray tee shirt, revealing an intricate, tattooed dragon, breathing flame.

"This is why," he said. "I'm a Dragon, now. My place is here. I owe the gang my life. I'm not going to turn my back on that."

"We need to get rolling," Makara said. "Where is this Sunset Gate?"

"It's on the south entrance of town, set up on the highway. There are some turrets there that can provide cover fire, in case the Blighters get feisty."

"Blighters?" I asked.

Michael looked at me, confused. "Surely you've seen them. The big scorpion reptile things with the pearly eyes?"

"Yeah, I know them. Just never heard that term before. We call them crawlers."

"Maybe they're only called Blighters around here," Michael said.

"You guys can catch up later," Makara said. "We have to get moving."

Michael nodded. "Right."

"We'll need to ferry the bikes across the canyon. Then we can travel the rest of the way to this Sunset Gate. Marcus and the Exiles can follow our trail." She looked at Michael. "Are Char and the Raiders here?"

"Char?" Michael asked. "Yeah, he's here. Arrived two weeks ago. He's camped by the Sunset Gate as well."

Makara nodded, then gave a sigh of relief. "Thank God."

Marcus's reaction, however, was completely different. "I can't stay by him. If I do, I may end up doing something I regret."

Makara gave another sigh, but this one was out of exasperation. "Marcus, you're going to have to let the past be the past. Give Char a chance to redeem himself. We don't have time for bickering."

Marcus held a hand on his pistol at his side. "I promise nothing. I hate Char. I hate him with everything I've got. And he will pay for what he did."

Marcus's face was passive, betraying no emotion, though I could feel the anger boiling beneath. For twelve years, he had nursed it. And it wasn't going away until he did something about it.

"I don't know how to handle this," Makara said, shaking her head. "Since the Raiders are already by the gate, you just might have to camp somewhere else."

Marcus's face reddened. "That's the treatment I get? After agreeing to help you?"

"This isn't helping," I said. "How are any of us supposed to work together if we can't even camp in the same spot?"

Neither Marcus nor Makara answered as both Samuel and Anna walked up.

"We've finished loading the first of the bikes," Samuel said. He looked at Michael, offering a hand. "Samuel Neth."

"Michael Sanchez."

"We need to get moving," Makara said, her tone insistent. "It'll be dark in a couple of hours, and I have to babysit two grown men to make sure they don't kill each other."

"Makara," Marcus began, "the Exiles will get priority over the Raiders. We joined you first. I will *not* have my brother..."

"Marcus," Makara said, dangerously, "we can talk about this when we land. You brothers will have to get along. If you don't, this group will rip apart before it even has the chance to take off."

Marcus fell into silence, crossing his arms. He was not happy.

"We'll put down somewhere distant," Makara finally said in the silence that followed. "Maybe half a mile from the walls, but not right next to the Raiders."

"You'll be out of range of our turrets," Michael said. "Trust me. You don't want that."

"Actually, I think I do," Makara said. "I don't trust anyone in Vegas until I can get guarantees."

"We're not going to shoot you," Michael said. "For one, I'll make sure of that. And secondly, we need all the help we can get.

The Great Blight has been getting rather nasty lately. If you are outside the range of our turrets, it will leave you open to attack."

Makara eyed Michael, unhappy with what he was telling her.

"The Raiders and the Exiles will just have to live in peace, then."

Marcus growled, but said nothing.

"Can you arrange a meeting between me and the other gang lords?" Makara asked.

"I will let Boss Dragon know," Michael said. "Although every gang in Vegas will know about you within minutes of your landing. Each one will want to meet with you personally."

"I don't have time for that. Can't I just meet them all at the same time?"

Michael smiled grimly. "There aren't too many summits, these days. Things are near a snapping point, and most think there'll be another gang war soon."

"I don't care," Makara said. "I have to get these gangs focused not on each other, but focused on what matters. This city will be dead in a matter of weeks – maybe days. The Great Blight is preparing its next move."

Michael nodded. "If I go to Boss Dragon personally about this, he might be persuaded. He's mediated such meetings before. We can take you inside the city to meet him."

Makara frowned. "I don't like that idea. I'd rather he come out to meet me."

"That won't happen," Michael said.

Makara sighed. "We'll figure this out. What gangs are there in the city?"

"Well," Michael said, "The Dragons are only one of six. There are the Kings, the Reds, the Sworn, the Diamonds, and the Suns."

"And now, the Angels," I said.

"And if you count the Exiles and the Raiders, that makes nine total," Anna said.

No one said anything, pausing to think about the repercussions of having nine violent gangs around one another.

"This is going to be a bloodbath, isn't it?" I asked.

"Let's go," Makara said.

With that command, everyone moved to *Odin*.

Chapter 6

After ferrying the last of the bikes across the gorge, we flew in a straight line northwest. The beginning of the city's outskirts passed below, a maze of crumbling, gray buildings, houses, and roads scattered with rubble. In the distance rose dozens of skyscrapers, shadows against the darkening sky – the remains of the Vegas strip. Those lights had been out for thirty years, now. The buildings, roads, and city lay before us in a sprawled grid, completely empty save for abandoned vehicles and debris that cluttered the streets. The entire city had stopped in one moment, frozen in time, left to rot – to be buried in dust.

Makara landed *Odin* north of a large interstate interchange, right in the center of a cleared highway. Dust shifted on the smooth concrete, covering mangled green road signs with red sand. Dilapidated buildings and department stores lined both sides of the highway, their broken windows, lack of paint, and bare appearance reminding me of skeletons. Graffiti coated the buildings' sides, florid letters in colors of purple, green, and red. The sun appeared as a red blotch to the west through the dust, sinking behind a tall skyscraper.

Ahead and to the north lay what Michael referred to as the Sunset Gate. A mountain of rubble rose before us, walling out the abandoned outskirts of town and sheltering what remained of Vegas itself – the tall buildings of the Strip, to our northeast, along with its surrounding blocks. The gate was a massive wooden construction, similar to the one I had seen guarding Raider Bluff.

To open, it would slide to the side, its large wheels on a track. The gate guarded the northbound side of the highway, while rubble completely blocked off the southbound lanes. On either side of the gate rose wooden towers, where turrets had been set up. Men stood there, watching us.

We stepped off the ship. In the distance, we heard the rumble of the Exiles' engines approaching. While we waited for them to arrive, the sun fell, covering the land in darkness.

Michael stood off a way, speaking on his radio. He was trying to figure out when, or if, we could come inside the walls.

The Exiles pulled up in a collective roar of engines, and parked their bikes along the overpass's railing. One by one, the bikes were shut off, and the men began setting up camp. As tents went up and a bonfire was built, I marveled at their efficiency. I just wondered where they had kept all these supplies.

I noticed that some of the men spoke together in groups and looked off toward the south. A short way out from the overpass were a couple hundred tents, in the midst of which burned dozens of separate fires. It was the Raiders' camp. Surrounding the whole thing was a crude, wooden fence that had been raised in a hurry.

Makara, too, stared off in that direction. For the first time in three months, she was going to see Char.

When our own fire was lit, Michael turned from his position and approached us.

"They're not sending anyone out tonight," he said. "Likely, they'll organize a summit to decide what to do about you, first."

"I need to meet with all of them as soon as possible," Makara said. "This can't wait."

"That will happen, but you have to give them time to react to this," Michael said. "I mean, a *spaceship* and thirty fighting men have just landed outside their walls. Wouldn't you be surprised if that happened?"

Makara gave a noncommittal grunt. "There is no time for waiting. The Great Blight is moving, and won't pause for anyone. Can't we go in tonight? Not me, personally – I have to meet with Char."

Michael nodded. "I'll try to work something out. Maybe if you give me a couple of your crew, then explaining what's going on to the Boss will be much easier."

"Take Alex with you," Makara said.

I hadn't expected to go in tonight, but I tried to take it in stride.

"Alright," Michael said. "I think the Boss will be fine with that."

"Remember, this isn't just about what he wants," Makara said. "I'm important, too."

"I'll protect your interests," I said.

"So, is that his real name?" Makara asked. "The Boss?"

"It's Elijah, but there are protocols," Michael said. "I've only been here two months or so, and everyone calls him Boss Dragon. I'm not about to call him something different. He's the last person I want to piss off."

"If Alex is going, then I'm going, too," Anna said, walking up. She turned to me. "I think you could use some backup."

I nodded. I was glad she was coming, and was surprised that she would rather come with me than see Char, whom she had once guarded. The moral support would be good, and to tell the truth, she was much better in a fight than I was.

"There will be absolutely no fighting," Michael said, seemingly reading my thoughts. "Things are tense enough as they are without starting another war. Besides, outsiders are required to leave weapons at the gate."

"That's not acceptable," Makara said.

"No harm will come to either Alex or Anna," Michael said. "What's important here is letting Boss Dragon know what's going on. He can update the rest of the lords on the situation."

"Fine," Makara said. "Both of you go. Samuel, Marcus, and I can hold down the fort here and meet with Char. Just try to get back by tonight."

"Maybe this is a chance for Alex to catch me up on what's going on."

I nodded. Even though Michael was from Bunker 108, where my father researched the xenovirus, the virus itself wasn't common knowledge. Only my father, Chan, and I had known about it in any sort of detail. And Khloe knew some, from what little I told her. To most people, these "Blighters," as they were called, were nothing more than monsters. Soon, all that would change when Michael and others learned about the true cause of the Blighters – the xenovirus.

Hopefully, what we had to tell them would be enough to get everyone to stop their fighting and work together. And not only work together, but join Makara and the New Angels.

We had a long road ahead of us.

***

Michael, Anna, and I approached the Sunset Gate. Two large torches blazed on either side, casting a feeble orange light on the thick wooden doors.

"Are they always on guard duty like that?" I asked.

Michael nodded. "These days, they have to be. The gangs have a pact where each donates the same amount of members to man the walls, so that no one gets too powerful. Attacks from the Blight happen almost every night. Usually, it's just a few crawlers that we can scare off with a few shots. Sometimes, there's more, and you have to worry."

"You must have a lot of ammo."

"We won't be running out for a while. Each gang has its own munitions stocked in its HQ. Any gang that doesn't, won't last long."

"HQs?"

"They're all close to each other, actually. Five of the six gangs are set up in the hotels and casinos along the Strip. Only one, the Reds, live outside city limits. They control most of the outskirts. Horrible place to be these days. The Reds have no walls, but they do have the most people. A lot of people live out there, in the slums. The Reds rule over them."

"Seems like a dangerous place to be," Anna said.

"You have to be a gang member, or good with one of the gangs, to be let inside city limits. If you aren't, you join the Reds and hope they give you a job that's better than slave. They have their own farms, and are seen as a threat by the city gangs. They've been upsetting the normal balance in the last year. Since farm space is so limited, the rest of the gangs work together to grow food out on what's left of Lake Mead."

We made it to the gates. Michael called upward.

"You going to let us in, or what?"

The man on the right-hand turret spoke. "Hold your horses, Sanchez. You're still not cleared with Boss Dragon. You were told to come *alone*."

"Maybe so," Michael said. "But I have two members of the Lost Angels, who will explain why they're here much better than I could."

"If they give up their weapons, then maybe. Let me call HQ."

The man turned his back and talked on his radio. While the guard was talking, I decided to use the opportunity to ask Michael more questions.

"I guess this place has slaves, too?"

Michael nodded. "Unfortunately, yeah. They are kind of a necessity. Without anyone to grow food, no one can survive. I mean, most everyone who doesn't fight has to work the farms, like my wife and kid. But the slaves get the most backbreaking labor."

"And where do you guys grow food? You mentioned Lake Mead, but that looked all dried up by now. Plus, it's really far away."

"A lot of water actually survived in Lake Mead, but not on the surface. We use drills to tap underground reserves. That water is used to grow crops, and a lot of it is transported back to town using trucks."

"Sounds like a lot of trouble," I said.

"It is," Michael said. "Especially these days. The crawlers come out at night, mostly, so there's a constant stream of traffic going back and forth between Mead and Vegas during the day. All supply routes are heavily guarded, as are the farms. By this point, the gangs are so used to it that it's hardly a second thought."

"What about the Great Blight?" I asked. "It can't be too far from the lake."

Michael nodded. "It's getting closer, expanding a few feet every single day. It's already at the western edge of the lakebed, and it's starting to cover the river."

"So, you don't use river water to drink?"

Michael shook his head. "No. I don't touch that stuff. People who drink it get sick, even if they boil it thoroughly."

The turret guard faced us again.

"Leave your weapons here," he said. "You're clear to go in."

Slowly, the gate rolled back, revealing a long stretch of empty highway. In the far distance, skyscrapers rose, shadowy in the darkness. Vegas's days of glitz and glamor were over. Somewhere distant, a crawler screamed in the night, reinforcing that this was now the new reality.

"Best to get inside," Michael said.

When we passed the gates, a guard appeared to my left, holding out his hands for our weapons. With resignation, I gave the guard my Beretta, and Anna gave him her katana and handgun. He cleared his throat. I realized I hadn't yet given him my knife. I handed it over, begrudgingly. I felt a lot less confident without both.

We walked past crumbling buildings, abandoned now for decades. In parking lots, metal shells of cars sat on the ground, stripped of tires and ornament. The rubble wall of Inner Vegas stretched around the city in a wide, haphazard circle. Beyond the highway lay the suburbs. After thirty years, the greater part had been swallowed by the desert. It was amazing what thirty years could do.

We talked little on the way. Michael told me that his wife, Lauren, and their daughter, Callie, were fine – such as fine was, these days. I'd only met Lauren once, a little bit before heading out on my first recon. She was a pretty, blonde woman, but I hadn't spoken to her much. Bunker 108 was small enough that you could know everyone, but large enough that you didn't know everyone well. Lauren definitely fell into that second category. The fact that she had also survived was amazing news. Perhaps I would get the chance to meet Michael's family soon.

Michael gripped his AR-15 tightly. The gun was old, but reliable, and its vast proliferation around the country, Pre-Ragnarok, made finding bullets and replacement parts easy even now. It was a gun I had used a lot for practice in Bunker 108, so I knew it well. It was the gun Samuel wanted me to use.

But it also reminded me too much of Bunker 108. Too much of my old life.

About fifteen minutes later, we turned off the highway onto Russell Road. The Strip was one block over, and the tall buildings rose into the sky, their tops obscured by darkness and dust. When we turned onto the Strip, dust swirled in eddies. On the median, hanging askew, was the sign: *Welcome to Fabulous Las Vegas, Nevada*. A few of the letters were missing; the faded sign was marred by graffiti, time, and dust. The median itself was empty –

the trees that once grew there had long been cut to the ground, leaving vestiges of stumps like wooden graves. On our left was a wide, empty lot, in the middle of which lay the remains of a massive bonfire. On the right rose some newer buildings, towering above like some long-lost, glamorous vision of the future – from back when people dreamed of a future.

We walked on. Michael pointed to a complex of buildings on our left.

"Mandalay Bay," he said. "Once a hotel and casino, now the Sworn HQ."

"Where do the Dragons stay?" I asked.

"The MGM Grand," Michael said. "It's just a few blocks up."

Without daylight, it was hard to see anything. But the buildings rose one after another, in their abstract, eye-catching shapes. It was hard to imagine just how many people there used to be. The wide walk that once bore tens of thousands of tourists was now emptied. As we passed Mandalay Bay, I noticed men with guns hanging out in front of the drive that led to the casino. They watched us pass in the night, ready for anything should we approach.

"The gangs mostly keep to themselves," Michael said. "Especially at night."

"It's dangerous to be out here," Anna said.

Michael nodded. "It is. But it's always dangerous in Vegas. You can't really help that."

We passed an intersection, an enormous parking lot, and mangled signs and traffic lights. On our left was a gigantic pyramid, unseen at first because it was black.

"The Luxor," Michael said. "The home of the Suns."

In the next five minutes, we passed several more casinos. Michael said nothing about them. I had thought Vegas would be more like...well, a city. Nova Roma had been a city. Vegas was more like a series of fortresses. We passed castle after castle, each the home of a different lord, his soldiers guarding the gates against constant attack.

And maybe that's what it was. As I walked down the abandoned strip, as the wind carried with it the dust of decay, I realized I was in a wilderness more than a city.

This impression of lords and castles solidified when we *did* pass a castle of sorts – the Excalibur Hotel Casino.

"The Kings' lair," Michael said. "We don't much like them. It's too bad that we're neighbors."

"Why don't you like them?"

"Their Boss, Rey, is trying to make a play for controlling the rest of the gangs. The Kings tie up all the trade, and they get more batts than any of the other gangs – Reds included. Rey is a businessman more than a gangster, but he's not afraid to get his hands dirty if he needs to."

Finally, on our right at the northeast corner of the intersection, was the MGM Grand – the Dragons' HQ. I felt the Dragons would have done well to name themselves the Lions. A wide, empty fountain stood in front of the massive building. In the fountain, a golden lion stood. Torches lined the circular walk around the fountain, leading to the front entrance. There, a couple of guards stood, talking softly. They looked at us as we walked alongside the fountain, to the building's front.

We paused before the doorway.

"Boss is inside," one of the guards said, a tall, muscled black man. He looked at Anna and me. "Which of you is Makara?"

"She isn't here," Michael said. "She's meeting with the Raiders. These are her representatives, Alex and Anna."

The Dragon raised an eyebrow. "The Boss won't like this, Michael."

"The Boss can wait until tomorrow, James."

The other Dragon stepped up, small of frame and white. "You better watch where your loyalties lie, Sanchez."

"Relax, Daniel," Michael said. "The Angels just got here an hour ago, and it's already night. What did the Boss expect?"

James eyed Michael hard. "To have his orders followed to the letter."

"I heard nothing about bringing Makara," Michael said. "It was originally supposed to be just me."

"Well, even if the one called Makara is not here," James said, "we will lead you in. Good luck explaining it to the Boss."

"Wait," Daniel said.

He stared off into the darkness, onto the boulevard from which we had come. Someone was walking around the fountain, obviously having followed us.

"Who goes there?" James shouted. "Reveal yourself!"

The man did not stop, or even slow. In fact, he broke into a dead run. A horrible wail pierced the night air, making my skin crawl.

"Howler!" Daniel said.

I reached for where my Beretta was usually holstered. Finding the holster empty, I cursed, and backed away through the doors of the MGM. James and Daniel stood in front, blocking the way into the building.

The Howler appeared from the darkness, his clothing ragged and mouth agape. Purple slime coated his entire body. He had a hole where his left cheek should have been, revealing a gray, lifeless tongue and gums. The completely white eyes burned, almost glowed, in the night. The Howler careened forward, arms outstretched.

James fired his rifle, nailing the Howler twice in the shoulder. The monster screamed in pain, but didn't slow. Michael raised his AR-15, firing a few shots. One of the bullets connected with the Howler's head, sending the thing crashing to the ground.

The body, now grounded, quivered and convulsed. The skin bloated and stretched, threatening to pop.

"Inside, now!" I yelled.

Everyone rushed inside the building, through sliding glass doors that already stood halfway open. Anna, Michael, and I were closer, and made it inside easily. James dove, his hulking mass shooting past me as he rolled into the hotel lobby. Daniel ran, but not fast enough. The Howler exploded, sending globs of purple goo sailing through the air. Daniel was caught in the torrential downpour of virus-infected sludge.

Daniel stared at us all. His eyes were wide, horrified.

Then he turned to run.

Recovering, James scrambled up, aiming his rifle into the darkness. He fired.

Daniel fell to the ground.

James panted, looking out into the night where his compatriot now lay dead. He turned back to us, his hardened face like stone.

"Go inside. Boss Dragon is waiting."

"Howlers are in the city!" I said. "Aren't you going to do something?"

James shook his head. "Howlers have always been in the city. Their numbers have grown, and they roam the city at night. I have never seen one on the Strip, though." He sighed. "It isn't a good sign."

Michael placed a hand on my shoulder, causing me to jump.

"Come on," he said.

We turned from the grisly scene, and walked into the darkness of the MGM Grand.

Chapter 7

Anna grabbed my hand, holding it tightly, as we followed James and Michael past the doors.

"You alright?" I asked.

"I'm more worried about you."

"I'm fine," I said. "I just thought this place was safe for some reason."

We followed the line of marble on the floor, between long-defunct slot machines, emptied cafés, and stained card tables. The screens of some of the machines were riddled with bullets.

"Nowhere is safe," Anna said.

I felt a chill pass over me as we went deeper into the darkness of Dragon HQ, lit feebly with lines of torches. I was beginning to regret our decision to come here. If it weren't for Michael, I would have walked out of this place in a heartbeat.

On our right was a series of large glass windows, through which I could see rocks and fake trees. A sign above the windows read "Lion Exhibit." I peered into the darkness of the habitat, but the lions, if there ever had been any, were either long gone or long dead.

"So, all the Dragons live in here?" I asked, as we passed a bank of elevators.

"Most Dragons do. The Boss lives in a villa on the premises. But with recent events he is staying somewhere that is more secure."

"Recent events?" Anna asked.

"The Kings tried to nab him a few weeks ago. Since then, he's insisted on staying in his penthouse."

"Doesn't it irk you to have to call him Boss all the time?" Anna asked.

Michael shrugged. "Not really. I've had a boss in one form or another all my life. I could have done much worse than the Dragons. I'm glad I came across them first, rather than the Kings or the Reds."

"What's so bad about the Reds?" I asked.

"The Reds are bad because they live outside city limits. It was actually a good thing for them at first, because being so distant made them safer from attacks. Now, though, they're an easy target for Blighters."

We stopped before the open doors of what used to be a fancy restaurant. Within the dark interior, torches burned from the walls, and a line of candles lit a table where a muscled black man in dark clothing sat. His face was hidden by shadow, but his forearms, in the light of the fire, were visible. On each one was a tattoo of a dragon, one light blue, breathing ice, the other red, breathing fire. They both seemed to glow in the darkness.

The hands raised, gesturing to nearby seats. "Sit."

Michael led us inside the restaurant, and we sat. Closer, we could more easily see the Boss's facial features. He was a big man, maybe in his late thirties. He wore all black – black pants, black shirt – which, coupled with his dark skin, made him blend in with the shadows.

"You Makara?" he asked Anna.

Michael answered for her. "She is meeting with Char and the Raiders. I brought two of their high-ranking members here to represent her."

"High-ranking?" The Boss gave a sideways grin. "What is this, *Lord of the Flies* with spaceships?"

I had to smile at that, even if it was an insult.

"She's about our age, yeah," I said. "We're not kids, though."

Boss Dragon snickered. "Yeah, alright. Of course you're not. The question is, why should I listen to you?"

Before I could answer and get us into any trouble, I felt Michael kick me under the table. "Actually, Boss, the New Angels were hoping to have the opportunity to meet with you, as well as with the rest of the gangs."

Boss Dragon eyed Michael skeptically "What kind of business would we have to discuss? If it's protection, that's already been decided. We're not letting anyone in until this Blight mess is over."

"Then no one is getting in," Anna said. "The Blight mess won't be over until Vegas is gone. Makara wants a meeting to decide what to do about that. And she has a plan to stop it."

Boss Dragon looked at her. "I don't care if it's about tea and crumpets. The gangs won't meet for any reason. Too much blood, and not enough water. No one will meet unless safety is guaranteed."

"We aren't going to try anything," I said. "We can meet somewhere that's open, so that there's no chance of an ambush."

"We could use the runway," Michael said.

Boss Dragon looked at Michael, as if wondering whose side he was on. "You said Makara has a plan. What is it?"

"We figured out how to stop the xenovirus," I said. "The xenovirus is what controls all the Blighters. And..." Anna looked at me, and I realized I probably shouldn't reveal too much, too soon. "Makara can explain the rest at the meeting. But one thing you should know is that the xenovirus and the Great Blight are a lot more powerful than you think. First it was Raider Bluff. Next, it will be Vegas."

Boss Dragon's eyes appeared troubled. After sitting in silence for at least a full minute, the candles on the table burning on, he looked at Anna and me in turn.

"I'll arrange a meeting. By tomorrow, every gang lord will know that Makara will be parlaying on the runways."

"We can let her know tonight," I said.

"Actually, you both will be staying here tonight," Boss Dragon said.

"I'm not staying here any longer than I have to," I said.

"I'm not taking you hostage," Boss Dragon said. "It's too dangerous to be out on the streets this late. I would be remiss to allow it."

"Staying is a good idea," Michael said. "Especially if Howlers are out."

I didn't like it, but I decided to trust Michael's judgment.

"Until tomorrow, then." Boss Dragon looked at Michael. "Escort them to some of our guest rooms. You are to stay with the Angels until the meeting is over. Keep me updated."

Michael gave a slow nod, and just like that, the meeting was over. We got up from our chairs and followed Michael out of the restaurant, toward the bank of elevators we had passed earlier.

"At least he agreed to set something up," I said. "We got what we wanted."

It was hard to tell if Boss Dragon was friend or foe, but for a gang lord, he didn't seem that bad. Michael led us up some stairs, taking us to the third floor. The interior was dirty, smelling of dirt and must. I guess that's what happened when a carpet hadn't been properly cleaned in over thirty years. The doors – at least most of them – were still intact.

Michael led us to the end of the hall, opening a door on our left.

"You can stay here," he said. "I'll come back for you in the morning."

Makara was going to be wondering where we were tonight. "Is there any way you can give Makara word about where we are?"

"Give me the right channel, and I can try contacting *Odin*."

I gave him the channel, and he brought the radio to his mouth.

"*Odin*, you have a copy?"

He waited ten seconds or so, before trying again.

"*Odin*, do you have a copy?"

"They must be off the ship," Anna said. "You can try again later."

"I'll try to let her know what's going on by tonight. As far as you guys stand, you have nothing to be afraid of. The Boss sees you as messengers, and he won't do anything to provoke Makara. Stay here until morning. We'll meet by the fountain. You can catch me up on everything then."

Michael reached out a hand. I shook it.

"Alex. It's good to see you alive. Try to stay that way."

He nodded to Anna, and walked down the hall.

We went inside the dark hotel room, and locked the door behind us.

Chapter 8

The next morning, Anna and I sat on the edge of the empty fountain out front while Michael went to find breakfast. He came back a few minutes later with some corn bars and water.

"Sorry for the small portions," he said. "We're being careful about food around here with the Blighters around; our supply could be cut off at any time."

"When is this meeting supposed to happen, specifically?" Anna asked, taking a big bite of her bar.

"Not sure, yet," Michael said. "Probably sometime this afternoon. I'll have my radio on me, so Boss Dragon will let me know the details when he arranges something." Michael turned to me. "Now that we have some time, maybe you can catch me up on everything that has happened. How'd you get out of Bunker 108?"

So I told him – the whole thing. I started with the fall of Bunker 108, and getting out with Khloe. That all seemed so long ago. The memories were distant, but all the same, the cold fear of that night was still there, along with the pain of losing Khloe and my father.

"Me and my family must have gotten out just before you," Michael said. "We headed for the motor pool and took one of the Recons."

"Smart," I said.

"It was one of the Recons that was already prepped with some supplies, so we were able to set out into the dust storm. We didn't make it far that first night. I only went far enough to feel safe before parking near the mountain."

"How'd you end up here?"

"I knew L.A. was bad, because of the Reapers, so I set off for Vegas from the start. On our way we ran into raiders and Blighters. We ran out of juice halfway, not able to find water to fuel the vehicle. We ditched the Recon and walked the rest of the way, making it to the Vegas outskirts a week after leaving Bunker 108. There, a Dragon patrol found us. Before they could do anything, they were ambushed by some Reds. I helped fight them off, and the Dragons right then and there led us into the city. They gave us food and water, and then I met Boss Dragon himself. He asked me to join up with him. So I did. Since then, my wife, daughter, and I are all staying here."

"Where are they now?" I asked.

"Everyone works in Vegas," Michael said. "They're out in the fields, on the lake. I don't want them to be out there, but there's little choice. Anyone who can't fight, works. I see them at night, though, when they come home."

I picked up the story where I'd left off. I had to tell him about Makara first.

"Do you remember when you were with me on my first recon, and we came across the man from Bunker 114?"

Michael nodded, his brown eyes haunted. "How could I forget? That's what started it all."

"Well, at Bunker 114, they were studying the xenovirus. One of their test subjects escaped, infecting the first person it encountered. The xenovirus just...spread. That person we found – he had escaped from Bunker 114, and was coming to 108 for help, or to warn us. I still have no idea why Chan let him in that night."

"So, what is the xenovirus?" Michael said. "I know from what you've said so far that it causes the Blighters."

"It's an alien virus that was buried in Ragnarok. It spreads the xenofungus. And now, it infects humans, turning them into Howlers. It created the xenodragons you now see flying around."

"How do you know all this?" Michael asked.

"Makara, Samuel, Anna, and me...we've been through a lot. After Khloe died, I wandered the Wasteland for about a week before running into Makara. There's something I need to admit – I saw her there, Michael. When we found that man, I saw her watching in the distance from behind a rock, but I didn't say anything."

Michael hesitated a moment, then finally understood what I was saying. "Why did you stay quiet?"

I shook my head. "I don't know. Something kept me. I guess it was the shock more than anything. Makara ended up hiding again, and it was only later that I learned that she, or at least some of the raiders she was with, killed that man. Makara said they found him on the road, and that he was sick at the time."

Michael's expression darkened. "If she hadn't had done that..." He looked at me. "If you had just said something..."

"I've thought about it a lot since then," I said. "I'm not sure if anything could have been prevented. I think CSO Chan might have been expecting that guy from 114. He sure let him in quickly enough."

"I don't know about that," Michael said. "I mean, wouldn't Chan have said something to us? He probably would have said something to me, the senior patrol leader. I knew nothing about a visitor from Bunker 114."

"Maybe not, then," I said. "Whatever the case, I feel like the CSO knew something we didn't. He might have known what happened at Bunker 114 even before we did."

"So, it really is gone?"

I nodded. "Yeah. There's nothing left. We've tried contacting other Bunkers, but nothing."

Michael was quiet for a moment. "I was hoping for some good news, there. I was hoping that me and my family could leave here, one day, and find another Bunker, somewhere. I guess that won't happen now."

"Whatever happened," I said, "Chan allowed that man inside Bunker 108. Maybe he saw it as a way to increase our understanding of the xenovirus. I didn't see that at the time, but looking back, I think that might be why he let him in. He wanted news of Bunker 114's fall. Both my father and Chan had no idea what would happen that night."

"And the rest is history." Michael shook his head. "It's amazing we survived. Without my family, I don't think I could have found the will to carry on."

"I was the same way, until I met Makara. Long story short, we ended up in Bunker 114 not too long after, when Makara learned that her brother, Samuel, had gone there to investigate its fall. He led a team out of Oasis, and all of them ended up dying except for him. Well, we got into the Bunker, and discovered something in its digital archive called the Black Files."

"The Black Files?"

I nodded. "It's just as bad as it sounds. The Black Files hinted at what the origins of the xenovirus were. And if we knew the origins, we might be able to find a way to stop it. But the Black Files weren't in Bunker 114."

"Where were they?" Michael asked.

"Bunker One."

"And you *went* there?"

"Yes, but it wasn't easy."

Michael smiled. "Damn, it seems like you've seen more fighting in your first week out of 108 than I've seen in my life."

"I'm surprised I'm still alive," I said. "But we discovered the Black Files in Bunker One, in Cheyenne Mountain."

"You just flat out *went* across the Great Blight?"

"Yeah," I said. "We had no idea what we were in for."

Michael shook his head again, eyes wide. "You've got brass balls, buddy."

"Well, it was Samuel's idea," I said. "I wanted to just hole up in Oasis, to be honest."

"So you crossed the Great Blight and found the Black Files. What happened after that?"

"Well, between all that I met Anna. She was Char's personal bodyguard in Raider Bluff, and she agreed to guide us to the Great Blight. She ended up keeping her path crossed with ours. Now she's here, helping us."

"Anna," Michael said, "all I have to say is, I'm sorry you met this guy."

Anna smiled. "Yeah, well, I've decided to just roll with it at this point."

"She's an expert katana user," I said. "Just wait until you hear about our vacation to Mexico."

"Interesting choice of word there," Anna said.

"I'll fill in the details later," I said, "but yeah, we made it to Bunker One, found the Black Files, and learned about the xenovirus. If no one stops it, the xenovirus will take over the world. So now, it's kind of our crazy mission to stop it. What's worse, there is this alien consciousness, located in Ragnarok Crater, called the Voice. We don't know exactly *where* it comes from, but it seems to be directing all xenolife."

"Well," Michael said, pointing westward, "I don't need any Black Files to tell me the world is being taken over. I see it every day."

"Marcus said the exact same thing."

"So, where does the spaceship come in?"

"About now, actually. After we discovered the Black Files, the Voice recognized that we were there, and sent an entire swarm after us. We managed to make it to Bunker One's runway alive, but we were completely surrounded. We were about to die, when out of nowhere, a spaceship came down from the sky, extending a ladder for us to board."

"Alright, *that's* a little bit unbelievable..." Michael said.

"Well, it'll make sense in a second. I'm leaving out a lot of details, but the spaceship turned out to be piloted by a man named Dr. Cornelius Ashton – the very author of the Black Files we had found. He had contacted us in the lab beforehand about getting to the runway. Anyway, we got into the spaceship, escaping the snapping jaws of death. Soon, we found ourselves living in a space city called Skyhome."

"Skyhome?"

"The U.S. Government constructed it during the Dark Decade," I said. "It was top secret, and intended as a backup for the President in case things on Earth went to hell. Which they did, but President Garland couldn't escape Bunker One in time. However, Dr. Cornelius Ashton did, back in 2048. He has lived there with a community of Bunker survivors since then, continuing his research on the xenovirus – such as he can."

"So, you've been in fallen Bunkers, the Great Blight, outer space...and then, Mexico?"

"That happened after. We were attempting to negotiate peace between Raider Bluff and Nova Roma. We had to meet Emperor Augustus to do that. But that didn't work out. Mixed in with all that were slavers, gladiatorial matches, and finally, the dragons."

"Holy shit," Michael said. "You are seriously a badass among badasses. You're not that same sixteen-year-old kid I took on his first stroll in the Wasteland."

"I've changed a lot," I said. "But all of what I told you leads up to why we're here in the first place. Augustus is moving out with his army to conquer the Wasteland. The bulk of it won't get here for a while, but there's a good chance that the faster part will – the part that has vehicles and horses. Ashton has his own spaceship, called the *Gilgamesh*. He has his own errands to run right now, otherwise you'd have met him. But Ashton keeps us up to date on Augustus's movements."

"So, that's why you're recruiting?" Michael asked. "To stop Augustus?"

I nodded. "We won't stand a chance against him unless we are united. Adding to the complexity is the fact that Carin Black is on his side."

"The Black Reapers are allied with the Empire?" Michael asked.

"As far as we know. Augustus led us to believe as much, so that is the current thought process. We hope to have all the Vegas gangs behind us, at which point we'll pick up anyone else willing to help along the way."

"Along the way? Along the way to *where*?"

"To Los Angeles."

Michael whistled. "That's a little ambitious."

"It has to be done," I said. "We need to take out Black before the Empire arrives. Together, they will be unstoppable. And if we free the L.A. slaves, we'll have a much larger army for it."

Michael didn't say anything for a while. I had given him a lot of information, and it would take time for him to make complete sense of it. Indeed, I had left a lot of information *out*, but I felt that I had given him enough to go on – at least, for now.

"I will do whatever I can to help you," Michael said. "But it won't be easy. If everything you say is true, then we need to get Makara to that meeting."

"We should go, then," Anna said.

We got up from the fountain, and walked away from the MGM Grand. Now lit, albeit dully, the ruin of the city was all more apparent. Las Vegas Boulevard was empty – we were the only three walking along it, though it was midmorning. It was something to be thankful for. For now, the gangsters were in their fortresses, which meant we could walk unimpeded down the dusty Strip. The hotels and casinos fell behind us, empty, forlorn, abandoned, layered with grime and dirt.

A massive, faded advertisement spread above the Strip itself, covering an enclosed bridge over the street between two of the newer casinos. It showed a man and woman wearing IUI glasses. IUI, shorthand for Immersive User Interface, had become increasingly prevalent beginning in the late 2010's. Such technology of the past was amazing to think about – glasses that displayed information, in real time, about whatever object the user happened to be looking at. Such power seemed unreal. If I found a pair of those glasses today, even if they hadn't been stripped of the batts, they would be useless. There were no more wireless networks to feed that information, no more information clouds to store all human knowledge. The only clouds now were the ones above, angry and red and perpetually blanketing the cold, bare Earth. If Ragnarok hadn't come, who knows that kind of world I might have been born into?

"You seem contemplative," Anna said.

"Just thinking about how much we've lost."

She nodded, pointing to the sign above. "I'd be caught dead before wearing a pair of those."

"Come on. You have to admit they *are* kind of cool."

"Whoever heard of a Google, anyway?" Anna asked. "These Old Worlders were very strange." She looked at me and smiled. "I'd rather look someone in the eye and judge that person for myself, rather than have some machine decide for me."

Anna did have a point. We walked further down the Strip, still empty of potential threats. I turned to Michael.

"So, when are you going to join with the New Angels?"

I had meant it somewhat jokingly, but Michael took the question seriously.

"I don't know. I would like to, but my allegiance is with the Dragons. They gave me a home and protection, and it's because of them that I'm alive. That doesn't mean I can't help you guys out, though."

I didn't see how Michael could be okay with working for a man who was known for violence, even if that man was more reasonable than I had expected him to be. I wanted Michael to realize that his place was with us. Then again, this was part of who Michael was. He was a soldier, and a good one. He was used to following orders, and was perfectly content with that. Such dedication, such simplicity in his way of looking at the world, was enviable. That dedication and loyalty to the cause was why Chan had appointed him an officer.

If Makara proved herself a better leader than Boss Dragon, then maybe Michael would join us.

"There is one thing I can let you know, though."

"What's that?"

"It's not much, but I can show you where I left that Recon."

"Yeah," I said, smiling. "That's not much at all."

Chapter 9

After getting our weapons back, we exited the Sunset Gate, walking up the slope of the overpass to where *Odin* had landed. The Exiles' bikes were lined up against the left-hand guardrail, and at the end of the line, I saw Marcus tinkering with his own bike's motor.

"What are you doing?" I asked.

"Replacing the hydrogen fuel line," he said.

I looked down at the motor, noticing there was a miniaturized pressure tank filled with several gallons of water.

"Do all the bikes run on hydrogen?" I asked.

Marcus nodded. "Conventional gasoline has a short shelf life, and is hard to come by. That's why any vehicle worth anything burns hydrogen." Marcus tapped the bike. "Pearl has been with me ten years now."

"Pearl?" Anna asked, a smile on her lips.

"That's her name," Marcus said, proudly. "But I got to get rolling. Me and some of the boys are doing some recon."

I wondered at the need of a recon at this point. It could have been just as simple as Marcus needing something to do. Or, more likely, he needed the excuse to get away from his brother.

"Good luck," I said.

"How did things go in town?" Marcus asked, mounting his bike.

I shrugged. "I got attacked by a Howler, but at least Boss Dragon agreed to set up a meeting. I guess it could have gone worse."

Marcus chuckled. "Guess so."

"We're meeting, probably, this afternoon," I said. "You might want to get back before that."

Marcus stared off into the distance, his sunglasses obscuring his eyes. "I'll try, but we haven't done any recon on the west side, yet. If the Reds are in town at that time, then it might be our chance to find something out."

"Be careful," Anna said.

Marcus started the engine with a roar, the high thrumming of the hydrogen tank sounding strange and otherworldly against the deeper sound. "Keep your wits about you, Alex."

Before Marcus kicked off, Anna spoke. "Is Char on the *Odin?*"

Marcus didn't answer, either because he didn't hear or because he didn't want to. Instead, he swerved his bike around, bringing up a cloud of dust, and headed down the overpass. Upon seeing their leader leave, six more Exiles rushed to their bikes, started them up, and left us in their dust.

"Well, there's our answer," I said.

Anna, realizing that Char had arrived, ran to the ship.

I turned to Michael. "She hasn't seen Char in several months."

"Neither have you, for that matter."

I shrugged. "I was only with the guy a couple days. I don't know him like Anna or Makara do."

We entered the ship, finding Makara and Samuel sitting with Char in the galley. Char turned, his cold blue eyes surveying us and not missing a detail. When his eyes fell on Anna, he smiled. The combination of that smile with the marred face was uncanny. It reminded me too much of a Howler.

"Anna," he said, his voice gravelly.

He stood, and Anna went to hug him.

"You seem well," he said.

"I'm glad you're alright."

Char chuckled. "It takes a lot to kill me, kid. Those Blighters will get what's coming to them, once we're done here."

Char stepped back from the embrace, turning to face me.

I reached out a hand. Char took it firmly.

"Good to see you alive, Alex."

I nodded. "Same for you."

The Alpha turned his eye on Michael.

"This is Michael Sanchez," I said. "We knew each other in Bunker 108. He was an Officer."

"An honor, sir," Michael said, reaching out a hand.

Char took it. "It is good to meet you, Michael. The New Angels are always in need of strong warriors."

"You joined up that quickly?" I asked.

"I am not as mercenary as my brother," Char said. "My people and I have nothing, but if we join the New Angels, we have a chance to get it all back. Besides, this Blight business needs to be taken care of. If we don't work to stop it, we'll all be out of a home, soon, and not just the Raiders."

"I'm glad to see you still alive," Makara said to Anna and me. "What did you find out?"

"Boss Dragon is organizing a summit of all the gang lords for this afternoon," I said. "It's the perfect chance for you to explain everything."

"Also, there are Howlers in the city," Anna said. "It doesn't seem like they're many, but one of them attacked us at the MGM Grand. All the gangs, apart from one, stay inside the walls, using the old casinos as fortresses. The only time they come out is for food and water – both of which are located on the lakebed."

"The Exiles reconnoitered that area earlier this morning," Samuel said. "There's another town over there, complete with a wall and everything. The water trucks were already running at that time."

"I say we go right for the jugular," Char said. "Take their water, and they'll come to heel."

"I want loyalty," Makara said. "Going after their water is a good way to set them against us. I need an army to conquer Los Angeles. If all goes according to plan, we'll get everyone out of here and leave the city for the crawlers."

"You have your work cut out for you," Char said. "Those gangs aren't moving. Not unless you give them a reason to."

"I plan on laying out my reasons." Makara looked at Anna. "Where do they want to meet?"

"The runways, from what Michael told us," Anna said. "The Dragons are going to meet us inside the gate sometime this afternoon, and then they'll take us to the airport."

From the look in Makara's eyes, I could tell she didn't like that.

"You'll be fine," Michael said. "Boss Dragon will be as good as his word in protecting you."

"I want my own men having my back," Makara said.

"They'll be fine with you bringing a few," Michael said. "They just don't want an entire army coming inside the walls."

"That means all of us will be with you," I said. "Marcus, too, if he's back on time."

"I wouldn't count on it," Char said. "He's still being a baby."

No one said anything to that. Makara probably hadn't spoken to Char about what we had learned from Marcus.

"Of course," Char went on, "we might find out the gangs would rather side with the Emperor. If that's the case, then we'll have to strike first."

That was something I hadn't yet considered. If the Black Reapers sided with Augustus, who was to say other gangs wouldn't as well? What Char said made sense. The gangs here had no reason to help us over Augustus. They were still trying to figure out what *our* motives were.

"Makara is right," I said. "They at least have to know why we're here, as soon as possible. If we can figure out the thought and motivations behind each of the gangs, that would go a long way."

"I like how you're thinking," Char said. "What do we know about them so far?"

"We have our source right here," I said, gesturing to Michael.

"Alex is right, in part," Michael said. "It will take explaining the situation with the Great Blight, the Voice, the virus...everything. None of the leaders are dumb, but it might help to condense that as much as possible. There are some gangs, like the Kings and the Suns, that probably won't listen, no matter what you tell them. They see themselves as too powerful, and they are used to calling the shots. Even so, it is a matter of the truth. Everyone already knows that it's only a question of time before the Great Blight finally tries to end this place. Raider Bluff is on everyone's minds here. Hopefully, you guys will be what finally gets them to move. Leaving the city might become the only viable option for them."

"Alright," Makara said. "We can use the threat of the Great Blight to remind them why it's important to work together. What else?"

"For the gangs that don't want to help, we can use a rougher hand," Char said. "Make an example out of them."

"How do we do that?" Samuel asked. "I don't want us to kill anyone needlessly, or do anything that leads to more violence."

"I can meet with those leaders one on one," Makara said. "You said the Suns and the Kings would give me the most trouble."

Michael nodded. "They are the two most powerful gangs in the city, along with the Dragons. Without at least two, you won't get anything done."

"So, we need to go after them," Makara said. "What are their leaders' names?"

"Grudge leads the Suns, and Rey leads the Kings," Michael said. "Grudge looks calm on the outside, but he can barely suppress the crazy. He's been known to kill men for no reason. He's wild and unpredictable. It's hard to imagine anyone being able to work with him. He's too power-hungry. If there's ever a war, it's very likely that Grudge would be the one who starts it."

"What about Rey?" Samuel asked.

"Rey is Grudge's complete opposite," Michael said. "In a way, he's more dangerous. He is calm, a natural businessman, and he is brutal when he doesn't get his way. He keeps a distant hand on things, letting his cronies do his dirty work. For all appearances, it looks like he plays nice. But he doesn't. He just plays the game well."

"And Boss Dragon?" Makara asked.

"Boss Dragon will be the easiest to work with of the bunch," Michael said. "He's tough, but he'll probably be the most willing to listen. I think if you met with him personally, then he would be interested in what you have to tell him. And the others – there is Cain, leader of the Sworn, a tough guy that commands respect of his followers, and then there's Jade, leader of the Diamonds. He's called 'the Weasel,' and you will see why. He wears that name like a badge of honor. He is slimy and amoral, and for those two reasons, he's dangerous."

"What do these gang leaders want?" Makara asked. "What can we say to get them to go with us to L.A.?"

"The Dragons, the Suns, and the Kings all want eventual control of Vegas, but they are using different routes to get there. The Dragons are weaker than the Suns or Kings, so they present a weak face and are just looking for the right opportunity to strike. The Suns use violence and terror to get ahead. The Kings like to play it cool and make batts, and can often use their money to get other gangs to help them."

"What about the other gangs?" Makara asked.

"We don't have time to be playing politics," Samuel said. "We need to get in there, say our piece, and hope this can get done the easy way. If not, we play Char's ace. We go after the farms and free the slaves."

"We win either way," Char said. "They care about their food, their water, and their slaves. And all of them are just a few minutes' drive away. We're not strong enough to take on one, or any, of the gangs directly. But if we go after the farms, we have a chance. If we offer those slaves freedom and put guns in their hands, that's army enough for me. Then we get the hell out of Dodge, and do the same to any other city we come across."

"That's part of the vision of the New Angels, anyway," I said. "Makara, you said the Lost Angels took control of L.A. back in the day because they offered freedom to slaves."

"My only reservation is, slaves are not fighters," Makara said. "Gangsters are. We can free the slaves, but training them up will take time. Time is something we don't have much of. Besides, who knows how well slaves would hold up in a fight?"

"I'll make fighters out of them," Char said. "I think you're sure of getting at least some recruits if you go straight for the farms. And if you need someone to train them..." Char chuckled. "I'm your man for that."

"How many slaves are there, anyway?" I asked.

"Marcus said two, maybe three thousand," Samuel said.

I nodded. "That sounds like a good number to me. That far outnumbers any of the gangs. Maybe all of them."

"It does," Michael said. "But I liked Makara's idea of trying to get the gang leaders to work together. Combined with Char's idea, it might be our way of gaining power in Vegas. If they at least know *why* we have come, then it won't seem like we are attacking those farms for no reason."

"I'm afraid all this might bite us in the butt," I said. "What if going after those farms gets them to work against us?"

"There's that risk," Char said, "but we're running low on options. It's go big or go home, kid. We need them to take us as a serious threat. And if we sit on our laurels too long, they'll realize that those farms are in danger. We need to move before they do.

Soon, they'll likely be arguing on which gangs get guard duty."

"That's how they've done it so far," Michael said. "No one gang ever gets control of the farms. They all send an equal number to watch over them; that way none of them gets the upper hand. It's the same with the walls and gates."

"How many guards are there in total?" I asked.

"Two, three hundred maybe," Michael said.

"That's more than I would have thought," Makara said. "But we have *Odin*, and *Gilgamesh* on retainer. That counts for a lot."

"There are a lot of slaves there," Michael said. "And not just slaves, but normal workers, like my wife and kid. The only difference between them and the slaves is that they get a ride back home at night. This is why I want to caution against such an attack. There will be casualties. Any time we kill, we're making all of us weaker, and the Blighters stronger." Michael shook his head. "Violence should always be the last option. That said, the slaves might rise up against the gangs. They're getting scared of the Blighters. They've gotten hit harder than Vegas because they're closer to the Great Blight. If offered a way out, they'd probably take it."

"That's all the convincing I need," Samuel said.

"Alright, then," Makara said. "We all need to be ready to head inside. Michael, when you find out what time, let us know."

Everyone nodded, satisfied at the consensus we had reached. What had once been just four was quickly growing into a full-fledged army. Two hundred strong – and maybe by the end of the day, we would be *two thousand* strong.

Despite what Michael had said about us not needing to worry, I felt going inside was as dangerous a plan as any we had concocted. It could be that this was all just a conspiracy for the gangs to take us all out in a pinch. We had to trust they were just as afraid of the Blight as we were.

Only, I didn't know how sure of a bet that was.

Chapter 10

A few minutes later, we were standing in front of the Sunset Gate. The tower guard went for his radio, letting Boss Dragon know we were on our way. Everyone in Vegas would soon know Makara was in town. They would know that the Angels were back.

"You're clear," the guard called down.

Slowly, the large wooden gates rolled open, sending up a thin veil of dust. The highway, twisted buildings, and rubble of the inner city were revealed, the towers and hotels on the Vegas Strip in plain view in the daylight. As we walked past the gates, the tower guard watched warily. He didn't ask for our weapons this time, for which I was grateful. Maybe he had been given specific orders *not* to ask for them, or maybe the scowl on Makara's face told him that asking was a bad idea. Either way, we walked forward along the deserted, dusty highway. In my hands I held my AR-15, per Samuel's instructions. If he wanted me to get back into the swing of using this weapon, I decided now was as good a time as any to start.

Using the rifle would take something of an adjustment, but I decided that Samuel, in the end, was right. There were situations where the rifle would be a better fit than my Beretta. It could shoot at long range, and thirty rounds per magazine meant I wouldn't have to reload as often. It also had the ability to go fully automatic. My Beretta definitely didn't give me that advantage. Still, I didn't want to use it. Pointing at Blighters was one thing. Pointing at human beings was another.

I slung the rifle over my right shoulder by the strap, and felt my Beretta holstered on my right side. With my combat knife on my left hip as well, I felt positively dangerous. I took a swig of cold water from my canteen, the taste metallic. The air had a nip to it, but it felt good. I wore enough layers to be protected from the harsh, dry wind.

My thoughts scattered when a group of six, toting guns, walked onto the highway from an on-ramp. We paused in our tracks. It was probably Boss Dragon and his escort, but it paid to be careful.

The lead man held up a hand in greeting.

"It's them," Michael said.

Makara stepped ahead, her hand not far from her gun. She wasn't taking chances, either.

"Let's go."

We walked forward, until we were about fifteen feet from the men. I recognized one of them as James, the man who had been guarding the MGM's front yesterday.

"The Boss is waiting on the runway," he said.

"Lead, and we'll follow," Makara said.

We walked in silence down the off-ramp to the street below, the remains of Mandalay Bay passing on our left. We crossed the beginnings of Las Vegas Boulevard and passed the marred "Welcome to Vegas" sign. On the other side of the Strip, we went around a decrepit wedding chapel.

I was beginning to wonder when we were going to come upon the airport, when we were there. Across a mangled fence lay a vast sea of gray tarmac, extending for what seemed miles. The red, faded light of the sky cast a crimson hue on the vast, open space. In the distance rose the airport itself, long and low on the horizon. Boarding tunnels jutted out from the complex, connecting only with empty air. A few tunnels, however, had planes next to them, abandoned now for decades.

REVELATION

We crawled through the fence where someone, long ago, had cut a hole for ease of access. We walked on, past desert ground and wispy, dead grass. We came across a row of hangars, their wide-open doors revealing planes gutted for parts. The hangars were like mechanical crypts, the planes dead things that would never fly again. The Vegas gangs had clearly already tried to get any part or tool that would be useful from these machines.

We walked on quietly, entering the vast open area of the runways. Red sand covered most of the gray tarmac, though the tarmac still showed through in places along with peeling yellow paint. It wouldn't be long before the desert totally buried the runways. It was eerily silent. The wind blew, carrying, always, the dust. The dust was a symbol of the disintegration, the burying. We now walked on the surface of an alien world, a world in which life was but a distant memory, a colorful dream that had only existed in imagination and not in truth. I could hardly imagine planes zooming down these runways, taking off, landing, in controlled chaos. And all that had just been thirty years ago. It felt like thirty centuries. After the lushness of the Empire, the absence of life in the Wasteland was a rude awakening.

Then, from beside one of the boarding tunnels, a vehicle made its way toward us, startling me from my thoughts. The vehicle glimmered in the dull, mid-afternoon light.

"That's him," James said. "Hold up here."

We stopped, waiting for Boss Dragon to arrive. As he approached, I had a bad feeling about this meeting. Even with the Dragons protecting us, the other gangs would probably outnumber us two to one. If anything went wrong, they could easily kill us. This rotting city was gangland turf, and as long as we were in it, we had to play by their rules.

As the vehicle's shape grew, I saw that it was a Recon – not the military grade, but more of a civilian knockoff. The main difference was that it didn't have a turret. We didn't have anything to fear from the vehicle itself, at least.

When it got close, the vehicle wheeled to the right, coming to a sudden stop about thirty feet away. The tinted windows made it impossible to see inside. The driver left the vehicle running for another few seconds before shutting it off.

Four men exited the vehicle, all bearing rifles. Boss Dragon exited last, his face hard and determined. He wore a pair of sunglasses, a black tee shirt, and camo pants. He had a rifle slung over his right shoulder.

Boss Dragon looked at Michael for a moment, wondering why he hadn't come to join his side of the circle. Michael didn't move, however. Boss Dragon looked at Makara.

"You Makara, then?"

"Yes. And you must be Boss Dragon."

Boss Dragon nodded his affirmation. "What do you got for me, Makara? Why do you want a meeting with the Lords of Vegas?"

"Because none of us will survive what is to come."

"Ah, okay." Boss turned his head, facing the east. "That Great Blight is getting closer, every day." He turned to face her. "That's what you're here for, isn't it?"

"Yes. In part."

Boss Dragon arched an eyebrow. "In part? What do you mean, 'in part'?"

"There's another threat. I suppose you know who Emperor Augustus is?"

"Yeah, I know who he is," Boss Dragon said, voice low. "He's the big, bad man in the south. He buys all our slaves. Don't see where he has room to keep them, though. Yeah, we know about Nova Roma. That's where the batts come from. You can ask Rey, Grudge, or any of the others." He smiled. "Guess you could say, Nova Roma's our lifeblood."

If these gangs were good with Augustus, then convincing them to fight him might not be in the cards.

"We just came from there," Makara said. "Augustus is coming here with an army. There's a good chance a big part of that army will be here in two months."

"Two months?" Boss Dragon. At last, Makara had said something that had caught him off-guard. "You sure about that?"

"I'm for damn sure. They might not be coming to Vegas, specifically. But yes. They are coming to the Wasteland. I formed the New Angels for two reasons: to stop Augustus, and to stop the Great Blight. But to do that, I will need an army."

Boss Dragon said nothing, gauging her seriousness. He folded his arms. He was an intimidating man, all the more so because of his size and muscle.

"Well," Boss Dragon said, "I think you're going to have a tough sell. Don't expect any miracles. In Vegas, we like to run our things our way. Men have tried for years to take control of this town. Tried, and failed."

"The Great Blight doesn't care about who runs this place," Makara said. "It only cares about killing." She gestured at all of us. *"We* know how to fight it. And unless the gangs follow us, then they're going to become part of *that.*" Makara pointed eastward.

Boss Dragon, instead of getting angry, nodded. "You're right. But tell me: when was the last time being right was enough?"

Makara didn't have an answer for that. I didn't know what she could say, either. Boss Dragon had hit the nail on the head.

"You have to think of what you can offer," Boss Dragon said. "Batts. Slaves. Those are the things that will get us to listen."

"I can promise nothing," Makara said. "Nothing, except freedom for the Wasteland."

"Freedom?" Boss Dragon smiled. "You are still young. Freedom is a fine idea, but Raine's time is past."

"Those are my conditions," Makara said. "I can lead the gangs to safety, and to victory. But I will need their loyalty."

"There are men in this town who would kill you for those words. You are lucky. I've always appreciated a good joke."

I watched the others, who had been staring silently at Boss Dragon, trying to decide whether or not he was a threat. Char and Samuel flanked Makara's either side, hands not far from their weapons. Michael stood by me, and Anna on my other side. We were all here for Makara, in case things turned nasty.

"When are the rest of them going to be here?" Makara asked.

"I don't know," Boss Dragon said. "They should be here now."

Well, that at least gave Makara time to think about what she had to say. Or, perhaps, to *not* think about what she had to say. She had the unenviable job of getting the gangs on our side, and not getting us killed in the process. And she had to stand on her own two feet to do so. Relying on any of us, or on Char, would make her look weak. She had to talk about the Great Blight and the Empire and hope that they, the gang lords, would all come to the same conclusion as we had.

But Boss Dragon's words echoed in my mind: *when was the last time being right was enough?*

Chapter 11

As the day wore on, the first of the gang lords pulled up. This was Jade, Lord of the Diamonds. He rode up in a long, dusty limousine, completely black. The limo idled for a moment before shutting off. Then Jade stepped out, decked in a cheesy white top hat and white suit. He bowed with a flourish, a slimy, yellowed smile spreading over his greasy face. His black hair was long and unwashed, so much so that I would not have been surprised if his hair was evolving its own life forms, far more deadly than the xenovirus.

I could see why Jade was called "the Weasel." Jade was, in short, a weasely man. Though probably in his early thirties, Jade already had lines etched into his face that bore testament to his constant, empty smirk. He was tall, and diamond rings graced all of his fingers. He had three men with him, similarly dressed, some wearing one ring, some two, but all wore diamonds. I wondered if the rings were the Diamonds' way of establishing rank. No weapons were visible outside their white suits, but I knew they each probably had guns in their jackets. They'd be stupid not to.

Jade snickered for no reason, and gave no greeting to Makara or any of us. He gave a slight nod to Boss Dragon. Boss Dragon crossed his arms, and looked like he was doing his best to ignore Jade's presence.

Jade and the Diamonds said nothing to us, talking only amongst themselves. From time to time, Jade looked at Makara with interest. Even so, he said nothing to her, and Makara said nothing back.

The next gang arrived about five minutes later. An all-terrain SUV surged from the direction of the Strip, throwing up a giant cloud of dust. As it neared, I could see one man with silvery gray hair, slicked back, standing in the sunroof opening. The man had ice-cold blue eyes. The vehicle pulled to a stop between the Dragons and the Diamonds.

"Cain," Michael said. "Lord of the Sworn."

Men piled from the vehicle, dressed in dingy military apparel. Cain sunk back into the vehicle from his perch and, shortly after, stepped outside to join his crew. I guessed Cain was probably in his late fifties. He was tall and well-muscled for his age. He had high cheekbones, broad shoulders, and a pale complexion. He stared at Makara, sizing her up. Makara just stared right back. He nodded and smiled, but said nothing, leaning forward with hands on his hips in an aggressive posture. Samuel, Michael, and Char stared him down, their hands not far from their guns. I slowly went for my Beretta as well. Somehow, Cain had a very dangerous air. Even Jade seemed nervous looking at him, touching the diamonds on his fingers, as if to draw some imaginary comfort from them. Boss Dragon watched Cain warily, saying nothing.

It was a while before anyone else arrived. The gang members talked amongst themselves, impatient. The two most powerful gangs, the Suns and the Kings, were absent. And of the Reds, there was no sign. They lived outside city limits, so it could be a while before they showed up.

Then, a cloud of dust formed in the east, at the end of a long runway. It was from the opposite end of the Strip. I supposed this to be the Reds, since the other gangs had their headquarters on Las Vegas Boulevard. It would make sense for them to approach from this direction. As the dust cloud approached, I saw that it was a train of motorcycles. Was it the Exiles? Marcus must have somehow figured out we were here, and was now coming to join the deliberations. That would have been fine with any of the New

Angels, but we were only allowed a certain number of people. If Marcus and the Exiles joined us, it would give us an unfair advantage, which would destroy the trust we were trying to cultivate with these gangs.

As the bikes neared, though, I saw that it was *not* Marcus and the Exiles. The vehicles were too lightweight, built for the speed of city streets rather than the harsh terrain of the Wasteland. The bikes were decked out in flashy colors of red, yellow, orange, and purple. Their collective high whine intensified as they drew close.

Then, the bikes circled around us, buzzing and humming like angry insects – or angry xenolife. As the dust rose, Cain shook his head, annoyed, while Jade's face reddened with anger. Boss Dragon's face was stoic, while Makara stood fast, betraying no emotion. I did my best to mirror her example.

Finally, the motorcycles pulled to a stop, between the Dragons and the Sworn. The lead man, who was short, well-muscled, with black hair, pulled off his helmet, revealing mischievous brown eyes. He was dressed in black leather, and a shadow of stubble covered his chiseled face. He grinned as he put down the kickstand and stepped off his bike. Immediately, the six men who had been with him followed suit.

"Sorry if I'm late," the man said. "Business."

Cain waved him away, but there was a slight smile on his lips. I could tell that they were friends. Jade gave no reaction, but it looked like he was trying to mask anger – and perhaps, jealousy. Boss Dragon gave a single nod of acknowledgement. I could tell that the man, whoever he was, was highly respected in Vegas.

"That's Grudge," Michael said. "Leader of the Suns."

Makara nodded. This was the guy Michael had said was a loose cannon. Now, though, he looked calm and in control. Respectable, even. But I knew not to trust that. I noticed, as the other riders took off helmets, that two of them were women. I was surprised. Up until this point, I hadn't seen any girl gang members.

Grudge walked across the tarmac, clasping hands with Cain. Grudge seemed genial and friendly. I wondered how he had earned the name, "Grudge" but it would be a while before I found out. Despite his easy smile, there was no doubting the element of danger the man exuded. I noticed the two Suns women gazed at him in an almost reverent manner.

Now that Grudge was here, there was one gang left – the Kings. The Kings were, by Michael's admission, the most powerful gang in Vegas, so it made sense that they would show up last to emphasize that point. As Grudge went back to his spot, I thought, not for the first time, that we were way in over our heads. Getting these gangs to do anything would be like herding cats. Maybe more like herding lions.

Another five minutes passed, each group talking amongst itself. The groups quieted when the sounds of engines approached from the direction of the Strip. The Kings were coming.

As they passed the security gate into the airport, I saw that they had no less than *four* Recons, all military grade, with turrets in the back. They gunned it for the circle, as if their aim was to run us all down. I noticed that the Dragon gang members clutched their rifles a little more tightly. At last, the Kings pulled to a neat, orderly stop, in the last space remaining in the circle of vehicles. They sat for a minute inside, tinted windows making it impossible to see within. For some reason, they were trying to drag this out as long as possible.

Then, they stepped out into the dull red sunlight. There were eight gang members total, two for each Recon. Then, exiting the passenger side of the back Recon came Rey himself – a tall Hispanic man who was probably forty years of age. He smoked a cigar, his eyes narrowing smugly as he watched the other gangs, like a king surveying his lords. He blew out a cloud of smoke, tipping some ash onto the runway. He wore a dark pinstripe suit that was immaculately clean, a pink rose pinned to his jacket. Where he had found that rose, I had no idea. It only added to his mystery, his power. It was not just Rey who wore a clean suit – it was his men, also – these elites who were a reflection of their lord. Like the rest of the gangs, excepting the Dragons, the Kings carried no visible weapons. The New Angels and the Dragons were the only gangs to openly show their guns.

Rey walked up to the circle, flanked on each side by his men. Rey was clearly the most powerful of the gang lords. Not only had he made the biggest showing of everyone there, he seemed the most in control – of himself, and of the situation. The other gang leaders looked to him, expecting him to speak first. Boss Dragon on the other side of the circle could not mask the scowl that came to his lips.

"Good afternoon, gentlemen," Rey said, looking pointedly at Boss Dragon. "And ladies. I first want to thank Elijah, Boss Dragon, for this gathering, because it was a long time in coming. It's a pity that the Reds cannot be here today, but perhaps that's because they're the Reds."

This elicited a chuckle from most of the gang members. It was an inside joke of some sort. I looked to Michael for direction, but he was focused on Rey.

"We have several matters of business to attend to, not the least of which is the presence of this new gang. First, we have the Raiders. Now, we have another group to deal with. As you all know, we have already spoken to Char, but with the arrival of these Angels, things have changed. So dealing with this should be the first thing on today's agenda."

The other gang members said nothing. I realized that Rey had, in a few sentences, managed to reframe the entire situation. Instead of Makara calling all *them* to deliberate on what to do about the Great Blight, it was now all about the Vegas gangs and what they were to do about this new nuisance called the New Angels.

Everyone waited a moment. Finally, Rey looked at Makara, with an expression that said that she was a little girl who was in trouble and needed to explain herself.

"You and I both know that's not what this is about," Makara said, with venom, "so quit playing games, because I'm not in the mood for them. The New Angels are not the threat here." Makara pointed eastward. "*That* is. *That* is why we are here. Let's just make that clear, Rey."

Rey looked bored. "So, you want shelter in our city? Get in line. We don't have the room, or the food. But if you have the batts or anything else to offer, we'll talk. In the meantime..."

"*No,*" Makara said, cutting him off. "We have no need of shelter. *You* do. You think these flimsy walls will protect you against the Great Blight?" Makara paused. "They won't. And you know they won't. They couldn't protect Augustus. They won't protect you, either."

Rey looked at the other gang lords, and smiled. "A lot of bark, this one."

Some of the gangsters chuckled, but most seemed to be taking Makara seriously. Noticing this, Rey's expression darkened somewhat before he was able to recover.

"What do you know about Augustus?" he asked.

"More than you think," Makara said. "And the same thing will happen here that happened to Raider Bluff and Nova Roma. It's just a matter of time until crawlers are roaming the streets."

Rey gave no reaction, waiting for Makara to say more. But Makara said nothing more. She was waiting for Rey to respond.

"She's Dark Raine's protégé," Jade said, from the Diamonds' part of the circle. He snickered, his demeanor becoming even more like that of a weasel.

"Dark Raine was a powerful man," Rey said. "But he is a ghost, now. The Angels are no more."

Grudge's face reddened, and he reached for his belt. Immediately, a dozen guns were pointed in this direction.

"Peace, Grudge," Boss Dragon said.

"I'm sick of the way Rey thinks he runs things here," Grudge said, withdrawing his hand from his weapons. "Like we're some sheep to follow his every word. No. That's not the way this works. Makara came here to say something, so let her say it, damn it. Quit acting like you're the one who called this meeting. I want to hear what she has to say about the Great Blight."

Grudge stepped back, having said his piece, but he was still fuming. I was starting to see why Michael said he was crazy. Rey arched an eyebrow, appearing bored, yet a bit more alert after Grudge's intrusion.

"Very well," Rey said. "We are not barbarians here. We are all here to ensure our mutual profit. And if there is a danger, like Makara of the Angels says…then it would be beneficial to listen."

He looked to Makara, ceding the floor.

"First of all, it's *New* Angels. Get the name right. As I was saying, there's a threat on the way. Not just to Vegas, but the entire Wasteland. I will deal with these threats in the order they are most likely to happen. First, there is the Great Blight. It is expanding, and it is only a matter of time until it takes out the city, just as it did with Raider Bluff."

"We will not fall," Cain said. "We have fought these dragons before, and have pushed them back every time. We are not easy prey for the Blighters."

"I didn't say you were," Makara said. "But you have not yet seen the whole strength of the Great Blight. They have legions of crawlers, howlers, flyers, and worse. There are the dragons, too, and then there is *him*. The giant dragon."

Apparently, all the gang members knew what Makara was talking about. They had seen the dragon.

"We call that one the Dragon King," Grudge said. "We have seen him, but have never fought him."

Rey said nothing. The gang members began talking amongst themselves. Makara spoke again, the men's voices fading at her words.

"Believe it or not, there are worse threats than this Dragon King. We have been into the heart of the Great Blight itself – to Bunker One. There, we discovered the cause behind the Blights. It is all controlled through something called the xenovirus. This xenovirus will take over the entire world, unless we do something to stop it."

The gang lords looked at each other, wondering if Makara's word was to be trusted.

"She's right," Char said, stepping in. "I outfitted them for their journey myself. They left Raider Bluff a little over two months ago, and this is the first I've seen of them since then." Char gazed at all the gang members, commanding their attention. "I thought them dead. She's already explained everything to me, about what they found out. I suggest you all listen. As soon as I heard, I pledged the Raiders to her cause." Char paused. "And my brother, Marcus, has also offered her the Exiles' services."

Rey smiled, looking around at the other gang lords. "Well, if the *Exiles* are following this girl, where do I sign up?"

Cain laughed, and Jade snickered. Boss Dragon and Grudge gave no reaction.

"There is no cure?" Grudge asked. "To the xenovirus, I mean."

It was hard to tell if Grudge was interested because he really was, or because caring was the opposite attitude to the one Rey was taking. The two men didn't seem to like each other at all.

"There is no cure, except to take out the thing that controls the xenovirus," Makara said. "It's called the Voice. The Voice makes the Blighters work together. It controls them like a general controls an army. It's based in Ragnarok Crater, and using the Blighters, the Voice is trying to conquer the world."

Jade giggled. "Why all this doom and gloom stuff, Angel?"

"*Quiet,*" Char growled.

Jade looked at Char contemptuously, a nervous giggle escaping his throat.

"Well, apparently, she has convinced Raider Bluff," Grudge said. "The Raiders were strong, until the Blighters got them."

"The same thing won't happen to us," Cain said. "We are too strong. We'll kick those Blighters back to the Crater, where they belong."

"The Great Blight isn't the only problem," Makara said. "The other issue is Emperor Augustus, of Nova Roma, and his ally, Carin Black, of the Reapers."

For some reason, this had the gang leaders much more interested than the threat of the xenovirus. They leaned forward intently.

"What's going on with Augustus?" Rey asked. "You act like you have seen him."

"He and his army are on their way to the Wasteland," Makara said. "We just came from there, and even got to speak with him at length. We learned a lot about what he wants, and what he hopes to gain by conquering the Wasteland. You can expect him, or at least part of his army, to be here in two months."

The gangsters looked at each other. Clearly, they had been unaware of this. Of course they had been unaware. Nova Roma was two thousand miles away.

"How large is their army?" Rey asked.

"The vanguard that will be arriving first – the one with vehicles and horses – will be several thousand strong. The rest...forty thousand."

A silence hung over the gathering. Makara had just shocked them all with that news.

"You are sure?" Cain asked, his blue eyes concerned. "You have seen this, personally? What do they plan to do with the winter?"

Makara nodded. "As far as what the plan is for the weather, I don't know. I'm only repeating Augustus's own words. He said two months, and my crew and I were there not one week ago. We barely escaped with our lives. The Novans are dealing with dragons, too, so maybe that will pen them there for a while. Then again, maybe not. With Carin Black on his side, we won't stand a chance if we allow both of their forces to join. The point is, we have to move quickly to counter this. If the Blighters don't get to us first, *they* surely will."

Everyone stood quietly, absorbing that thought. Rey appeared troubled. Troubled, because finally someone more powerful than himself was coming along – and that changed everything.

"All this is the main reason I'm here," Makara continued. "Not because *I* need protection. You all do. We need to save this city from the Great Blight, because there are lots of fighting people I can use to strike back at this thing. Carin Black is strong, and if Augustus gets here in two months, as he said he would, their alliance will make them unstoppable."

"How are we supposed to stop that?" Grudge asked.

"The answer is simple," Makara said. "We have to cross the Wasteland and attack Los Angeles head-on, and conquer Black's stronghold before Augustus can join up with him. We need to find settlements along the way, tell them what we know, and get their help. We have two months to do this."

Silence reigned once more – silence, save for the out-of-place snicker from Jade. Cain shot the Weasel a murderous look, which at once silenced him.

"Forty thousand..." Rey said.

"We cannot fight that," Cain said, blue eyes blazing. "Even with every fighting man, woman, and child in the Wasteland...we cannot fight that. Even if we kill the Reapers, it is hopeless. At best, we can produce ten thousand men. Maybe twenty."

"We do have several advantages," Makara said. "Because of *Odin*, our spaceship, we have time on our side. Augustus had not thought that we could return in time to prepare, because he did not know about *Odin*. The speed of the ship means we can communicate easily, and transport groups of men to where they need to be, quickly. The New Angels also have another spaceship, the *Gilgamesh*."

As she spoke, Rey's eyes glazed over with greed. He wanted those spaceships.

"We have plans to liberate two more, housed in Bunker Six," Makara said. "Four spaceships will allow us to crush a large part of Augustus's army, or set up flanks he cannot possibly defend against. His army does not have the same level of technology as we do. They have guns, but not enough to equip all of their soldiers. If you go down to Nova Roma, it's almost like stepping back in time hundreds of years. That's part of the reason Augustus wants to conquer the Wasteland. The Bunkers have tons of weapons and supplies that simply cannot be found anywhere else. If we get to the Bunkers first, then Augustus's army will be all the weaker for it."

The gang leaders looked at one another.

"You know their locations?" Rey asked.

"We know the locations of several," Makara said. "And it would be easy to find the locations of the rest, once we access any of their servers. We know of two Bunkers to the north which might actually still be online. With their help, we could bolster our numbers even more." Makara looked at each of the gang lords in turn. "We have time. If we make all the right steps to prepare, we can set ourselves up in such a way that Augustus can be crushed before he even begins. It's all about preparation. We have all the resources. But do we have the drive? The unity?" Makara paused, letting that sink in. "Those are the only two things working against us."

"Even if we did do all that," Jade said, now serious, "what makes you think we will win? Nothing ever goes the way you want it to. If all those things line up perfectly, sure...maybe we can win. Maybe not. I'm just going to say it, right now, because I'm sure you all have already thought about it." He paused, flaunting a smile. "We need to join up with Augustus."

Several of the men grumbled. We had assumed these Vegas gangs would want to be free of Augustus as much as we did. It turned out that they were more mercenary than that.

"I don't want any foreign king telling me how to run my gang," Rey said. "I'll take the Empire's batts, but that is as far as I will go. The Wasteland is *ours*."

"Augustus is powerful," Jade said, almost soothingly. "How can we stand up to that when it comes? We can't. It's best to join up with him, while we still have a chance."

"He is over two thousand miles away," Grudge said, face reddening. It looked like he had a mind to use his gun. "If we have time to prepare for his attack, why would we join him?"

"I agree," Cain said. "But I won't follow this girl. Cain and the Sworn go their own way."

Then, all the gangsters were arguing over what to do next. Our chief fear had been quashed – they were actually taking Makara seriously. It was funny how they took the threat of Augustus and Carin Black more to heart than the Great Blight. To them, crawlers and dragons were unruly critters that only needed to be slapped a few times so that they could get back to business. To the Vegas gangs, other people were the more tangible threat.

"And who will lead this expedition to Los Angeles?" Grudge asked. "I don't trust *any* of you enough to walk three miles, much more three hundred."

"That is why Makara leads!" Char shouted.

Everyone stopped short in their arguing, looking at Char. Now that he had everyone's attention, he hurried to speak before anyone else could get in another word.

"The Raiders and the Exiles have already sworn their loyalty to the New Angels. You do not have to do the same. You can march with us, as allies, to Los Angeles. We will take Carin Black out before he even has a chance to prepare. Once there, the wealth of the city will be open to us all – batts, slaves, whatever you want."

"*No.*" Makara stepped up. "I will not allow slavery. This is the rebirth of the Lost Angels, and neither Raine nor I would stand for it."

"Well," Jade said, "tough luck, lady. Slaves are part of the deal. We want the whole city...don't we, boys?"

Rey nodded. "The whole city. If you are going to take Vegas from us, we want to own Los Angeles. It is a fair trade. For all our risk...for our gamble...we need to have a reward that's worth it."

"Apparently, your survival isn't rewarding enough?" Makara asked.

Rey shrugged. "It's not about our survival. It's about *you* needing *us*. You need our help to fight Black, and Augustus. You only get it if you give us what we want."

"Augustus is just the first step," Makara said.

Rey arched an eyebrow. "Really. Well, what other services do you require?"

"The Great Blight is going to destroy Vegas soon. It won't stop at Vegas. It won't stop until the whole world is swallowed and everyone is dead. If anyone wants to survive this, we have to attack the Voice. We have to attack Ragnarok Crater."

No one said anything. This was bad news, and they didn't want to accept it. I could see them now, looking for flaws in Makara's argument, wanting it not to be true.

"We can show you the Black Files, if you want," Samuel said. "We can give them to you to read for yourself. They were authored by the Chief Scientist of Bunker One, Cornelius Ashton, and are the most advanced study ever done on the xenovirus. Read them, if you do not believe me."

"I don't need to read that to know this world is going to hell," Cain said. "More hell than usual, anyway. We can talk about that when we get there. Right now, let's just focus on the Los Angeles expedition."

Rey scowled, not liking where this was going. He had still not accepted.

"I probably don't need to point this out," Makara said. "But I will, anyway. The Great Blight will ruin your food and water supply, even if the Blighters don't attack first. You'll be forced to leave the city behind, with or without me. You can either do it with my help, with my resources, or without them. But if you come with me, you have to do it on *my* terms. No slaves. You can take all the batts you want from Los Angeles. Just leave the innocents alone."

Rey was used to getting his way. He had long since cast aside his cigar. He reached a hand out, and a crony handed him a new one, lighting it for him. After taking a few puffs, Rey turned back to Makara.

"This can be negotiated," he said. "If I am going to leave my home behind, I want a better deal than I have right now. You understand this, don't you? L.A. is rich. I am game for trying to take it down. Hell, it could even be fun. It'd be nice to turn our guns on someone else besides our Vegas brethren."

The other gang members smiled at that.

"But unless you give us a reason to go, besides survival...we won't go. Surviving isn't a reason for survival. You need something else. I want batts. Power. Slaves. They make the world go round."

Makara eyed Rey hard. The rest of the gangsters were behind him, now. If she said no, then the gangs would not follow her to L.A. It didn't matter how logical she was being about their survival depending on her. Even though they knew that, they wanted more.

"Fine," Makara said. "We will parcel out the city once it's ours. We'll each get territory inside that corresponds to our respective size and power."

Rey nodded his assent. "That sounds fair."

The other gang lords' eyes glistened with greed. They saw Los Angeles as a fat sheep ripe for the slaughter. It wasn't the best motivation, but it was the best we could expect of men like these. They would only be loyal as long as they believed they stood anything to gain from conquering Los Angeles. It also created a whole new problem. After Black had been taken out, the gangs would turn on each other, once more, fighting over the best territory. Even now, I was sure they were all planning for that eventuality. It was all a game to them. It was a game they all had to survive, first.

"I want to remind you that it doesn't end with the conquering of Los Angeles," Makara said. "You will have to defend what is yours when Augustus comes. By that time, we should be strong enough to resist him. And the Great Blight grows. Its menace will never end until we destroy the Voice. After Augustus has been defeated, or has agreed to help us, we can attack the Great Blight and bring down the Voice. Only then will the xenovirus be rendered moot. Only then will the invasion be stopped."

"What is it, anyway?" Grudge asked. "This xenovirus. Where did it come from?"

Of all the gang leaders, Grudge was the one I liked the most, despite Michael's warning. He actually seemed interested in our mission against the xenovirus, and how to stop it.

"The Black Files, which we found in Bunker One, confirm that the xenovirus is of alien origin," Samuel said, answering for Makara. "It's their way of killing us all off before they get here to take control of the planet."

Grudge nodded. Then, he smiled. "We might do their job for them before the end, huh?"

"I hope not, Grudge," Makara said. "That's something to think about. Fight all the wars you want when this is all said and done. I don't care. Until then, we work together. Agreed?"

One by one, the gang leaders nodded their agreement – Jade, Cain, Grudge, and Boss Dragon, who had been quiet all afternoon – and finally, Rey. Though Rey nodded like the rest, his eyes said he was going his own way. There was nothing we could do about that for now. It was done. As done as done could be, anyway.

"So," Char said. "When do we start?"

"It will take time, to prepare for our departure," Rey said. "We'll need to gather food, vehicles, slaves, supplies. We won't find much on the way, so we'll need to empty the storehouses."

"Should we combine our supplies, or each go separately?" Cain asked.

"I'm not sharing," Jade said, with a nasty look. "I don't trust any of you."

"We share supplies," Makara said. "Essential things like food, water, even bullets and guns. For one, it's easier, and second, I want to get it into your heads that we're working together now."

"This can be discussed later," Rey said. "I have things to take care of right now."

He turned back for his Recon, along with his cronies. After they started up the hydrogen-powered vehicles, the tires squealed on the tarmac, leaving us in a cloud of dust.

"We will be in touch, Makara," Cain said, with a nod. Where the blue eyes once mocked, now they held some measure of respect.

Makara nodded, and Cain turned away. He and his associates piled into their SUVs, and after starting their engines, headed back to the Strip.

Jade flashed a toothy, slimy smile before sliding into his limousine and riding away. It left only Grudge and his bikers. Grudge took a step forward, causing both Char and Samuel to reach for their guns.

Grudge held his hands up. He turned his eyes on Makara. "You did better than I would have guessed. Maybe they're all out for themselves...and I'm not saying that I'm not, either. But you have me convinced about this xenovirus thing. Those buggers have always made my blood run cold. I just want you to know...I've got your back, is all."

Grudge looked aside, embarrassed.

Makara nodded. "I appreciate that, Grudge."

Grudge's face was blank for a moment. Talk of loyalty or not, he was still dangerous. If he wanted to be in good with us, he had to prove it first.

"You'll see, Makara," he said, mounting his bike.

He held up a fist, causing all the other Suns to climb onto their own bikes. Then, in a swirl of dust, they sped off down the runway in the direction of the airport.

Boss Dragon came forward. "That was well done."

"Well, they've agreed to go, so at least that much is done. I didn't get everything I wanted, but..."

"Hey." Boss Dragon stared at Makara hard. "Nobody does, kid."

Char eyed Boss Dragon. "You have to prove yourself too, buddy."

Boss Dragon turned his eyes on Char with disgust. "I made this gathering happen and gave Makara my protection. What more proof do you need?"

"I'm a skeptic," Char said. "It'll take more than a few favors to impress me...or Makara, for that matter.

"Alright," Boss Dragon said. "I feel you." The Boss looked at Michael. "You sure about joining up with these New Angels then, huh?"

"Well, nothing's official yet, but I would like nothing more."

"You're one of us," Makara said. "Who says you can't be both a Dragon and an Angel?"

Boss Dragon gave a crooked smile. "You're right. You've been a huge help to me. But the Angels need you. This stuff about the xenovirus...me and my gang will do what we can to help. You have me convinced. Let me know what I can do. The Dragons will go with you, all the way to Ragnarok."

With that, Boss Dragon held up a fist and pounded his chest. The other Dragons, Michael included, did the same thing. It was a like a pledge.

"I appreciate that, Boss Dragon."

"You are my equal," Boss Dragon said. "You can call me Elijah from now on."

"Alright, then...Elijah. As long as any of my men can do the same. We Angels are all equals of one another."

Elijah nodded. "Just like Raine, then."

The way Elijah said that made me think that he had known Raine as well. It was strange that there had been an entire gang, the Lost Angels, whose legacy lived on long after their fall. It made me wish that I could have met Raine. And it made what Carin Black did, when he killed Raine, all the more egregious.

I then realized that this wasn't just about saving the Vegas Gangs or stopping Augustus. It was also righting the murder of Raine, a righteous man, and resurrecting the legacy of his gang, the Lost Angels. In just a few months, Makara was going to get her chance for vengeance and justice when we attacked Los Angeles. Raine's death had changed her life, had made her become the person she was now. It was hard to say, but if Raine hadn't died, maybe we wouldn't be going through all this right now. Maybe the Wasteland would already be united. Maybe, even, the Great Blight would be dead.

Well, I doubted that last one for sure. Things were coming to a head, more now than ever. We were all going to get the chance to finish what we had started.

Killing Black would be closure for both Samuel and Anna, as well, whose lives had been destroyed from the Los Angeles takeover – Samuel, for the same reasons as Makara, and Anna, because her settlement had been invaded by the Black Reapers when she was a kid. That had caused her and her mother to wander the Wasteland for survival, had caused her to start training on the katana.

So many things had happened because of the death of one man. And so many more things were left to happen, to be decided.

As Boss Dragon and his men piled into their Recon and drove away for the Strip, Makara faced us.

"Come on. We got what we came for."

We turned from the runway, making our way to the Sunset Gate.

Chapter 12

It was evening, and Anna and I stood on the overpass, about a hundred yards from *Odin*. We leaned over the railing, watching the glowing red sky shine off the western buildings of outer Vegas. The buildings gave way beyond to desert and jagged hills and dunes, all the color of blood.

"This place is done," Anna said.

She was right. It was only a matter of time. Out there, behind our backs to the east, an entire army of Blighters lurked. It was far too quiet. They were planning something big. I felt it. It was all going to come crashing down, soon.

I was worried that we were not going to be able to get everyone out of here fast enough.

"Makara was actually able to convince them," I said. "I was half-expecting to die back there."

Anna smiled. "Only half?"

"Alright. Maybe it was a little more."

We gazed together at the sunset. The blood-red colors intermingled with the desert ground, and the sun sunk beneath the final line of the horizon. Not the sun itself, for it was blocked by thick, bulbous clouds. When the sun's glow finally disappeared, the land was covered in darkness.

"Do you think we can stop it?" I asked.

Anna didn't answer for a moment.

"I don't know. I'd like to believe so. We got further than I thought we would today. I really did think there was a good chance we wouldn't live to have this conversation right now." She smiled. "I think we can, though."

She grew quiet, and I didn't know why. I looked at her, searching those eyes that stared off at the fading horizon. There was sadness there I didn't understand. I wanted to ask her what it was, but the words never formed. It was a deep sorrow that made me ache to see it. I wished I could make it go away, to see her smile again.

I turned her to face me, and saw that she was crying. I kissed her. Sometimes, words were not enough to show someone how you felt. Some things, like love, could only be expressed fully when you threw your all into it – your mind, your spirit, your movement.

Her lips moved against mine. It felt she was kissing me so as not to lose me. I didn't understand what that meant, at least, not at that moment.

She parted from me, and looked me full in the face. I laid my head on top of hers, felt her hair against my cheek. I never wanted to let go. I wanted her to know that I never would.

"I'm here to stay," I said. "I promise."

She shook with sobs. Before I could even ask what was wrong, she spoke.

"I know you do," she said. "But sometimes, the wanting isn't enough. Sometimes, fate has other plans."

"Anna, what are you talking about?" I asked, softly. "It's true. Wherever you go, I'll go with you. Even if you were to go off running to the east, I would follow you there."

She laughed into my chest. "Would you?"

I held her by the shoulders, looking her in the eyes. "Of course I would. You're my Sweet Pea."

She smiled. "Sweet Pea?"

"What, you've never heard that before?"

She shook her head.

I laughed. "Sometimes, I forget how sheltered you surface dwellers are. You've got to get down with the lingo."

"I've never heard it," she said. "I like it, though."

"No more sadness," I said. "We have to enjoy this. It's rare to find someone like this, in a world like this. It's almost enough..."

I trailed off, and she looked up at me. Her eyes questioned, wanting me to go on. But even I wasn't sure enough to go on.

"Almost enough for what?"

For me to believe in something larger than myself.

"I'm not even sure," I said. "I hope that the more time I spend with you, the more I can find out."

"That makes two of us, then."

I took a deep breath, holding my arms out to the breeze. Anna looked at me, not saying anything. I had no idea what the gesture meant.

It takes courage to open up to a world that isn't worth opening up to. That courage is part of our humanity, part of our noble defiance – and all we can do is pray that it's worth it.

And I wasn't going to let the promise of pain stop me from trying.

***

We now sat in the darkness, against the freeway railing. We could have been anywhere in the world, and I would still be perfectly content, because I was with her. We talked about a lot of things, saying everything unfiltered, whatever came to mind, judging nothing, loving everything. We talked that way for an hour, the best conversation I'd ever had with anyone.

Somehow, though, the conversation turned to the weather.

"Why is it so warm?" I asked. "For December."

Anna said nothing. Maybe it was just the warmth of her body against mine. She settled her head onto my chest.

"The Wasteland has two seasons," Anna said. "Cold, and colder. The colder just hasn't hit yet."

"It's almost 2061 now."

"The months and days don't matter much on the surface," Anna said. "We've gone past that. The last tolling of any consequence was the impact of Ragnarok. Since then, no other pendulum could ever shake us."

"That's...very poetic. And dark."

She shrugged. "It happens sometimes."

"Poetry?"

She snickered.

"What's so funny?"

"Nothing. I just thought of saying something really cheesy. Like, 'poetry is life.'" She paused. "Something like that."

"That's not cheesy."

She leaned up against the railing of the bridge, so now we were shoulder to shoulder. If there was anything Anna could do, it was surprise me. She was smart, decisive, strong – and when she was quiet, she was probably thinking of things I could never understand. She became lost in moments, moments she couldn't be shaken from. But then, her eyes would find me, connecting to the world once again. I wanted to hold her in those moments, let her know she wasn't alone in them.

"I wonder if the Great Blight has something to do with how warm it is," I went on. "You think? I noticed the same thing when we were in it. The fungus is alive, isn't it? Maybe it radiates heat, somehow."

"It's possible," Anna said. "I'd never really considered that. It would make sense, though."

Thousands of square miles of Great Blight, all of it producing heat, would add up. Warm, in the Wasteland, was just a relative term. Right now, it was only slightly above freezing. All the tales I'd heard of the cruel Wasteland winter didn't seem to be true, at this moment.

"The winter will fall like a hammer," Anna said. "You'll see. Every year, it comes at a different time. It's just late in coming this year. There'll be this great cloud of dust, and it will storm for about a week. Then, it will leave behind air so cold that it'll freeze your blood."

"Literally?"

Anna gave a small laugh. "No, not literally. But you'll feel it. Sometimes, it's so cold that you cry. You want to stay inside those days, with plenty of firewood and stew. That's when raiders take to drink, living in the bars and inns of Bluff. At least, that's how it used to be."

With Raider Bluff gone, things had definitely changed.

"And we'll be crossing the Wasteland while all that happens?"

Anna nodded. "Not much choice in the matter. This place is dead, either way. We will be, too, if we don't go soon."

She leaned against me, and I wrapped my arms around her. Feeling her warmth made winter seem like a faraway thing.

"If we're going to L.A, we'll be passing your home, won't we?" I asked.

Anna nodded. "Last Town is right on the way, guarding the pass into the city. Last time I saw it was when the Reapers took over for good, and they laid it to dust. I hear they've rebuilt it, though. It's a fort now, and all the trade has to go through there to make it inside L.A." She sighed. "It'll be hell trying to take it down."

From the south came the roar of approaching engines. I looked in that direction to see a dark cloud of dust advancing toward us.

"Marcus," I said.

We both stood, walking toward the approaching bikes. As they drew close, I saw that something was off. More of them had left this morning than four. I could swear it.

"Only four are coming back from that patrol," Anna said. "At least six or seven left, right?"

I waited a moment, just to be sure there were fewer Exiles returning. Without doubt, there were only four coming back.

"I'll get the others," I said.

I ran to *Odin*. We were in for some bad news.

***

As everyone on *Odin* ran down the boarding ramp, Marcus and what was left of his patrol walked up to the base of the ramp. Marcus hadn't been away so long because he had been trying to avoid Char. He had been fighting for his life.

"Crawlers?" Anna asked.

Marcus shook his head. "The Reds. They ambushed us in west Vegas, and we didn't have time to react. They took out Flex and Wedge. We gunned it back here, and they chased us a good way."

Makara's face darkened. "Wait. You were attacked by the Reds?"

"Yeah."

Marcus's clothes had somehow become tattered during his escape. His men stood beside him, silent.

"They just shot at us," one of them said. "No warning or anything. They want a war."

"They just attacked, for no reason?"

Marcus shook his head. "They might have thought we were attacking. We were just scouting, though. We never wanted this to happen."

"The Reds have always been more violent than the others," Michael said. "Why do you think Elijah didn't invite them to the summit? There's an agreement where the entire west side is theirs. But the east, that's for the rest of the gangs. That's where the water trucks are."

"They thought you were attacking," Anna said. "That must be it."

"We can't stand for this," Marcus said. "They killed two of my best men! We're down to just twenty three now, and..."

"Marcus," Makara said.

Marcus quieted, and looked at Makara. She stood for a moment in silence, commanding his attention.

"You're right. I cannot allow this to go unpunished. If the other gangs get wind of this, they'll think us weak if we just let this happen. We're going after them. Tonight."

Everyone turned to look at her, unbelieving at first.

"Are we really going to attack them?" I asked. "Shouldn't we be focusing on other things?"

"No," Makara said. "Like I said, word of this will reach the gang lords by tomorrow. I want them to know we don't take this kind of thing lightly. We attack them, let them know not to mess with us like this. We'll take *Odin*, load it up with our best men, and go. Raider style."

Char smiled, and Marcus made a fist. For a moment, the two brothers' eyes locked. It was the first time they had looked at each other with anything other than hostility since they had gotten here.

"If you think this is the best move for the group," Samuel said, "I won't stop you. You're the leader of the New Angels. As long as this doesn't interfere with the main mission, I can get behind it."

I looked at Samuel, unbelieving. Was I the only one who thought this was a bad idea?

"We can't be serious about this," I said. Everyone turned to look at me. "We can't waste more men and bullets on this. Leave the Reds to the Blighters. We're getting out of here in a few days, anyway. We need to be preparing to leave this place behind."

Makara looked at me, weighing my words. Anna was quiet, and I could tell that she wasn't sure what to think. She was a Raider, at least by association, so she at least knew of their culture for retribution. When a rival gang pushed you, you pushed back twice as hard.

Makara heaved a sigh, then turned to Michael.

"Michael, what can you tell us about the Reds? Numbers? Weaknesses?" She paused. "Where the hell are they, even?"

"Well, they're a large gang, led by a man named Lucius. They have a lot of territory, and are very possessive of it. They are mainly on the west side of town, in the suburbs. They have their own farms and slaves, separate from the rest of the Vegas Gangs. They are probably as strong as the Kings."

"If we took them out, would anyone inside miss them?" Makara asked.

Michael shook his head. "Most of them would be glad. Only Jade and the Diamonds have dealings with the Reds. Contracting slaves, that sort of thing."

"That settles it," Makara said. "They're done."

"Settles *what*?" I asked. "We can't just attack them. We'll lose a lot of men. We can't get drawn into a war when we're already in one. This just makes us weaker to the Blighters."

"Alex, let me explain something to you," Makara said. "Marcus is one of us. One of us got attacked. If we do nothing, we appear weak. The Reds, right now, are probably preparing a defense. We have to hit them before they're ready. If we leave them be, they'll be a thorn in our side. You think *they* aren't going to leave Vegas when the rest of us do?"

That gave me pause, because it was something I hadn't considered. The Reds weren't to be trusted, and having them picking on us while we were on the run was a very real threat.

"Besides," Makara said, "making an example out of the Reds will make the other gangs think twice before crossing us. I'm not proposing an all-out attack. Just a fly-by in *Odin*. Some guys on the ground taking some easy shots. Should take five minutes."

"Seriously?" I asked. "It'll take longer than that."

Everyone watched as Makara and I faced off. She didn't have me convinced. It just surprised me that I was standing alone. Anna looked at me, wanting to support me, but knowing she couldn't. She agreed with Makara.

"I'm behind whatever you decide," I said to Makara. "You are the leader of this gang. I just think this won't be as quick and easy as you think."

Makara stared at me. She hadn't changed her mind, either.

"She's right," Char said. "I know how men like Rey and Grudge think. We must go after the Reds. And the sooner, the better."

Marcus stared up at his brother. Up until now, I had not seen them speak to each other. For a moment, it looked like Marcus *was* going to say something to Char. If the two brothers would end up on speaking terms again, it would almost be worth going after the Reds. For some reason, though, it just felt like the wrong move.

Marcus turned to Makara. "I will lead the assault. Lucius and the Reds will not live to see the morning."

"We're not committing to an all-out war," Makara said. "Just a fly-by. We'll need everyone on the attack."

"An all-out war is what you'll get if you do this," I said. "Whether you like it or not."

Makara clenched a fist. "I need you to follow my orders, Alex. I am not messing with you. I'm in charge here, and this is *my* decision. Is that clear?"

I was doing all I could not to yell back at her. "Is this how we run things, then? Remember, if it weren't for me, this wouldn't exist. It was *my* idea to put you in charge. You better listen to me, Makara. I know what I'm talking about."

"You do? I don't think so. You're just some sheltered Bunker kid who doesn't know how the world really works. Leave the war and politics to me, Char, and Marcus."

"Both of you," Samuel said. "That's enough."

Makara looked at me, her eyes still angry. Though Makara could be harsh, sometimes it was just too much.

She calmed. "I'm...sorry. I shouldn't have said that."

"It's true, though," I said, quietly. "Maybe I really don't know what I'm talking about."

"Come on," Marcus said. "We can't worry about hurt feelings. We need to organize this attack, and do it right now."

Makara looked my direction. I could tell she felt bad. I could honestly say I preferred her feeling angry.

"Everyone, on the ship," she said. "And Alex. This *won't* be a war. You'll see. This is just saving face. That's it."

Marcus's expression told me it was more than that, but accepting Makara's lie was just a way to save *her* face. It was stupid. She had put me in a position where I had to accept her decision, or be a jerk.

"Whatever," I said. "If we're going to do this, we do this. I can point and shoot as well as any man. I just don't have to like it."

"That's fine," Makara said.

She sighed, clearly not happy. What she had to realize was that we couldn't get bogged down talking about my emotions. Emotions happened, and they made a mess. We had to ignore it, at least for now. More important things were at stake.

I looked from Makara, to Marcus, to Char, and finally, to Michael. I couldn't believe how quickly this was all happening.

"They have their HQ in this large office building," Marcus said. "I saw them park a lot of their bikes out there. If we raid that thing, we can deal a lot of damage."

Makara was only half-listening to Marcus. She looked to me instead.

"If not attack them, what do you suggest, Alex?" Makara asked.

I could tell it pained her to say that. I just wished she would stop. She wanted an out, wanted to give me a chance to think of something better. I could come up with the perfect solution, right now, and it wouldn't change a thing. Everyone looked to me, as if my opinion mattered. It didn't. I'd already heard the truth. Makara was in charge, end of story.

"Honestly, I have no idea if there's anything we can do," I said. "I just think it's a bad idea to make a decision in haste...especially one that will cost lives."

"We're already in this, kid!" Marcus shouted, his face red. "I don't care what anyone here says. I lost two men tonight. The Exiles go, with or without help."

"Marcus," Char said, arms crossed, "you need to stand down. You're not in charge, anymore. This is still an open question. Let the kid have his say." He looked at me, and nodded. "I'd say he's well earned it. We need to listen to skeptics."

Marcus's face, once crimson, was now pumice-gray. He was so angry he could not find words. His cold blue eyes gazed at Char, murderous.

"I'm not taking a counterattack off the table," Makara said. "I just want to hear all of our options. We can't ignore members of this group who disagree. That's not who we are. What I said earlier...it wasn't true. I don't want anyone to think I'm not willing to listen."

I shook my head. "I've already said what I've had to say. Do with it what you will."

No one said anything for a while. During the deliberation, many of Char's Raiders and Marcus's Exiles had made their way closer to the ship in order to hear the plans.

"This gang is pathetic," Marcus said. "You were all ready to avenge one of your own, until this kid whines about not wanting to get his hands dirty. If you're in a gang, you get your hands good and bloody. There's no other way to run a gang. Otherwise, you're just in a club."

Disgusted, Marcus turned from the ship, leaving us in silence. I had no answer for Marcus. Maybe the New Angels weren't *really* a gang, at least not in the traditional sense. All the same, I couldn't think of any way to solve the problem the Reds had caused without violence. Maybe I was just being petty. Besides, the Reds wouldn't understand anything *but* violence. Violence was the language of the streets. If we didn't learn how to speak it, we weren't going to make much of an impression.

"I've made my decision," Makara said.

We all looked at her. This time, I said nothing. Looking into her eyes, at that sense of resignation, I knew what she had decided. And I hated the fact that we would have to kill again. I didn't want to kill, but there was no way to avoid it. It was easy to point my gun at the crawlers and Blighters. Those things had no souls. It was harder to point your guns at living, breathing people, even if they were the ones attacking you first.

Makara turned to face everyone, distant Exiles and Raiders included.

"We will attack tonight."

The Exiles and the Raiders, who had once been staring each other down, now looked at Makara, their faces blank for a moment. Then the men broke into smiles.

Maybe attacking was bad in my book, but if it got the Exiles and the Raiders to stop hating each other, maybe it was worth it.

"If we're really doing this, we have a lot to go over," Michael said.

Marcus nodded, his expression relaxing.

"We can make our plans in the ship," Makara said. She looked out at the crowd. "As for the rest of you, suit up. We're leaving in two hours."

Several of the men whooped and cheered as the rest scattered for their tents. I watched as everyone went to the ship, not quite ready to join them. It still felt wrong. We were focusing on petty vengeance rather than the end goal – and everyone was just falling into line. Maybe, like me, they didn't agree. Makara had a lot of weight on her shoulders. She had a lot of hard decisions to make.

She could be wrong, but she could be right, too. Who was I to say what was right or wrong? The lives of thousands of men, both within the city and without, both inside the New Angels and outside it, depended on a nineteen-year-old girl. It was insane.

I sighed, and walked to the edge of the bridge, staring toward the Great Blight. The sky was dark with night, and I couldn't see much further than a few blocks of buildings. I almost wished the Great Blight would attack, as crazy as that sounds. It would get us focused on shooting the Blighters and not each other. I shook my head. We were doing this stupid attack because Marcus was dumb enough to ride into the Reds' territory. Did every life demand more blood to be spilled? Would it really be seen as weakness if we did nothing, and kept doing what we were supposed to be doing? I didn't understand the gang mentality. This attack made us no better than Rey, Grudge, or any of the lords we had met this afternoon.

I was just one voice, though. Makara wouldn't listen to me when everyone else was already behind her.

"You coming in, or what?"

Anna joined me at the railing. She looked into my face, but I just kept staring out.

I turned to look at her. "Do we really have to do this?"

"It's looking that way."

"I don't understand why. That's what makes it so hard."

"I don't understand, either."

I turned to her. "Then why are you just going along with it?"

"I'm not sure how I feel about it. I can see both sides. When you see both sides, you just go where the momentum leads you."

"I'm fighting the tide, then."

Anna nodded. "That was brave. It's hard to stand up for what you believe in, especially to your friends."

I shook my head. "I was just saying how I felt, because I feel like this is the wrong choice. I know this is going to bite us in the butt."

"Maybe it will. At this point, though, we all just have to go along with it."

"I don't want to be any part of it. This isn't right."

Anna was quiet for a moment. "You can't control everything, Alex. Sometimes…sometimes you have to do things you don't agree with. That's the way the world is. It's messy."

I was beginning to think Anna was right.

"You can't control everyone," she went on. "I've made lots of mistakes in my life. Mistakes that have led to men being killed. It's a lot to put on a seventeen-year-old."

I laughed bitterly. "Are we really so young?"

Anna said nothing, reaching for my hand. She was smiling.

"It's not the end of the world," she said.

I smiled, gesturing out to the Great Blight. "Actually, it kind of is."

Anna rolled her eyes. "You know what I meant. Come on. Let's go inside. Makara needs to know that you support her, even if you don't agree with her."

I nodded. "Whatever she decides, I'm there, for better or for worse."

"And Alex…"

I looked at her. She squeezed my hand.

"I'm here for you, too. Alright?"

I smiled. "Alright. I'm not going to let you guys go without helping out. I'm a New Angel, too. Even if we disagree on some things, we always have each other's backs."

"Come on, then," Anna said. "We're missing out."

Chapter 13

Over the next hour, we made our plan of attack. We were going to attack by both air and land – Marcus and the Exiles from the south, the Raiders from the north, and *Odin* from the sky. The ship would fly silently through the night, and drop each group off north and south of the Reds' HQ under cover of darkness. The HQ, according to Marcus, was a tall office building, maybe fifteen stories high. Once the Exiles and the Raiders were in position, they would open fire, hopefully drawing some Reds into the open. *Odin* would then fly down from the air and do its work.

It sounded positively bloody.

When the ship was loaded with the attack team, about two dozen Raiders and Exiles, the New Angels' inner circle were situated in the cockpit, ready to take off. I didn't feel any better about it, but I was behind my team, even if I felt the team was doing the wrong thing.

I just hoped we wouldn't lose too many men. Once the attack was over, *Odin* would rush to the rescue of the Raiders, who would be on the north side of the HQ. They would have a harder time escaping because they would be cut off by the building, meaning that they needed to be picked up first. After the Raiders were extracted, *Odin* would pick up the Exiles, who would be falling back to the south before the Reds had time to regroup. The Raiders numbered twenty, and the Exiles about ten. Only the best were selected, and the rest were staying behind to hold down the fort.

It sounded like a good plan, in theory.

I was assigned to the Raiders' group, along with Michael. Everyone else was assigned to the Exiles, who were less numerous. Makara and Anna were to remain on board, providing a steady rain of lead from above.

At last, we lifted off from the overpass. The city and its dark buildings fell away below us. Makara turned the ship toward our goal in the west. We flew over the south wall. Marcus and Michael both pointed us in the general direction we needed to go. I got a sick feeling in my gut that wouldn't go away, and it only became more intense the closer we got to the west side of town.

It was quiet when the dash lit up red, on and off, with a continuous beep.

"It's Ashton," Makara said.

"I'll answer." Samuel reached his hand for the transceiver and answered the call. "Ashton. Everything alright?"

"I'll say. I got my parts out of Bunker Six, but it wasn't easy. The place was infested with crawlers. Luckily, I found my parts before they found me." When no one answered him, Ashton spoke again, concern in his voice. "Hello? Anyone there?"

"Sorry, Ashton," Makara said. "You caught is in the middle of something."

He paused. "The middle of what? What's wrong?"

"Look, don't take this the wrong way but...can we call back later? We're in the middle of an operation."

"Humph. You're dodging my question, Missy. I don't like it."

"We're just...about to attack one of the Vegas gangs. It's necessary. Don't ask questions, because it will take too long to explain."

"Huh. I see." There was a long pause. "Well, you need to turn your ship around."

"What?" I asked. "Why?"

I was eager for any excuse to turn away from this attack. Hopefully, Ashton would deliver the goods.

"I know I've been out of the loop for a couple days, but what I have to tell you changes everything. I've discovered something that needs to be addressed immediately."

"Alright, I'll bite," Makara said. "What did you find out that's more important than making sure our hold on Vegas is secured beyond the shadow of a doubt?"

"Oh, trust me," Ashton said. "I have you beat. You see, when I got out of Bunker Six, I set up the wavelength monitor, just to test it out once I was up in the air. And in the process, I found out there is another Voice."

No one said anything for a moment. What Ashton just said didn't quite register.

"Another...what?" Samuel asked.

"Or at least, what I *think* is another Voice," Ashton said. "It has a different wavelength, coming from a different direction. But the pattern is so similar that it can't be anything else. That means there is *more* than one Voice controlling the xenovirus. It means we have to take out two of them, instead of one. And the thing is, right now, we have a chance to take out this second one, a chance we might not have ever again."

"Wait," Samuel said. "You are there, right now?"

"Yep. And it's a doozy, let me tell you."

"Where are you?" Samuel asked.

Ashton hesitated before answering. "About fifty miles east of you."

"I'm sorry..." Makara said. "What is it?"

"I don't know, but it needs further investigation," Ashton said. "I'm pretty sure that this...thing...I'm looking at is the source of the second Voice. I need you all here, pronto. There's this huge spire, just rising out of the Great Blight. The air is clear, as well as the ground." He paused. "I'm landing first, to get a closer look. I could learn something that could help us for when we attack the other one, in Ragnarok Crater. But I need you guys here in case things get dicey."

We looked at each other, hardly believing what Ashton had just told us. If there was another Voice, that meant we had two to kill, not just the one. And more might pop up out of nowhere. That meant this xenovirus might never get killed, if new Voices could just replace the old ones.

"Ashton," Makara said. "Do *not* land. Are you crazy? You could be attacked the second you set foot on that xenofungal field."

"Don't worry," Ashton said. "I have my gas mask, and plenty enough for everyone. This is a chance for research we might never get again."

"Let me talk," Marcus said. "Ashton, this attack is not going to be interrupted for anything. Whatever you're talking about, it can wait."

"I'm not so sure," Makara said. "If the Voice is not being protected, we might have a chance to do some real damage."

If that were true, then this would be a key time to strike. We already had the men and weapons on board. We were already in the air. If it was fifty miles way, we could be there in less than fifteen minutes.

"Do we have gas masks?" I asked.

"A dozen or so," Samuel said. "Ashton collected them over the years."

"*Gilgamesh* has about twenty," Ashton said. "How many men on board?"

"About thirty," Samuel said. "Enough masks for everyone."

On our first trip to the Great Blight, gas masks were not a precaution we had taken. We had gotten lucky. When Makara and I had gone to Bunker 114, I had passed through my first Blight. Just as we were about to reach the Bunker, the xenofungus had released some sort of spore that knocked us out. The only reason we were still alive was because Samuel happened upon us and pulled us into the safety of the Bunker.

"What are your coordinates?" Makara asked.

"I've already uploaded them to you," Ashton said. "Just open it up, and the ship can autopilot itself here."

"We're not doing this," Marcus said. "We have to finish what we started."

Makara held up a hand, silencing him. "And you said that it's fifty miles east of us?"

"Yeah, I'm hovering above it right now, trying to get some readouts. I'm not going to pass up this opportunity."

Makara turned her head to the side, concentration on her face. I'd seen that look before, and seeing it now scared me to death.

She was about to do something crazy.

"Marcus, we can come back and do this later. The mission against the Great Blight comes first."

"No, we're not," Marcus said.

But Makara wasn't listening. She veered the ship around, one hundred and eighty degrees. Everyone cried out as they were forced to the ship's side.

"We'll meet you there, Ashton," Makara said. "On our way now."

I was relieved. It seems strange to say I was relieved at going to the Great Blight, at the center of this new Voice, rather than what we had been doing.

"Makara, I hope you're doing the right thing," Char said.

"I am. I've got thirty fighting men on board, and the chance to deal a critical blow to the Blighters before they know what hit them." Makara increased the ship's speed. "I'm not going to pass up that chance."

Anna stared at her from the copilot's chair. "You're serious, aren't you?"

Makara nodded. "I am. I'm sure about this. The Reds can wait. This can't."

"You are sure?" Char asked.

"Of course I'm sure," Makara said. "How many times are you knuckleheads going to ask me that? Fighting the Blighters is what we're here for. It's what we do."

"What about the Reds?" Marcus demanded. "What about my fallen soldiers?"

Makara didn't answer for a moment. "We'll deal with that. As soon as we're done with this."

"No, that's not good enough!" Marcus said. "I refuse to help with this!"

"If you help us out here, we'll go after the Reds. I promise. They won't get away with what they did."

Marcus growled, realizing he wasn't going to win. In one moment, everything had changed. It was par for the course as far as I was concerned.

Char stepped up. "Hey, Marc, listen. You've got to hang in there. It'll just be another hour before…"

The fuse that had been burning all evening suddenly lit in a powder keg of anger. Marcus threw his arm back and swung wildly at his brother. Eyes widening, Char took the hit right in the jaw, spinning around and falling into Makara's seat, right across her lap. As Makara's eyes widened, Michael grabbed Marcus, pulling him off his brother. Meanwhile, Samuel grabbed Char, pulling him back.

Makara grimaced, and after putting the ship on cruise, stood up. "I will not have this on my deck! We are here to fight the xenovirus, first and foremost. Everything else is secondary. If that's a problem with anyone here, you can get the hell off my ship!"

Marcus's anger wasn't spent, yet. His arms and hands shook in an effort to control himself.

"You're a coward!" he shouted. "I knew you would back out."

Makara pointed at Marcus. "Someone, get him under control. We *are* going after the Reds. Plans change, Marcus. That's how it works. We might not get this opportunity again for a long time."

Just then, a shadow swooped past the windshield and behind the ship. A baleful roar shook *Odin's* interior.

A xenodragon.

"Anna, engage the auto-turret."

"Roger that."

"This is insane," Marcus said. "We need to turn back, now!"

"I'm not going to let one of those things scare me away," Makara said. "We're almost there."

The LCD showed the dragon, a dark mass in the night, chasing us from behind. The auto-turret fired, lighting the creature's frame in quick, successive bursts. The creature screamed, then ducked to the side, out of range of the turret.

"Keep following his trail, Anna," Makara said.

"I'm trying," she said. "It's getting away. Flying north. It's out of range."

"Why north?" Char asked.

I hoped the answer that came to my mind wasn't correct. "Probably to get some of his buddies."

That comment shut everyone up.

"Why are we doing this?" Marcus asked. "Why are we risking this *entire* mission? Just so some old man can do his research?"

"No," Makara said. "We need to blow this thing up. This spire Ashton talked about could be the source of this Voice. We need to take it out, now, before it can do any damage. It might even be the thing that will control the attack on Vegas."

Everyone grew quiet at that. Could it really be a coincidence? If this Voice had sprouted here recently, it could very well be for the purpose of attacking Vegas.

Marcus crossed his arms, but I could tell that even he could see her point.

"What's the plan when we get there, Mak?" Samuel asked. "If that thing comes back?"

"We land. We scout around, and see what there is to see. I want everyone who's going off the ship to wear a gas mask. I'm not taking any chances. We need to keep our eyes peeled for danger. Ashton wants to go on the ground and do some research first. I'm fine with that, as long as it does not endanger anyone in the group. The first sign of trouble, we're out of there, and we're blowing this spire to smithereens."

"Alright," Marcus said. "Fine. I see I'm not changing anyone's mind, so we can go on and find out what we can. But I'm holding you to what you said, Makara. We go for the Reds after this."

Makara nodded. "I won't forget, Marcus. They will pay for what they did to you and your men."

Marcus stepped back, placated, at least for now. The xenodragon was all but gone, lost in the darkness of night. I could see nothing outside. We were below the cloud layer, and no light made it through from above.

Makara switched on *Odin's* twin floodlights, pointing them down to the surface. The lights revealed alien, pink terrain that passed in a blur. We flew over jagged hills and twisting canyons, all covered with the sick, pink growth.

"About three miles out," Makara said. "Prepare for landing."

Marcus had gone back to the galley, probably to let his men know about the change in plans. Hopefully, they wouldn't take it half as bad as he did, or we were going to have a mutiny on our hands. Char went with his brother, to make sure that Marcus wouldn't start anything. I thought their being together was a bad idea, but no one else seemed to think anything of it.

"I've never been in the Great Blight," Michael said. "Can't say I've ever *wanted* to be in it."

"We'll be fine," Makara said. "Get in, do what we need to do, get out."

"Should be easy," Anna said, shaking her head.

"This could be our chance to learn about how the Voice works," Samuel said.

"Thinking like a scientist," I said.

Samuel nodded. "It's the chance Ashton and I have been waiting for."

From the galley came shouts and protests. The Exiles were not taking the news well. Marcus yelled, trying to calm his men down. It sounded like a losing battle.

"At least he's not instigating them," I said.

"They can bite me," Makara said. "Here we go."

She veered the ship down. I grabbed onto the wall, my seat having been taken by Char.

Then, it was in front of us: the spire Ashton had spoken of. It was a gigantic, organic swath, twisting and rising into the dark sky. The spire was tethered to the ground with thick, trunk-like struts growing out of the xenofungal bed. The spire was about five hundred feet tall, if I had to guess, and it ended on top in a series of jagged, cruel spikes – not unlike antennae. The entire thing was a deep purple color – the same color as the blood of the xenolife we'd had to kill all too often. The surrounding area was empty of tangible threats. Too empty. I didn't trust how easy this seemed so far, despite that dragon. It had merely flown off. Why? Was there something so nasty about this thing that even a xenodragon was afraid of it?

Apparently, similar thoughts were passing through everyone else's minds. It was Samuel who broke the silence.

"It looks like a radio tower. From that top, a signal can be projected and communicated to the entire xenoswarm. This thing is dangerous. It needs to come down."

"*Gilgamesh* has the missiles," Makara said. "*Odin* doesn't."

"Where is *Gilgamesh*, anyway?" I asked.

"We're about to find out," Makara said. She nodded to Anna. "Put Ashton on the line."

Anna fiddled with the communicator on the dash, opening the channel.

"Ashton, you have a copy?" Makara asked.

"Yeah, go ahead."

"We're here."

"Yeah, I see you up there."

"What's your location?"

"I'm at the base of this thing," he said. "Come on down. It's safe."

"You're *down* there?" Makara asked. "Ashton, I thought I told you to stay put until we got here."

"I want to study it up close. *Gilgamesh* is parked just a few feet away. If anything pops out, I can just take off."

Makara mouthed the word "stupid."

"Alright, we'll meet you down there," Samuel said.

Samuel's eyes shone with excitement. He hadn't had the chance to study xenolife directly since his time at Bunker 114. Seeing him look at that strange, creepy spire, as weird as it might sound, reminded me of a kid looking at a new toy.

"We just need to blow it up," Makara said. "Forget the research. That thing looks evil."

"Not before we have Ashton's go-ahead," Samuel said. "I'm curious to hear about what he's learned so far."

Makara sighed. "Fine. But we're blowing it up as soon as you guys are finished."

Samuel held up his hands. "Fine."

I was more inclined to agree with Samuel, though I could also see Makara's point. If that thing was transmitting another Voice, destroying it quickly might be a good idea. Then again, if we could learn about this spire before destroying it, it might help us out in the long run.

"All I know is, that thing creeps me out," Michael said.

Anna nodded her agreement.

"We'll get in and out of here," I said. "Won't be anything to it." At least, that's what I hoped.

As we circled around the spire, lowering to the xenofungal floor, I couldn't help but stare. The spire was thicker toward the bottom, a series of thick, twisting vines rooted in the xenofungus. The vines interlocked in a complex braid, circling around and around to form the spire's trunk. The trunk shot up in the sky, until they turned into the series of thin needle points that rose even higher. Samuel was right. The spire looked like it was designed to transmit something. There was no doubt in my mind that if this thing were destroyed, this second Voice would not be able to transmit itself over the air.

But I also remembered what Samuel had said about the Black Files. The xenofungus itself was a communication device. That meant as long as the Blighters were connected to the Great Blight, they could still take orders from the Voice. The point of the spires, then, assuming there were more than one, was the ability to transmit those orders over the air, beyond the reach of the Great Blight. Maybe the other, smaller Blights were part of the main xenofungal network as well, somehow.

All I knew was, the xenofungus was starting to seem less and less like simple fungus, and more like something intelligent. Something that could think and communicate. That's what made this fungus and the virus that spread it so scary. It was able to think and adapt, and that made it all the more dangerous.

Maybe it even knew we were here, right now.

Makara set *Odin* down next to *Gilgamesh,* which was parked on a level bed of xenofungus right before the xenofungal spire. Ashton, for now, wasn't in sight.

Makara left the ship running, keeping the power on low in case we needed to get out of here quickly.

"I'm giving us thirty minutes to find out whatever we can," Makara said. "Then, we're blasting this thing."

Samuel's eyes told Makara that thirty minutes would not be nearly enough time. Makara raised an eyebrow, causing Samuel to sigh.

"Fine. Let me grab my instruments."

The rest of us left the cockpit and headed for the galley. There, Char's and Marcus's men stood, talking quietly. None of them appeared happy. Michael and I went to the armory, and started to distribute what few gas masks we had. There were enough for everyone in the main party, plus a few of the Raiders, to have one. The Exiles refused to budge, feeling cheated out of their attack on the Reds.

"I can go to *Gilgamesh* and bring the other gas masks here," Michael said.

"I'll help," a nearby Raider said.

Another Raider stepped forward. Michael led them off the ship, and into the xenofungal field. Many men stepped back, afraid that the very air would poison them. I knew that wasn't likely, but being overly cautious was better than being overly zealous.

I fit my own gas mask over my face. It felt awkward there, and I hated the heat it produced just covering me. My breaths came in and out as hisses, and the straps dug into the back of my head. I pulled my hoodie up, getting ready to enter the Great Blight.

When the gas masks from *Odin* had been distributed and put on, Makara stepped forward, pressing the exit button to the blast door.

"Remember," Makara said, half turning and her voice warbling from her mask, "we're here for thirty minutes. Anyone who doesn't have a mask, stay here until Michael returns. Char, have everyone who goes outside set up a perimeter around this side of the spire. If anything comes, call out, and we're out of here." She nodded. "This might be our only chance for a long time to deal some damage to the invasion. Let's not screw it up."

The men looked at each other, grumbling. They didn't understand fully why we were here, even if Marcus had explained it – and I doubted he had done so fully. I wondered how many of these men knew the full purpose of this mission, or even of the New Angels. That was something we had to fix as well. We just hadn't had time to explain everything yet.

"Hold on a bit longer, guys," Makara said. "What we learn here tonight could help us out in the long run in our war against the xenovirus."

"*Could?*" another man asked.

Makara rolled her eyes. Well, I couldn't see her eyes roll in that gas mask, but I knew her well enough to know that she had probably done so. "Right now, the coast is clear, so let's get out there and do our jobs. Stay alert. Any sign of trouble, let me know immediately. No shooting at *anything* unless I give the order."

The men looked at her another moment before she left the ship, walked down the boarding ramp, and into the Great Blight. Samuel rushed off the ship after his sister, loaded with a large backpack filled with scientific instruments. Several of the men that already had gas masks also filed out, pistols and rifles in hand.

"This is a bad idea, isn't it?" I asked, my voice metallic.

Anna nodded. "Yep."

I followed her out the blast door, into the place I had been lucky enough to escape the first time.

Chapter 14

Anna and I silently strode out onto the bed of xenofungus, joining the Raiders and the Exiles in the dark night. The wind, warm and moist, crawled against my skin like the exhalation of a beast. The fungus beneath was squishy, sticky. It had been months since I had stepped on it, and just feeling it again made my skin crawl. I gazed out, away from the spire, seeing an endless field of xenofungus out to the point where my view was cut off by darkness. Several, smaller towers rose into the sky like alien trees, each one a good distance from the other. It seemed like their growth, or construction if you prefer, had been planned.

While Marcus and Char directed their men to set up a perimeter, Michael and his assistants handed out gas masks to anyone who was still without. It turned out that a lot of the men hadn't listened to Makara's order to stay in the ship until they got a gas mask. Once done, Michel joined Anna and me in walking toward the gigantic spire. Straining my neck, I could hardly see the top. The most disturbing part about the spire was knowing it was alive. We walked closer, until my feet were nearly touching one of its slimy, gnarled roots, as thick as a tree trunk. Several of these roots grew out of the fungus at the spire's base, twisting and turning and knotting together as they shot into the air above. The spire's entire base was wide – far larger than any tree I had ever seen. It was more similar in size to one of the skyscrapers of Vegas.

We found Makara and Samuel standing at the bottom of the spire, a good way off, staring up at something at the top of the roots, before they made a sharp turn upward. As I approached, I realized what they were looking at – or rather, *who* they were looking at.

"Ashton, you shouldn't be up there," Makara called, the gas mask dimming the loudness of her voice.

Ashton, however, heard, and waved a hand dismissively. He, too, was wearing a gas mask. At least he had taken that precaution. Rather than Ashton coming down, Samuel began to climb up a particularly large root – one that led directly to Ashton. I couldn't help but notice how the root palpitated as Samuel climbed up – as if it knew it was being climbed on. The entire spire seemed to give a barely audible groan, and the fungus vibrated beneath me. Was it communicating? Everything grew still once more. Once again, the warm wind buffeted my side, pushing me into Anna.

"It's not right here," she said.

I grabbed her hand. I wanted something to remind me that she was there in the darkness. With my other hand, I held my Beretta. We were in a dangerous spot, but I felt we were so deep into this that backing out was not an option. Likely, crawlers were setting up a circle and just waiting for the signal from this spire to ambush us all. I stared upward, noticing now, in the darkness, that the spire had a slight, greenish glow to it. The green glow allowed me to see the entire structural lines rising up and to see its branches webbing outward from above. Thin, spindly things, like hair, waved in the breeze, growing on the branches' undersides. Membranes, maybe. Some sort of antenna.

Samuel now stood next to Ashton. Together, they crouched low, and began to confer and take measurements. Samuel reached into his pack for some sort of tool. A scalpel, maybe. Once he pulled it out, he began digging into the root of the spire. Ashton, meanwhile, began to take pictures, the flashes of his camera like unworldly lightning.

All I could think, as they got to work, was that it was way too quiet.

I looked behind at the Raiders and Exiles, who now formed a solid perimeter around our half of the spire. Each guard was paired off with another, gazing into the darkness, ready for something to come at us. But as the minutes crawled on, nothing attacked. The fact that nothing did, the fact that Samuel and Ashton continued to work in peace far past our allotted thirty minutes, was the strangest and most terrifying thing of all.

When a full hour had passed, Samuel and Ashton had worked their way around to the opposite side of the spire. Makara went after them. Michael, Anna, and I followed silently, and the guards circled around in order to protect Samuel and Ashton from the new direction.

Ashton and Samuel paused on the other side, speaking quietly. The wind blew again, from the south, carrying with it the faint smell of rot. I looked to the south, imagining that something horrible might be lurking there. But I only saw a line of jagged, rotting hills, maybe half a klick out, covered with infected trees. Above, the clouded sky was dark, letting in no light. I wondered how it was that we could see, before I saw that it was not just the spire that was glowing – everything covered with the fungus was. It was faint, but it was there. I had assumed at first that it was just the light being reflected. But no – it was coming from the fungus itself.

Samuel and Ashton were now climbing down from the spire, picking their way carefully down a large root. Now, close to us, they knelt and slid the rest of the way down, landing softly in the xenofungus.

"Learn anything useful?" I asked.

Ashton nodded. "I think so. I'll learn even more when I take these samples back to Skyhome."

Samuel stared back at the spire, craning his neck upward.

"Any idea on how to bring this thing down?" Makara asked.

"Bullets wouldn't do any good," Samuel said. "You might injure it, but it would only heal."

Ashton gazed at the spire sadly. "Do we really have to kill it?"

We all looked at him as if he were crazy.

"Ashton, this thing is too dangerous to keep alive," Makara said. "I don't care how much research you think you can squeeze out of it." She nodded, affirming what she had just said. "It goes down tonight."

Ashton didn't answer. We continued looking at the spire. Almost imperceptibly, it swayed with the breeze. It was a living thing – maybe even a living consciousness. It was almost peaceful. But was that feeling true, or did the spire just want us to feel that in order to catch us with our guard down?

These thoughts were fuzzy. I was finding it very difficult to concentrate on any one thing. It was late, and the tiredness from the day was finally beginning to hit me. I wanted nothing more than to crawl into my bunk and sleep the night away – and perhaps a good portion of the day as well. I stifled a jaw-cracking yawn, leaning up against Anna for support.

That's when she fell down into the xenofungus.

"Anna!"

I knelt on my knees, finding Anna's eyes closed. Was she asleep?

That's when I noticed that Michael and Makara were also dreary-eyed.

Through the haze, I could think of only one other time I had felt this way – at the entrance to Bunker 114, where the xenofungus had released sleeping spores. But – this wasn't supposed to be affecting us. We were wearing gas masks.

Apparently, the masks were not enough. These things had found a way to beat them.

"We need to get out of here," I said.

As Samuel tried to wake up Anna, Makara and Michael nodded dully, just now reacting to what I had said. I looked upward, noticing that the spindly limbs at the top of the spire were shaking in the breeze. No, not in the breeze. There was no wind, at least not now. They were shaking of their own will, and what fell from them was a fine, glowing dust that was percolating into the air. It was covering everything – the fungus, my clothes.

My hands.

That was how, then. The thought barely registered as I fell to my knees. I twisted my torso in order to call for help from the men guarding us. But none of them were there. It was then that I noticed that they, too, had fallen to the fungus.

I realized, then, that this was the end. We would fall asleep, and never wake up. I held Anna, her long, soft hair fanning out over my arms. Her eyes were still closed. Above I heard a rustle, not from the wind, but from the spire as it continued to rain the glowing dust onto us.

Michael was next to fall to the fungus with a thud. Makara and I locked eyes for a moment before her gaze faded. She folded to the ground, collapsing to the fungus.

I looked upward once more, my vision fading. As I snuggled against Anna, the top of that ominous spire was the last thing I saw before darkness overwhelmed me.

***

What followed was a darkness so long and absolute that I couldn't be sure how long it lasted. Days. Weeks. Months? Surely not that long, but if it had been months, it would have made no difference in my perception of it. I drifted between consciousness and dreams, or dreams and death. I was in no state to tell the difference between one and the other. I saw alien images and colors that I could have never imagined on Earth. I was a flying bird, zooming across a pink landscape under a bright sun and purple sky, over faded ruins of a far-future Earth where the xenovirus had already taken over everything. I swam in deep, warm water, where I could see the xenovirus evolving, billions of years ago, in a primordial, alien sea, on a planet orbiting a star countless light years away. Where did it come from, this xenovirus? Were these dreams a message, or were they the imaginings of the sleeping spores?

Something Samuel said, seemingly an eternity ago, came to me:

Foolish thing – to run into a xenofungal field without the proper breathing equipment. If I hadn't come along, you would have been dead. Or worse.

We *did* have the proper breathing equipment, but the spores must have gotten in some other way, through my skin. Through the fog of dreams I remembered the glowing dust settling on my hands. But this thought slipped from my mind as sand slips through a crack. It just didn't seem important, now. Not anymore. I saw the effects of the xenovirus, infecting a thousand worlds across our galaxy. Why was it doing this? Why was it expanding? Why did it want to destroy everything?

Or did it want to save it?

I didn't know where this thought came from. All the same, it felt...right. But it *couldn't* be right. It was killing us, all life. It turned humans into ravaging monsters. It was twisting animals into warped versions of themselves. And some creatures, like the xenodragons and crawlers, did not seem to be of Earthly origin at all. How could it be saving us if it was killing us?

It was a wonder that I could comprehend anything when my head felt so addled. In my dreams I found a conscious lucidity that was hard to explain. I felt I suddenly knew everything there was to know, and that this knowledge would disappear as soon as I awoke. It was hard to tell if this was a feeling, or if it was the truth. It felt like the truth. These swirling dreams were my new reality. Strange as it might sound, this question wasn't important at the moment. What was important was discovery, of finding answers to all the questions that had been haunting me ever since the xenovirus killed everyone I held dear.

I walked forward, finding myself on Earth again. I was in the Great Blight, walking toward a line of hills under a boiling, crimson sky. At the top of one of the hills, a lone figure stood, brown cloak and hood swirling in the wind. I walked toward him, unnaturally fast, my gait seeming to take me a mile with each step. The man turned, and walked away – to the north.

I followed, and was soon running. I wanted to scream at him to wait, but no words came. Instead, I ran, fueled by a panic I didn't understand. If I lost him, I felt *all* was lost. Somehow, I knew catching up with the man would help me discover all the answers to the questions that had been maddening me for so long. I sprinted, finally making headway. The miles melted behind as I charged north, across flat plains spread evenly with xenofungus, past copses of deadened trees cocooned in pink growth and dripping slime. I passed lakes and rivers of pink fluid that cut their paths through the fungus, some of the liquid funneling into tiny crevices within the surface, dripping down, who knew how far. I ran and ran through thick, pink trees growing claustrophobically close. Then, as I burst from the trees, there was the man, standing at the top of a ridge.

I climbed the ridge, and walked up to stand beside him. Something told me not to look at him. Not yet. Instead, I stared straight ahead. I saw that I wasn't on top of a ridge. The ridge made a wide circle, round and round, like a rim, until it was lost to my sight. A bowl spread out before me, so wide that all of its edges were lost to sight.

Ragnarok Crater.

Within that crater I saw nothing but an empty field of pink, countless rocks and boulders, covered with the xenofungus. No, *not* rocks and boulders. They were the fragments of Ragnarok. An entire, fiery mountain had crashed down from Heaven, had rent itself into Earth, had created Hell. Sometimes, I wondered if it really had fallen down, the Rock – if the world *really* had ended like this, or if it was only one massive lie, designed to keep all of us

Bunker dwellers underground. From what I saw before me, it was all too real. Though I knew this was a dream, in my lucidity, I knew that this existed. This was real.

Swarms of flyers spiraled out from hidden holes in the ground, from between the cracks of crumbled, jagged mountains. Moving out of their holes, at lightning speed, were crawlers – thousands of them. With high and painful shrieks, they charged toward where the man and I now stood.

The man half-turned to me. "This is the fate of the world should you fail, Alex."

That voice. I could not place it, though it sounded so familiar – both in its tone and seriousness. At first, I thought it was my father. I don't know where this thought came from. Then, with realization, I remembered where I had heard it.

It all hinges on you, Alex. You have wondered, more than once, what your place is here. I am telling you now. Without you, this mission will fail. Without you, the world will fall and everyone will die.

I could finally find my words and speak.

"You are the Wanderer."

I turned to look at him, but the Wanderer's face was masked in shadow. The terrain had somehow become dimmer, the clouds thicker, and the darkness deeper. The Wanderer gave a slight smile, nodding in wordless reply. From my position, only his right eye was visible. It was completely white.

I stepped away. He was one of *them*.

But something kept me from running, even as the swarm of flyers and monsters rolled toward us in a Blighted tide, white eyes glowing. Though his eyes were white, he wasn't on *their* side. Though infected with the xenovirus, he was not a Howler. He had not fallen under the xenovirus's spell. He was something else. And I wanted to find out exactly what that was.

"The time is coming soon," the Wanderer said. "Everything is changing. And you will be the one to stop it."

"Stop what?"

He gestured outward, and with a sweep of the hand, including everything now attacking us. "This. This invasion from another world. Though a thousand worlds shall fall, one will remain. It is a prophecy as deep as energy. This cannot be altered. It was written from the beginning, in the fabric of everything."

I understood little of what his cryptic words actually meant, this blending of prophecy and science. I was beginning to think that they were one and the same – that the deeper we came to the infinitesimally small, the closer we came to the truth of reality. Was that truth God? Prophecy? Fate? I couldn't have said.

The crawlers and flyers were dangerously close, now. Still, we remained standing, to be consumed in pointless sacrifice.

"I want to do whatever I can to stop them," I said. "We all do."

He smiled. "You will get your chance, Alex. You must merely be patient. You must merely be open to the possibilities – to what the lords of fate place before you."

I had no idea what that meant, and didn't have time to think about it. A crawler, twisted and with three white eyes glowing, sailed through the air ahead of the swarm, on course to crash into me. I could only watch in horror as that twisted face gnawed at empty air, as its long claws curled in the expectation of entering my flesh. The end of my life was near, but still, I stood calm, defiant.

In a roar and beating of wings, a completely white dragon swooped right in front of me, striking at the crawler with extended claws. The crawler gave a wretched scream when another dragon, this one colored red, appeared on our left, giving a bone-shaking roar that stopped the frontrunners in their tracks. Both dragons swirled toward the ground, landing between us and the oncoming horde.

"We must go," the Wanderer said.

The dragons lowered their wings. The Wanderer ran forward, climbing onto the back of the white dragon. He meant to fly on it. Once mounted, the Wanderer looked at me with white eyes, expecting me to do the same.

Unthinking, I ran to the red dragon, scrambling up its leg and onto its back. I settled between two ridges there, and found myself surprisingly secure. I held onto the ridge in front of me. The hard, scaly skin was warm to the touch. No sooner was I settled than both dragons took flight, beating their wings and lifting off from the ground, where the crawlers writhed in a teeming mass in the spot we had vacated. The fungus and Crater fell away. We angled south as the sun victoriously burst through the clouds.

I smiled, wondering if any of this was real. I knew it was a dream, but it felt more real than reality.

We sped on, going even faster, the air sharp and revitalizing. Soon, the spire appeared in the distance – no longer sinister, but welcome – like returning home. I didn't understand this sentiment, because I had never had a home in my life. Even Bunker 108 had felt unreal – humans weren't meant to dwell underground, surrounded by gears and machines and bolts.

I suddenly had an outward vision of myself, riding on the dragon. It was such a strange sensation that it knocked the wind out of me. I saw myself, eyes staring ahead intensely toward the spire to the south.

And my eyes were completely white.

Chapter 15

I shot up in bed in a dark room, fear and panic clutching my heart. Cold sweat ran down my bare chest.

"Alex!"

It was Anna. I felt her hand on mine before I even had a chance to realize where I was and what was happening. A moment of chaos passed, where I didn't know or understand anything. There was a deep pulse, a thrumming, surrounding everything. It was a moment before I realized that this sound and vibration was *Odin,* flying through the air.

"What happened?" I asked, my voice parched.

Anna reached for a nearby canteen in the darkness, and held it to my lips. I felt the cool water enter my mouth. I drank a good long while.

Anna didn't answer me for a moment. "I'll get the light. I'll tell you everything."

"No. Don't. Keep it off, unless you want to split my head open."

My mind was still spinning. The images I'd seen were a maelstrom, overwhelming me, keeping me pinned. I had no idea where to start – whether I should try to connect to that reality, or this one.

Anna sat down next to me, the cushion of her stool swishing. She held my hand again.

"I'm glad you're awake," she said. "You were out for the longest time."

"How long?" I asked. "Spores, right?"

I could see Anna's head nod in affirmation in the darkness. "They got in through our skin. Maybe through the mask, too. But yeah. We were all out for a long while, but all came to with the morning. You, though...you stayed unconscious. We moved you onto the ship. We didn't lose anyone, but we also weren't attacked. Makara gave the order to blast that damn thing to pieces."

At first, I didn't know what she was talking about. Then I realized that she was referring to the spire.

"No," I said. "You shouldn't have done that."

I didn't know why I felt so strongly about that. I was remembering my dream. The spire was the last vision I'd had, apart from the fact that my eyes were –

I closed my eyes.

"Alex?"

No. It was just a dream. It wasn't real. Still, I kept my eyes closed.

"So, it's really gone?" I asked. "The spire?"

"Yeah. It is."

Anna wasn't telling me something, and it was driving me crazy.

"You never told me how long I was out."

She hesitated. "Two days, Alex."

I sat up straighter in bed, opening my eyes. "Two days? We should have left that thing alone. It wasn't what we thought, at all. Is Vegas still there?"

Anna didn't answer me, and her lack of an answer was answer enough.

"I didn't want to shock you," she said. "Not at first. You've been through a lot."

I felt coldness crawl over me. Another city, gone. The second largest one in the Wasteland. Thousands of people dead, in a couple of days. And I had been asleep during all of it.

"That's why we're in the air, then," I said. "That's why we're not helping."

"Makara and the gang lords gathered who they could," Anna said. "A couple thousand, maybe. Thousands more died. The farms were the hardest hit."

The farms. Michael's wife and kid would have been there.

"Michael's wife is fine," Anna said. "So is his kid. They're both on the ship, safe." She sighed. "Much more so than everyone else. They're all heading west. *Gilgamesh* and *Odin* are hovering above them, to keep the air clear of any dragons, if they come."

"Have there been any?"

Anna shook her head. "No. Not now, at least. They attacked the city, and there was nothing we could do. When we shot that spire thing down, it made them all go haywire. The only thing we could do was try to evacuate everyone. Luckily, Rey and some of the other lords had already prepared a lot of supplies and trucks. The water trucks are filled, and will help water the people and fuel the vehicles...at least for a little while. They won't last forever, though."

"How long?"

Anna paused. "A week, maybe. Even with the amount we have, we're going to have to find another water source, soon."

I said nothing, and could only be shocked by how much things had changed. I realized then why that spire had been empty of Blighters. It wasn't because it was trying to trick us. It was trying to protect us. In the dream, something strange had happened. The Wanderer, with his white eyes, had been infected with the xenovirus. But he was not dangerous. At least, I didn't think he was. And the feeling I got, when we had ridden the dragons back to the spire...

My head swam. We rode *dragons*. It was just a dream, but it had felt so real. It was messing with my mind, now, so much so that I knew, without a doubt, that destroying that spire was a mistake. It had unleashed the swarm.

"It's really gone, then?"

Anna nodded. "We're probably ten miles west of Vegas now. Everyone's been kept going by force. I don't know how much time we have until the swarm starts to follow…"

I shuddered. Everything had changed so quickly. I felt *I* had changed, though I hadn't been awake to witness any of the attack's horror. I had been here, sleeping, while everyone had been down there, dying.

"I guess everyone in our group is alright?"

"Yeah," Anna said. "It was the farms that got hardest hit, like I said. We rescued a lot of the farmers. Many were left behind."

I squeezed her hand. "Are *you* alright?"

"I don't know," she said, after a moment. "I'm still trying to decide that."

"I can't imagine what it must have been like. Did the gangs make it out alright?"

"Yeah," Anna said. "Makara, Char, and Marcus hold the reins, for now. The fact that they were *right* is giving them some leverage with the gang lords. Who knows how long that will last, though? Rey and Jade want to go their own way, and Cain is thinking of going with them." Anna sighed. "None of them understand that we can't be fighting each other right now."

"They'll probably agree to work together," I said. "At least for now. Without unity, they can't have L.A. Now, out of their home, they have no choice but to press on."

"I hope you're right." She leaned down, kissing me on the cheek. "I was afraid you'd never wake up. At first, we thought you were dead. Your pulse was so slow. You should have seen how worried Makara was."

I laughed. "I don't believe you."

"It's true."

"Where is everyone?" I asked.

Anna was looking at me, not answering. Something had changed. Even in the darkness, I could tell that she had tensed.

"What's wrong?" I asked.

A sudden fear clenched my chest.

That was when Anna screamed.

Before I knew what was happening, she rushed to turn on the lights. I was blinded, and covered my eyes with my arm, so as to shield them.

Footsteps sounded from the corridor. Michael slid open the partition, running into the room.

"What the hell is going on?" Michael asked.

Anna was crying. Crying at *what*?

It wasn't long before I got my answer.

"His eyes..." Anna said. "He's turning."

I turned my head to the side. I knew I was in the clinic, and if that were so, on my right there would be a mirror. I faced myself toward it, not daring to open my eyes.

Then, slowly, I opened them, and wanted to scream myself.

Anna was right. My eyes were completely white.

***

I stared at my reflection dully for a moment, wondering how it had happened. But the image didn't lie. My vision wasn't any different than what I was used to, except perhaps my sensitivity to light was sharper. Looking at the reflection in the mirror was like being stared at by one of *them*. The eyes – I couldn't think of them as *my* eyes – stared back at me empty, vacant. There was no doubt. Like the crawlers, like the dragons, like the Wanderer – I was infected.

No wonder Anna had screamed. No wonder she had run.

Michael still stared at me, his expression shocked.

Samuel and Makara were next to run into the room. I kept my head turned. I wanted to hide. I didn't want any of them to see.

"What's going on?" Makara asked.

I dreaded what would come next. I didn't want anyone to know, neither her, nor Samuel, nor anyone else. Anna's reaction was enough pain for a million lifetimes.

I knew, however, that I would have to face this sooner or later. I turned my face upward, and opened my eyes.

Everyone gasped.

"I'm infected," I barely managed.

No one said anything for what seemed an eternity. I heard Char and Marcus speaking outside the door, their enmity now forgotten. I wondered who would be the first to draw their gun.

Samuel suddenly took charge. "Makara, find us a spot to land. Now."

"Where?"

"Anywhere! Just hurry. Bring the army to a halt. Anna, call Ashton. Tell him to drop everything and come here.

Anna didn't move.

"*Go!* You want to help him, don't you? There might still be time."

She ran out of the room.

Time? There was no time. Once infected, there was nothing now preventing me from becoming a Howler. All the same, wouldn't I have transformed by now? Anna said it had been two days since the spire. Usually, it took no more than two hours for someone to turn.

What the *hell* had happened to me?

With Anna and Makara gone, Char and Marcus entered and stood against the wall, saying nothing, ready for anything. I sat up in bed, shaking my head. I was glad that both of the women were gone. For some reason, they were the last ones I wanted to see me like this. My gaze first found Samuel, who just looked at me as if to confirm that what he saw was real.

"Holy cow," Michael said. "She wasn't kidding. White as a Howler's, only the rest of you is normal."

"I have no idea what happened," I said. "I had a dream, where I found the Wanderer, and his eyes were the same way. Maybe I'm more like him than the Howlers."

I remembered something the Wanderer had told me – not in the dream, but when we were in the cave, on the way to the Great Blight. He said he had gotten lost in the Great Blight, and that he became...different. His eyes had been clouded then, as well – yet not completely so, as mine were now. But in the dream, they had been dead white

"Well, you haven't turned," Samuel said. "It's been two days since we were all knocked out by that spire. You were in a deep sleep the entire time. Maybe the spores affected you differently. The thought that you would turn never came to any of us."

I still didn't know what Samuel was talking about. Why me? As far as I was concerned, we had *all* been affected by the spores. Was I the only one with whitened eyes, the only one that was turning?

Beneath me, I felt the ship veer and dip to the ground below. Makara was landing.

"What do you remember, Alex?" Samuel asked.

Everyone waited for me to speak. Marcus slid shut the clinic's partition door behind him. As I watched the brothers, something seemed different between them. During my sleep, they had come to some sort of understanding. I guess being attacked by an army of crawlers was enough to do the trick.

"I remember flying to the spire, and you guys collecting samples," I said. "That's it. Then, nothing. I found out about Vegas from Anna, before she..."

I couldn't make myself go on. Everything felt broken with her, now. I had no idea how long I had left in the world. Samuel just needed whatever information I could give him, if I didn't make it through this.

"As you said, the spire released some sort of spore that knocked everybody out," Samuel said. "None of us woke until morning, but you stayed out. You were still alive, but in a coma so deep I didn't know if you were ever going to come out of it. I kept those thoughts to myself, however. Anna, though...she never left your side."

I didn't want to think of Anna. I didn't blame her for screaming at me. I would have done the same. That realization didn't make the pain go away, however. It just made it worse.

"When we came to our senses, we flew away from the spire," Samuel went on. "Makara decided we needed to destroy it. I didn't argue." Samuel shook his head. *"Gilgamesh* shot off a couple missiles at the spire. It went down easily enough."

"What happened then?" I asked.

"Well, it didn't change your state. Your eyes stayed closed, and you stayed in your coma. But everything else changed. As soon as that spire went down, all hell broke loose. The swarm – dragons, crawlers, birds, behemoths, and other monsters besides – they came out of nowhere. Many had been buried in the fungus, dormant. We took off for Vegas, the swarm on our tail. We had to get the city population moving before it was attacked."

For a minute, my changed eyes were momentarily forgotten as I focused on Samuel's story.

"What happened next?" I asked.

"The swarm attacked Vegas. They didn't stop for anything. The farms were the first struck, but luckily we had time to move everyone behind walls, taking a large supply of food and water while we were at it."

"Yeah, Anna told me as much." I turned to Michael. "Glad to hear your family is alright."

Michael gave a single nod, but said nothing.

"That night, and for the rest of the next day, we fought. The gangs gathered, such as they could, against that storm. It didn't matter who was who anymore. We were all just fighting for survival. We battled over the next two days, trying to let anyone who couldn't fight get a good head start. Finally, at the last minute, we turned and fled. The city was gone. We left by the west gate last night, leaving that city to its fate. The swarm is still in the city. There are people there. I guess they won't be people for long."

Those words chilled me. Two days, and it had all gone to hell. Now, we had a force of two thousand people out in the middle of the desert, in the dead of winter. Food, water, and supplies were low. We had to make it to Los Angeles under these conditions, and not only that, but conquer the city.

It seemed impossible. And it was even more so for me, if the virus had its way with me. I would never live to see how it all turned out.

"You said killing that spire caused all this?"

Samuel nodded. "It appears so."

Then, a thought came to me. Maybe the spire wasn't directing the Blighters, as we thought. Maybe it was holding them back. Protecting us, even. Calming them. However, that thought didn't make any sense. Or maybe the Blighters had been so angry to see their spire fall that they had to attack. That was the likeliest option. Only...

I remembered my dream, such as I could. Those dragons had rescued me, for some reason. It wasn't just a silly dream. It was real. There had been a message there – a message from the Wanderer. What was he trying to say, aside from the fact that my eyes were white now, like his? *That* had been real enough. Unfortunately, I didn't have any answers. Answers were what we needed, but I didn't see any way to find them. The Wanderer, wherever he was, was not about to walk into our camp and explain everything.

If my eyes were white, like theirs, did that mean I was somehow part of the xenoswarm? I didn't know who I was anymore. Maybe I wasn't even fully human. I didn't understand why all this was happening, why it had to be me. I remembered the Wanderer, and his prophecy. It all hinged on me, somehow. Those were his words. What did my current state have to do with *that?* If I was going to die before I had the chance to play my part, what good was any of it?

"I'm not going to turn," I said, with sudden realization. "While I was asleep, I dreamed about many things. But it was more than a dream. I learned things about the virus, about xenolife, even about where it all started. Even though I learned all this, there is still so much I don't know. Somehow, I have to find out."

Samuel and the others said nothing, merely staring at me. I had no idea if they believed me or not. Maybe they thought I was crazy.

I went on. "I met the Wanderer. He took me to Ragnarok Crater, and showed me what was going to happen to the world if we failed. Showed me what has already happened to a thousand other worlds before ours."

"This has happened before?"

I nodded. "You were right about the dragons. They aren't from here. They're from somewhere else. Somehow, the xenovirus still has genetic information taken from other planets. The dragons are one example. The xenofungus is another." I looked at each person in turn. I could tell that my eyes were throwing them off. Those hardened, grizzled men had difficultly looking into them. "There is more to this than we think," I said, ignoring the fear I saw. "When you guys killed that spire, it unleashed something."

I paused as the ship slowed its descent, falling toward the ground at a steady rate. We were about to land.

"Go on," Samuel said.

"I don't even know what I'm saying," I said. "I just think that whatever happened to me is different from the Howlers. Different from all the other monsters we've fought. After all, the Wanderer had the same eyes as me, and he wasn't a Blighter. Do you remember?"

Samuel said nothing, only looked at me. I could not discern what he was thinking. He looked to the side, unsure what to say.

Char and Marcus just sat, listening.

"Are you two good now?" I asked. "I haven't seen you throw punches at each other in the past five minutes."

Char hesitated a moment before answering. A slight smile came to his lips. A large, black welt swelled under his right eye, above the marred side of his face. "It's a work in progress, but the attack on Vegas is giving me a new perspective. Seeing all the gangs fighting together instead of with each other for once is something I thought I'd never see. As far as what happened back then, with the dam...well, it's a long story. It was wrong. Hopefully, Marcus and I can come to terms about that."

"What happened to the Reds?" I asked.

Marcus shook his head. "That attack never ended up happening, as you can imagine. The Great Blight changed all that. I assume they are still back in Vegas. Either that, or they went off on their own."

Samuel turned back to face me. "Whatever happened at the spire, just seeing and speaking to you now, you are clearly not a Howler. Something else happened, something we can't explain, yet."

They all paused, looking at me. In unison, all of their eyes widened in surprise.

"What?" I asked. "What's happening?"

Marcus pointed to the mirror. "See for yourself."

I hesitated to turn. Looking in that mirror the first time had left its scar, a scar I didn't want to reopen.

When Char nodded at me, a thin smile on his face, I turned, and looked.

My eyes had resumed their usual brown color.

Chapter 16

I didn't feel any different, but there was no doubt. Reflected in that mirror, my eyes looked as normal as they ever had been.

I got up from the bed. I was still dressed in my clothes from two days before, though my boots had been taken off. I stared in the mirror, looking for any sign that my eyes had been white just a moment before. But there was nothing. They looked completely normal.

"What the hell...?"

"I don't know," Samuel said. "We'll keep an eye on it." He paused. "Pun not intended."

Anna burst back into the room. "I just spoke with Ashton, and..."

She looked up at me, her eyes widening. I looked down and away. She took a step toward me.

"Alex, your eyes are fine!"

"Yeah. They're back to normal, now."

Before Anna could speak again, Samuel cut in. "I'll need to take a blood sample." He looked at Anna. "Sorry, but I have to get started immediately. I want to have at least something to update Ashton with by the time he gets here."

"Well, he said he'd be here in just a few minutes," Anna said. "He's not far."

Samuel reached for a syringe in one of the clinic's white cabinets. I winced as he stepped closer, wielding the instrument like a knife.

"Careful," I said.

"Hold out your right arm."

I held out my arm, closing my eyes. The needle pricked my skin, and I felt a numbing sensation as my blood was drawn. After a few seconds, the sensation ended. I opened my eyes. Samuel dabbed my skin with some alcohol, and covered the skin-prick with a bandage.

"Well," he said, looking at the syringe. "That's interesting."

I didn't see anything at first. But there was something off about my blood. It was darker than usual, having a violet hue. It reminded me of the purple blood the monsters had. It was proof that this wasn't over – that I was far from normal.

Everyone frowned as they stared at the sample.

"I don't feel any different," I said. "I feel normal. Healthy."

"This can't be good," Samuel said. "Clearly, you are infected with xenovirus. But this strain isn't the Howler strain. It's something else."

Everyone looked at me, as if I were going to transform into a Behemoth at any moment and snap off their heads.

"Seriously," I said. "I feel fine."

"We believe you, kid," Char said. "Things can change quickly, though. We're just being careful."

Makara stepped into the doorway. She looked at me, her reaction much the same as Anna's.

"Holy...what happened?"

"He's back to normal," Anna said. "We were afraid for no reason."

"Now, hold your horses," Char said. "It isn't over, yet. Not until the doctor gives us his word that it is."

"He'll be here, soon," Anna said. "I know Alex will be fine. Right?"

She looked down at me hopefully, but I didn't know the answer to that. Maybe she was just trying to make up for her reaction earlier. I wanted to tell her it was okay, only the words wouldn't come.

"We'll wait and see," I finally said. "I have no idea what's next, only I *think* I'll be fine."

Anna looked at me, seeming to accept that answer.

"While we're waiting on Ashton, we have things to take care of outside," Makara said. "There's an entire army out there that needs to know what the agenda is."

"The nearest settlement is two days away," Marcus said. "Let's hope they can make it until then."

Makara sighed. "We can discuss that outside."

Makara left with the leaders of the Raiders and Exiles in tow. That left me, Samuel, Anna, and Michael in the room.

Michael stepped forward, his brown eyes earnest. I noticed, for some reason, that he was wearing that same camo brown that we both had been wearing on my first foray in the Wasteland, months ago. It seemed like another lifetime. Things had been so different, then.

Michael looked like he was going to speak, but he said nothing. Michael was your guy when you needed something done. But now, no one knew what to do about me. We were just waiting for something to happen, even if that was me snapping.

"What's next, then?" I asked.

"Makara's just trying to keep everything from falling apart," Anna said. "Which is due to happen at any moment."

"I guess Jade and the Diamonds are causing trouble."

She shook her head. "You have no idea. If only that weasel had died back there with the rest of them."

It was difficult to wrap my mind around the fact that Vegas was gone. It must have been harder for Michael and the gang lords to comprehend it. It had been their home. And now, the xenoswarm was on our trail. They would pause at the city, but it was just a minor hurdle. How soon until the crawlers caught up with us? Could we reach L.A. in time, getting inside before we were overwhelmed?

"Is the basic plan still the same?" I asked. "Go to L.A.?"

Samuel shook his head. "We don't know. We're trying to restore order, trying to get all the gang lords to agree on the same damn thing." He clenched a fist. "It isn't easy. And there is still a lot of stuff we have to do beyond all that. Visit the northern Bunkers. Talk with Ohlan and Oasis, and any other settlement that might listen."

"What about Julian?" I asked.

It had been over a week since I'd seen him – which seemed like no time at all. But with the amount of things that had happened between now and then, it might as well have been months.

"Julian and New America, too." Samuel said. "And at some point, we'll have to return with Ashton to Bunker Six. I want those other ships to work with. They'll give us an edge we'll need in the upcoming battles."

That meant more trained pilots. Maybe Skyhome could help out with that.

"What about Bunker 108?" Michael asked.

Michael's mentioning our old home brought up horrible memories; visions of exploding bodies, severed limbs; memories of my father, bathed in purple blood; Khloe, buried under the red sand. A whole Bunker, my Bunker, had become Hell in a single night.

"There will be weapons there," Samuel said. "Supplies. We would be remiss to pass it up. It's right on the way."

"I know," I said.

"We'll get there when we get there, Alex," Michael said.

"If I get there."

"Hey," Char said. "None of that talk, alright?"

I supposed he was right. "What's our next stop, then?"

"Well," Samuel said, "Makara, Char, and Marcus have their sights set on a settlement in the southwest. Called Pyrite, if I remember correctly."

"You do," Michael said. "I passed it on the way here."

"Why there?" I asked.

"We need to get everyone supplied and fed. It takes a lot to feed the amount of people we have. There won't be a steady supply of food until we are in L.A., safe. Which means we have to move quickly."

"What about Skyhome?" I asked.

"Skyhome has a little extra food," Samuel said. "It grows enough to sustain its current population, but that's about it. Its hydroponics are designed to support only a hundred people. We have to support two thousand, and that number is likely to grow."

"Pyrite's a small town," Anna said. "Though it's been a while since I've seen it."

"It still is," Michael said. "But they have farms."

"We're just going to steal from them?" I asked.

"We're going to ask, first," Samuel said. His face was grim. He was determined to succeed, whatever the cost.

Samuel still believed that getting to L.A. and taking down Carin Black was the best way to stop the xenovirus. I was no longer convinced of that. After what I had seen, the mystery behind the xenovirus had only deepened. Yes, what I had seen was in a dream. But my white eyes hadn't been. Somehow, I was infected, but I wasn't one of them. Once again, I was left with more questions than answers.

If there *was* an answer, it wasn't to the west, with L.A. It was to the *east*, with the Great Blight.

The only problem was that an entire army of Blighters stood between us and that answer. And if I told the crew what I really thought, they'd think I was crazy.

Outside, I heard the roar of an engine. *Gilgamesh* was here.

"Ashton," Anna said.

She stood up from the stool she had been sitting on, casting me a worried glance. I tried to let her know I'd be fine. I avoided the temptation to look in the mirror again, to make sure my eyes weren't white. I never wanted her to see me like that again.

Anna left the room, and Samuel still held the syringe filled with my blood. I could see the purple tinge to the red. It was undeniable. Something about me had changed genetically.

When Ashton got his hands on that vial, we would all find out the truth.

* * *

Ashton arrived not too long after, toting a medical bag and wearing a white lab coat. As he entered, he offered a sympathetic smile, a smile that seemed empty of meaning. Seeing his medical bag and lab coat, for some reason, scared me more than a gun would have. His blue eyes were serious, and he brushed his long, wild hair out of them. The wrinkles on his brow and at the edges of his eyes were more pronounced than ever. He forced a tired smile.

"How are you, Alex?" He asked, pulling up the stool Anna had vacated.

"Fine," I said, eyeing the bag. "Considering the circumstances."

Ashton's attention turned to the blood sample Samuel now held out to him. Ashton took it, holding it up to the light. His eyes focused. He flicked the vial twice with his index finger.

"Yeah, that's a bit strange," Ashton said. "The first thing I need to do is put it under the microscope. I can then confirm that the xenovirus is there. I will need to cordon off the *Gilgamesh* until I am done. It should be safe to handle, as long as I don't spill anything, but in case something happens, I don't want to risk infecting anyone else. Alex...you will come with me. Understood?"

"You think I'm going to turn."

Ashton paused a moment before answering. "If you were going to turn, you would have done it by now. It's been two full days since the spire. I think you are in control of yourself. Obviously, we'll need to investigate this as much as we can. We need to keep an eye on things, and make sure you don't display any symptoms typically found in Howlers..."

"What about the eyes, though? That's a symptom."

"That's what we're working to discover, Alex. It is likely a new strain of the xenovirus. Something that is different from the one that causes the Howlers, or the Behemoths, or anything else for that matter. Whether it's dangerous or not, we cannot say now."

"How could it not be dangerous?" I asked. "It's the xenovirus."

Then, I thought, what about the dreams I'd had, visiting alien worlds and running into the Wanderer? Despite the danger present, these dreams had been almost...peaceful. It was strange, because the xenovirus was a thing of violence, of blood, of conquest. Maybe my perception of those dreams had everything to do with my being infected with the xenovirus. If the xenovirus was a part of me, then of course I would think of it as unthreatening. Wouldn't that be inevitable?

Then again, maybe I was just going crazy. A lot of questions haunted me. Questions barely remembered, yet important all the same. The Blighters *had* been behaving strangely in those dreams. The xenodragons had allowed the Wanderer and me to fly on their backs. Was it all a trick, a sham, something designed to let my guard down?

The xenoswarm was coming. If we stayed here, they would be upon us, soon. That swarm would leave a wake of destruction as it chased us across the Wasteland. It wasn't just Augustus's army we were chasing, now. We had to deal with the far more tangible threat of being ripped apart by a crawler, of being speared by a dragon's talons or pecked to the bone by a cloud of flyers.

"Alex, I need you to come with me."

Ashton had been looking at me for a while, along with everyone else. I felt like an animal in a zoo.

"Can you stand?" Michael asked.

"I think so."

I put my feet on the deck. I found my boots sitting nearby. Samuel moved to help me put them on, but I brushed him away. I could do this myself. I slipped one foot in, then the other, and began to lace the boots. I still wore my pants and my shirt. My hoodie lay on the counter to my right side.

I went to it and pulled it on. I was standing, my legs stiff from lack of movement in the past two days. I stretched, expecting to feel a bit different. I gazed in the mirror, one last time. My eyes stared back, questioning, wondering. Afraid.

I *really* had to pee.

"Bathroom," I said.

They parted for me as I went to the lavatory. As I let loose, I didn't even look down. A full minute later, I reached to flush, surprised to see yellow in that bowl rather than purple. I wondered, while I had been out, who had been cleaning up my messes. I just hoped it wasn't Anna.

I washed my hands, drinking deeply from the tap. I gazed at myself at the mirror, at my thin face, my haunted brown eyes, my shaggy hair. I looked, and felt, crazy.

I sighed, turning for the door. I had to put all this aside for now.

Ashton was waiting for me in the hallway.

"Let's go," I said.

Chapter 17

We entered the bitterly cold air, air that I felt could freeze the marrow of bones. When I took my first breath, it was like being punched in the gut. It was so *cold*, cold beyond my wildest imaginings. Men and women were camped out here, *sleeping*. How many would live to see the dawn?

Both ships were parked at the top of a low hill. Below, I could see massive fires – hundreds of them – burning in the night. The people huddled in their tents and crude shelters, in their cocoons of blankets, warm breath fogging the frigid air. Wood smoke hung in the air, not from trees, but from scavenged buildings and the ruins of civilization. Civilization, I guess, wouldn't mind getting a little more ruined.

My face and ears were numb by the time Ashton and I reached *Gilgamesh's* boarding ramp. We didn't go up the side boarding ramp. We used the wider, lower one, directly in the ship's back. I hadn't even known about this one until recently. It led directly into the cargo bay, and parked in that bay was a Recon, facing out.

"That's new," I said.

"Michael showed us where he left it," Ashton said.

His tone of voice said that this detail wasn't important. Given what had just happened to me, I didn't blame him.

Still, I was curious. As we entered the bay, Ashton pulled out a small remote, clicking it. The door began to shut behind us, and warm air blasted out of a vent above. The air warmed my chilled bones. As the door continued to close, I followed Ashton to the right side of the Recon, past barrels of supplies, tools, clothing, gas masks, and fuel. This was the main difference between *Odin* and *Gilgamesh*, aside from their obvious disparity in size. *Gilgamesh* had a large cargo bay that could be accessed from the outside, a cargo bay large enough to store an entire Recon.

At the end of the bay, Ashton led me up a short set of steps, directly into the galley. The door shut behind us. The air was now comfortably warm.

I turned right after Ashton, toward the clinic. I realized that this was the first time I had ever been alone with Ashton. I didn't know why, but it put me on guard. I had no idea what he was going to do to test me.

We stepped inside the clinic, a near mirror image of *Odin's,* except that it was slightly larger. I almost expected Makara or Anna to come running down the corridor right now. I wanted either of them here right now...especially Anna. I wanted to let her know that everything was alright. She would probably be turning over her reaction to me in her head, and I needed to let her know that was pointless, so we could go back to how things were.

"Sit down," Ashton said. "This should only take a moment."

I sat down on the neatly-made bed. Ashton went to the clinic's other side, where a microscope was set up. The clinic was large enough to double as a small lab.

"What are you doing now?" I asked, to break the silence more than anything else.

Ashton donned a face mask, then dripped some of my blood from the vial onto a clean petri dish.

"Looking for signs of xenolife," he said.

It was quiet again. I fiddled with my hands. I always hated the feeling of not doing something. It made me think too much, worry too much. And now I had a lot to worry about.

"Hmm. We've got xenolife in here. That's for sure."

I looked up from my hands. "What kind?"

"Just a minute." Ashton squeezed one eye shut, peering through the microscope with the other. "The basic structure is all the same. Only I can't tell anymore unless I can compare it with what we already have in my database. I'm going to need to return to Skyhome to analyze it. When I compare with what I already have on file, I can be absolutely sure that it's something new."

Hearing him say that made me wonder what I was doing here. If he could just take my blood sample home and analyze it there…

"Wait…" I said.

I realized exactly why I was here. He didn't just want to take a blood sample to Skyhome. He wanted to take *me*.

"I'm not going back to Skyhome," I said.

Ashton looked at me. "This is necessary, Alex. I hate to take you away from this, but this is an opportunity we can't pass up. Coupled with what I discovered from the spire, this might be just what we needed. We will be able to find out if…"

"…If I'm dangerous?"

I was standing, now. I felt dangerous. And angry. I didn't want to be taken from here.

Ashton backed into a corner, his eyes wide. "Alex, there's no need to…that's *not* what I meant!"

I calmed myself down. "I'm *not* volunteering for this, Ashton. You have my blood sample. If you need anything else, I'll give it to you. I can't leave here. I'm needed."

He looked at me. I could tell he was trying to think of what to say next, wondering what the magic words would be to get me to agree. There were no magic words, though. Nothing could get me to agree to this.

I heard the blast door to the outside sliding open beyond the clinic, then footsteps running down the corridor. Ashton said nothing as Anna appeared in the doorway.

"Anna, he's trying to take me back," I said.

Anna didn't say anything for a moment, but she didn't have to. Her silence said everything for me.

"Ashton told us that, and...we all think it's best, for now."

I couldn't believe it. The feeling of betrayal welled up, so much that I thought I was going to break down right there.

"This can't be happening."

"You're not well," Anna said, her eyes full of concern. "Surely, you can see that much? I'll come with you, so you don't have to be alone."

I sat down, too weak to move – too weak to resist, or shout, or be angry. The wind had been taken out of my sails.

"You don't have to come with me," I said. "You'll probably be more useful here."

I didn't look at her, and I didn't want to see the pain in her eyes. Worse, I was more afraid that there wouldn't be any pain there. That nothing I said or did mattered. Apparently, that was how it was going to be. They had all decided this, behind my back, in the past ten minutes.

"Why?" I asked, unable to mask the pain.

"We knew you wouldn't agree," Ashton said.

"You were afraid I would attack you."

"No, of course not," Anna said. "Aren't we allowed to make mistakes?"

"Seriously?" I asked, at last looking up. "You're trying to make me feel guilty? *You're* the one who made the mistake. *You* are the one in the wrong."

Anna pursed her lips, crossing her arms.

"This is decided already," Ashton said. "It'll be best for you, too. You can't be here when the xenovirus is living inside you." Ashton gazed at me intensely. "Get that in your head. The xenovirus is living *inside* you. It has transformed your blood and your eyes. That much is clear. Do you *really* think your being here is the best idea right now? Yes, you are not a Howler. No, you are not violent. But there's nothing that says you won't be, in time."

I couldn't argue with him. No one could predict what was going to happen to me.

"I'm coming with you," Anna said. "We'll get this taken care of, and come back to Earth."

Ashton said nothing in response to that. I knew it probably wasn't going to be that simple.

I couldn't bring myself to look at either of them. I wanted out of this room. Out of this mission.

Out of everything.

I sighed. If everyone wanted me out of the way, then there was little point in staying here.

"Take me to Skyhome, then."

***

I felt betrayed, not just by Anna, not just by Ashton, but by everyone.

"We don't know what to expect, Alex," Anna said. "This wasn't easy."

"It's not that you made this decision," I said. "It's that you kept me out of it."

Neither responded. Maybe I was being stubborn, but I still deserved to be part of major group decisions like this. Maybe they didn't trust my ability to reason, anymore. Maybe they thought the xenovirus would make that impossible for me.

It was clear from Anna's stern expression that she had already steeled herself against any protest I might make. They all had. I wasn't going to leave this clinic on my own, not until everyone was sure that I wasn't going to turn on them.

"The others aren't even going to see me off, then?"

"I told them to hang back," Ashton said.

"Why? In case I get dangerous?" I glowered at Ashton. "These are my friends, and you're keeping them from me. You think I'm going to snap and kill everyone."

"You *could!*" Ashton said. "We don't know what will happen to you, and until we find out, I'm keeping as few people around you as possible. It's enough that the old geezer gets to risk himself. I told Anna to stay away, but here she is now, against my orders." Ashton quieted. I looked at Anna, and saw from her eyes that what Ashton said was true. Ashton continued, quietly. "She's not disloyal to you. Quite the opposite."

"I would never hurt any of you," I said, looking at Anna. "Least of all Anna."

"Yes, you are in control now," Ashton said. "But for how long? These are questions that need answering immediately. We are going to Skyhome; end of story."

It was settled, then. Anna and Ashton were taking me hostage while we left everyone else behind in the cold desert, all so Ashton could play scientist. I knew, deep down, that nothing was wrong with me. What was frustrating was that I couldn't get *them* to see that. All they saw was a potential Howler ready to snap.

And I can't say I blamed them. I was to become a lab rat, and then what?

"This isn't right," I said.

They both looked at me, willing me not to move or do anything rash. I could believe one of two things: what they were saying, or what I was feeling. This feeling within me was so much stronger than all their words. I almost wanted it to be the opposite. Going along with what they wanted would be easier. But I *knew* I was right. I had dreamed the answer, and I knew this answer to be true. The Wanderer had spoken to me in that dream, that revelation. I had to believe in myself, and that was all that mattered.

"We're doing this all wrong," I said. "You need to listen to me."

Anna and Ashton moved to block the doorway. I ignored them.

"The xenovirus," I said. "We have it all wrong. There's more to this than its trying to take everything over. There's a reason, and I'm going to find it out."

I was standing, now. Anna just looked at me, her eyes pleading with me to sit down, just as I had been. But I couldn't just sit. I had seen too much.

Everything hinged on this.

My vision swam; Anna's and Ashton's forms became wavy and ill-defined. The rest of the room swirled, and then stabilized. Without even looking at myself in the mirror to my side, I knew. My eyes had changed.

I had to get out of here.

I walked forward.

Anna reached for her katana, drawing it out.

"Stay back."

Her eyes were afraid, pained. I didn't want her to look at me like that.

"Let me out," I said.

Anna stood in front of the doorway, refusing my request. She thought she was helping me. She thought she was right. I thought I was right. I knew, from her eyes, that she would never kill me. Her drawing that katana was a useless gesture.

"Don't do anything, Alex," she said. "I'm warning you."

She looked at Ashton quickly. Ashton reached into the cabinet.

"What are you doing?" I asked.

"Just stay still, Alex."

"What are you doing?" I asked again.

Ashton retrieved a syringe, filled with a clear liquid. Probably a tranquilizer.

"*No!*"

In unison with my roar came a great howling from above, the tremendous sound piercing through the ship. Ashton covered his ears as Anna closed her eyes, the horrible shriek shocking us all with its sound. A gust of wind swooped past the ship.

A xenodragon had come.

Anna looked at me, as if I were to blame for this.

"What do we do?" she asked Ashton.

Then, *Gilgamesh's* side was pummeled by a colossal force. The lights flickered as we were sent tumbling to the deck.

This was my chance. I scrambled to get up before either Anna or Ashton could. Fate had provided an escape, and I was going to use it.

"No!" Anna screamed, grabbing my leg.

I fell to the hard deck, doing my best to crawl away. Anna was strong, though. She reached, trying to pull me back into the clinic. I could hear her katana blade scraping on the deck.

"Now, Ashton!" she yelled.

In my peripheral vision, Ashton fumbled for the syringe, which had rolled away toward the wall. Time was running out. I didn't want to hit Anna. Instead, I twisted myself, wrenching free of her grasp.

She shrieked in frustration, crawling forward. I gasped, scrambling up and aiming for the blast door.

I stumbled again when *Gilgamesh* shook beneath me, only this time I didn't fall. I pressed the exit button, and the door hissed open. I ran down the ramp into the cold, dry air. Screams filled the night as the dragon circled in the darkness above. Shots fired from around the camp, echoing across the desert flatland.

As soon as I ran away from the ship and into the dark night, the dragon wheeled around, coming straight for me. I wasn't afraid, though. I merely stood still as its form slowed and two legs came down, alighting on the ground gracefully. It stood before me, staring down at me with white, peaceful eyes. It seemed strange to think those eyes peaceful.

I knew, instantly, that it was here for me, and I knew what came next. I reached out a hand, stroking the dragon's neck. The light pink scales seemed to vibrate at my touch.

"Alex!"

Anna stood on the boarding ramp, her katana drawn. Samuel and Makara were circling around from *Gilgamesh's* front. They, too, stood in shock as they saw me touching the xenodragon. Michael slid to a stop, a cloud of dust rising before him.

I looked into the dragon's eyes, feeling it understood everything without my needing to utter a word. My friends continued staring from beside the ship, doing nothing, as I walked around to the dragon's back. It remained on the ground, waiting.

The yells of men sounded in the distance. Several crested the hill, toting guns that they now pointed at the dragon.

"No!" Anna shouted.

The men didn't listen. They shot, spraying the dragon's side with bullets. The dragon cried out in pain, but I imagine those bullets were more akin to the stings of angry insects than any sort of death-blow. Those scales were like armor, and it would take more than conventional bullets to pierce them.

Then I understood why the dragon was here. It was going to fly me away.

I felt that this was inevitable, and I had no reason not to try. It was now or never. Going back would mean returning to Skyhome and being Ashton's lab rat for who knew how long. If I really felt I was right, I had to prove it, and that meant flying this dragon wherever it was pleased to carry me.

I crawled up the dragon's leg, settling onto its back, between the two ridges I knew were there. It was just as it had been in my dream. As soon as I sat, the dragon gave a roar and cast off, flying away from the ship, leaving behind the curses of men and gunshots and fire and chaos. The wind was cold, but I leaned forward, and the dragon's warm body helped shelter me from the elements. Below, I could hear Makara and Anna yelling, could hear Samuel and Michael shouting, chasing after me. It was futile. They were already becoming smaller with darkness and distance.

I wondered, for a moment, just what the hell I thought I was doing. A moment of doubt overcame me as I rose into the darkness on the back of this gigantic beast, this dragon that could turn upside down, right now, and end me forever. It was a terrifying thought, and I clutched the dragon's ridge in front of me more tightly. Then I calmed. I didn't feel like I was in any sort of danger. Now, out of the camp, I felt safe. Wherever this dragon was taking me, it was where I was supposed to be.

The dark ground passed beneath. I wondered if Anna and Ashton had been right, after all. If they had been right, the xenovirus was now leading me to my doom. But if the virus wanted to kill me, this dragon could do it, right now. The fact that it didn't meant I was being carried somewhere for a reason.

Another thought struck me. Maybe it wasn't killing me because I was part of the xenoswarm.

And that thought didn't scare me as much as it should have.

Chapter 18

I had fallen asleep at some point on the back of the dragon, its body keeping me warm even as the cold wind buffeted against me. I opened my eyes, forgetting for a moment where I was, what had happened. It all came back as I watched the rosy sunrise in the east, glowing on the edge of the Great Blight. Or was it the Great Blight itself that was glowing?

The dragon glided low to the ground. The Wasteland below was empty and forlorn, a dark spread of shadows, dunes, and mesas. There was no sign of the city of Vegas, either ahead or behind. We were flying straight for the Great Blight. For what purpose, I couldn't guess.

I pulled myself upright on the dragon's back, the muscles in my back stiff and my eyes weary. The dragon beneath reacted to my stirring, heaving a long sigh as it beat its wings against the wind.

Almost there, it seemed to say. I didn't know if that was what it was really saying, or if it was just my imagination.

The realization of everything that had happened suddenly struck me. I was *flying* on a dragon. I was infected with the xenovirus. I was flying into the Great Blight. The events of the night seemed unreal. Still, no matter how hard I tried, the feeling of betrayal wouldn't go away. If my friends had all had their way, I would be in Skyhome now. But I had run away, and now found myself here, flying toward the Great Blight. Maybe to my death.

I had only myself to blame. Maybe I was as insane as they thought I was. Maybe the virus *had* changed me.

We passed the pink border of the Great Blight just as the sun fully rose, obscured behind layers of luminescent, crimson cloud. The light spread its fingers, igniting the entire eastern horizon with a fiery glow that belied the cold, dry air. The light illuminated the pink, alien trees that poked through the surface of the fungus like wispy hairs. Tall, pink grass waved in the wind like fields of grain. Sticky pink pools and rivers flowed toward lower elevations, bleeding through the fungus. It was beautiful in its own surreal way.

The dragon took me even lower. In one of these pools, I could see several crawlers soaking below the surface, dormant. Was this how the monsters were birthed? A flock of birds flew like a swarm of insects from a thick stand of xenotrees, spiraling toward the sun in an organic whirlwind. The xenolife should have attacked me on sight, but they ignored my presence on the dragon. Another sign of my change, perhaps? Maybe I really was one of them, now.

We flew a while longer, the sun doing little to warm the chilled air. I wrapped my hoodie tighter. I wondered if my eyes were still white. They had to be. I wondered how long it would be until my transformation would be complete.

"Where are we going?" I asked the dragon.

I didn't know why I asked it that. The dragon couldn't answer, so I guess I was just trying to break the silence and loneliness. The dragon gave no reaction, merely flying on in a straight line, due east. I remembered my dream, and thought, with dread, that I might be flying to Ragnarok Crater. If *that* was where I was headed, then I could never expect to get out alive. Maybe I was being taken hostage for some reason. But that didn't seem right. Why even bother with that when these dragons were programmed to kill? Apparently, these dragons also had a penchant for ferrying sixteen-year-old kids to who knows where.

I got the beginnings of my answer as the dragon flew upward, above a steep rise coated in alien purple and pink. Once above, I saw the ruins of the spire *Gilgamesh* had shot down. It was gray, lifeless, its many roots blasted, tangled, and disconnected from the nourishing fungus. I didn't know if it was my natural, human feeling, or the virus within me, but I felt sad at the sight. The fungus appeared to be thicker around its base – perhaps trying to heal it? Pink goo flowed from the spire's base like blood, down to a valley in the south, where it collected in a small lake. Maybe it wasn't merely *like* blood. Maybe it *was* blood.

The dragon drew closer to the spire. With a high-pitched cry that shook my bones, it extended its claws, alighting on the ground. It folded its wings, and knelt. We had come to the end of our journey.

I hesitated only a moment before hopping off, the xenofungus beneath my feet padding my fall. As I stepped onto the eerie fungus, it glowed beneath my weight, fading over time to its normal color. *That* hadn't happened before. I couldn't help but feel that it was its way of registering that I was connected to its network.

I tried not to be freaked out by that. I walked forward, to the spire. I gazed at it for a moment, its dead, twisting mass bewildering. What was I doing here? Was I to be punished for being part of the team that destroyed it? I turned back to the dragon, but its white, featureless eyes gazed back at me empty, answerless. The large beast gave a slight shiver, grieved at the sight of the spire. Could these monsters feel? I had always thoughts of them as unthinking beasts, caring only about killing. Maybe they were more than that.

I turned back to the spire, noticing a change taking place at its base. The roots began to twist. I took a step back as they unraveled, revealing a dark opening that led deep into the thick mound of xenofungus that supported the spire. It was just wide enough for me to enter.

I hesitated. I waited, for a moment, for something to come out. The dragon gave a low growl, urging me onward.

"Easy," I said, beginning to step forward.

I felt fear grip me as I moved toward the opening. I had bad memories of going underground, so I was more than a bit hesitant. It was completely dark within, but it was clear that it led down. I realized, upon entering, that those very same roots could close in on me, trapping me beneath the surface. But I saw no other option at this point, so forward I went.

I walked down the slope, into darkness. As I had guessed, the roots curled shut behind me. As soon as they did, the walls of the tunnel began glowing pink, offering just enough light to move onward. The tunnel sloped, spiraling toward the right.

I began walking. There was a creepy deadening of all sound. Immediately upon each new step, the sound of any squish was absorbed by the walls. The air was cool to begin with, but as I walked on, spiraling lower, it became hot and stuffy. I was crawling into a living thing, and that thought made me shudder.

I walked for about five minutes in this way, wondering when, or if, the spiral would ever end. When at last it did, I gasped at the sight before me.

I had entered a cavernous chamber, covered on all sides by xenofungus. Before me was a wide, pink pool, strangely clear and pure. Stalactites of xenofungus hung above, dripping yet more pink slime, filling the pool. The pool could probably be more accurately described as a small lake – it stretched far, and various inlets jutted out of my sight, deeper into the space, everything glowing pink from the fungus itself. Strange as it might sound, it was beautiful in its own alien way. The surface of the fungus gleamed, like crystals.

I noticed a small island out in the middle of that lake. One person sat on it now, back to me, under the branches of a silvery tree, the roots of which traveled down the sides of the island, burying themselves deep within the lake. I called out, but the surrounding xenofungus and pool shimmered, absorbing my words long before they could make it to the island.

I would have to go there myself.

I stepped to the pink shoreline, my boots just inches from the strange liquid. It looked viscous, like water, only it didn't move. The entire surface was still as glass. I bent down, and reached my hand toward the surface. I touched it. It was warm, and the liquid wrapped itself around my fingers. When I raised my hand, the liquid slid right off, back into the pool, joining the still surface of the pink lake. It might have been even *more* fluid than water. Each molecule of the stuff was obeying its own command, knowing when to stick together, and when to dissipate. Maybe, at its basic level, the liquid's smallest components were *alive*.

I didn't really want to swim through something that was alive, but I saw little choice. I believed I was meant to talk with that man on the island, and to do that, I had to step into the pool and swim to that island. I did so now, the organic goo surrounding and compressing my body. I panicked for a moment as the pool constricted around my chest, pushing the air out of my lungs. Then the pressure was released, and I could breathe again. This stuff could very well kill me, if it wanted.

I swam outward, toward the island. After a few moments, the liquid of the pool only just began to soak my clothing. It was easy to stay above the surface – the liquid pushed me upward, obviously much denser than water. Its current pushed me along, so much so that I could probably have ceased all motion and it would have carried me straight to the island. Ripples rather than waves emanated from my position, bouncing off cave walls, advancing ahead toward the island. When I was halfway there, the first of my ripples made it to the island's shoreline. The man's form stiffened, but he gave no other reaction.

I knew who it was, long before I arrived. It was the Wanderer. I increased my speed in order to meet him. *He* was the one who would give me answers to all the questions that had been haunting me. The glittering walls of xenofungus were strangely peaceful as I swam along, nearing the island.

I gasped as something grabbed my foot. A cold, fearful sweat poured from my body, but subsided when I realized what it was. My foot had merely touched the lake bottom. I placed both of my feet on the ground, surprised to find that it was much shallower than I had anticipated. I stood, the slime trailing off me in waves, rushing back to join its larger part in the pool. Within moments, the entire upper half of my body was completely dry. I stepped the rest of the way out, and the rest of the slime flowed off me, crawling down my skin and clothing to be absorbed into the xenofungus. It tickled a bit, making my skin tingle. I rubbed my arms, trying to remind myself what *normal* felt like.

Thankfully, the sensation left as the goo fell away, and I realized that *everything* in here was alive. It was a startling realization. I wondered if even the air I breathed – warm and pungent with a spicy, alien scent – was filled with xenolife. It was truly like being on another world.

The Wanderer still had not turned. He was garbed in the same brown robe and hood I had seen him wearing over two months ago – the very same I had seen in my dream. I climbed up the incline of the small island and stood just a few feet behind him. The silver tree's limbs hung above me, a blending of Earth and non-Earth. It was like no tree I had seen before. Its bark was pure, glittering silver, and its delicate trunk rose from the xenofungus gracefully. Spindly limbs protruded outward, beginning perhaps twenty feet high, from which more limbs grew, sprouting thin, pink leaves that had glowing silver spots. It gave a sweet, natural aroma – something I could not place, but that was familiar. Whatever it was, it was a familiar smell, full of a sad, ancient reminiscence I didn't understand, something buried primordially deep, something so true as not to have words. It was like remembering the happiness of childhood from the perspective of an adult – bittersweet longing, smelling a dream, or reality as it was meant to be.

It was hard to describe, but I could see why the Wanderer had chosen this spot for his meditation. I thought about trying to get his attention somehow, but I merely stood, trusting that he would sense my presence. I had a feeling he knew I was there. I could only speculate as to why he summoned me.

The Wanderer finally stood, turning to face me. His eyes, like mine, had gone completely white, set in his wrinkled, ancient face. Long, white hair was obscured by the hood of his robe, and his long white beard gave him a sagelike, and perhaps even a wizardly, appearance. The beginning of a smile was on his lips.

"I was worried you would not come," he said.

I said nothing in reply. I was overwhelmed by so many questions that I did not know what to ask first. I did not know if it was even *okay* to ask.

"I had nowhere else to go."

The Wanderer nodded, indicating the ground. We both sat across from each other, legs folded. He looked at me, waiting for me to go on.

"So, I'm one of you guys now, right?"

My voice had no problem carrying, now. The fungus and the air did nothing to impede its progress. I realized then that speech is a peculiarly human form of communication. These creatures had no need of it. They had the xenovirus and the xenofungus to communicate with each other in their own language – if it could even be *called* language. Sound might be involved in their communication, but it was nothing like what we called "speech."

"I told you this long ago, Alex. That it all hinged on you. Do you still believe that?"

I wasn't sure, anymore. Now that I was infected, I probably wouldn't be fighting alongside my friends anymore.

"I don't know if I believe that," I said. "That's why I'm here. I want answers. I want more than what I saw in that dream."

The Wanderer nodded, expecting me to say that. So he had dreamed it, too. It was a reaffirming sign that I was not crazy.

"You will get your answers, Alex. Though they might be a bit...overwhelming. It is the nature of truth to be overwhelming." He paused a moment, looking into me with those eerie, white orbs. "You are *Elekai*, now."

I paused for a moment at the unfamiliar word. *"Elekai?"*

The Wanderer nodded. "And when you and your friends destroyed the Xenolith, you dealt us *Elekai* a mortal blow."

"The Xenolith?" I frowned. "You mean the spire?"

"I imagine you thought you were helping. But it's just another setback. We will rebuild, somewhere else. We will run, before *they* come."

I had no idea what, or who, the Wanderer was talking about.

"You mean, the Xenos? Samuel calls them that. *Are* they coming? And if they are, when?"

The Wanderer looked at me quizzically. He and I were talking about completely different things.

"They are already here," the Wanderer finally said. "The Xenominds. The first is in Ragnarok Crater. The second..."

The Wanderer paused, looking at me. I was confused for a moment, until I realized who the second one was.

"You are the second," I said. "You are the New Voice."

The Wanderer smiled, nodding. "I am not *the* New Voice. Merely *a* Voice, because we are many."

My mind spun as I thought of the implications. The Wanderer had told me that he was not just a Voice, but that there were more of them. If that was true, then we could never find them all. And even if we did, more would rise in their place. We couldn't just kill these spires – these Xenoliths, as the Wanderer called them – and be done with it. This invasion would *always* have direction if there were more Voices to contend with.

Worse, I was an unwilling participant in it – infected, but not completely turned. It made no sense.

"You mentioned the *Elekai*," I said. "What does that even mean?"

"Alex, *that* is the crux of this whole thing. When you understand what it means to be *Elekai,* then you will know everything you need to know to stop this. To save this doomed planet from its timeless fate."

I sat, listening, and the Wanderer began to explain.

This was going to be a long story.

Chapter 19

"For millions of years, on hundreds of worlds, there was war – a war very much like the one playing out now, on this world. A war that has happened ever since the rise of the Xenominds, three hundred million years ago."

Three hundred million? How could this be *that* old? Nothing existed that long. It seemed impossible, ridiculous on its face. But I needed to listen, all the same.

"There were always two sides of the Xenominds. There were the *Elekai*, the Gardeners. And then there were the *Radaskim*, the Destroyers."

I stared at the Wanderer, blankly, not comprehending anything he had just told me. I didn't even pretend to understand.

"You're going to have to repeat that. What is a Xenomind, exactly? You've mentioned it a few times now."

"Forgive me," the Wanderer said. "A Xenomind is what you would call a Voice. It is a higher consciousness that acts as a communication hub for all the xenolife under its thrall."

"So, it *is* real," I said. "Ashton and Samuel were right. If we can take out this Voice…"

The Wanderer held up a hand. "Let me continue. There is more to it than that."

I nodded. I supposed that was probably true.

The Wanderer continued. "Think of the *Elekai* and *Radaskim* as alien tribes. Each side has its own Xenominds, who in turn have their own goals and motivations. The Xenominds would be like gods to your eyes. The xenolife under their control follows their directives without question. Some Xenominds allow their xenolife a great deal of latitude, allowing even sentience. This is all beside the point I'm trying to make. I'm only trying to illustrate that there is great diversity of values and goals among all Xenominds. Not all of us are bad, and in fact, many of us are good, and do not want this to happen to Earth." The Wanderer paused. "We *Elekai* want to save it."

"Okay, let me get this straight," I said. "There are lots of Xenominds, and they are at war with each other? Even on Earth?"

The Wanderer nodded. "There are two Xenominds on Earth. I am the *Elekai* Xenomind. And to the north – in Ragnarok Crater – is the Xenomind called Askala, who leads the *Radaskim*. This is the one you call the Dark Voice. This is who you are fighting."

I had to pause a moment to think. It was difficult for me to comprehend that there were two sides of this. I had always thought of the xenovirus as a single entity, trying to conquer the world, as Samuel and Ashton had always said. That in itself was confusing enough: we were being colonized, so that when the aliens came, they would find us gone, and a world ready to receive them, shaped to their specific needs.

The Wanderer was saying the opposite was true. There were no "aliens," no equivalent of humans coming in their starships to colonize this world. The aliens were already here, and they have been fighting their own war against each other for millions upon millions of years across the cosmos.

"You said there were two sides," I said. *"Elekai,* and *Radaskim*. Can you explain the difference?"

The Wanderer nodded. "It is key that you understand both sides, and what they want. That said, one side cannot exist without the other. Both are encoded into the xenovirus, which infects *all* xenolife, regardless of its allegiance. However, one day there will only be one side. And this is a war the *Radaskim* are winning.

Probably *will* win, in the end."

This was a lot to take in, but I did my best to follow. "So, there are two alien sides. The *Radaskim* are the ones who are killing everything, spreading the Blights, trying to take over the world? And the *Elekai* are trying to stop the *Radaskim* from doing that?"

The Wanderer nodded gravely. I had a feeling that I had only scratched the surface, even after everything the Wanderer had just told me.

"The *Radaskim* seek perfection in all things," the Wanderer went on. "They kill in order to attain that perfection. Their xenofungal networks contain genetic information of a thousand races, all now dead, across hundreds of worlds. They live in perversity, creating new monsters in their pools. When you see crawlers, or the dragons, or the birds turned by the virus, you see the creatures of a thousand worlds, evolved and perfected by the xenovirus. If genes are incompatible, the xenovirus finds a way to make them work. The Warrens, in Ragnarok Crater, is where most of this is done, where most of these creatures are birthed and evolved. The *Radaskim's* goal is to create an unstoppable army, using the genes of the worlds they conquer, against unconquered worlds. And they only get more powerful over time. So far, no one has been able to stop them, on any world. Not even the *Elekai.*"

"Why are they here, then?" I asked. "Why are they killing us? You said they want genetic perfection. *Why* do they want that?"

I remembered asking the Wanderer why we were being attacked, over two months ago when we had run across him in the Wasteland. I hadn't even known the xenovirus *was* alien, then. The Wanderer had not given me a direct answer to that question, then, and I wasn't sure if he was going to give me a direct answer now.

"You speak of the Eternal War."

I didn't realize I'd spoken of the Eternal War. I waited for the Wanderer to explain.

"The Xenominds are ancient beyond compare," the Wanderer said. "They are old – older even than many stars. They can exist for so long because they are not bound by a single body. They are comprised of many elements of life, elements that can replace themselves as they wear down. By this definition, they might not even *be* alive by human reckoning. They grow and evolve themselves over the eons, albeit slowly. As long as xenolife persists, they do, too. Any information they acquire is stored in the fungus.

"But even as old as the Xenominds are, they are in a race against time. You see, because they *are* so old, the Xenominds experience time much differently. A hundred years is but a breath to them. Communicating over the vast light years between star systems, which would take many human lifetimes, is just a thought to them. All this means that the End, for them, comes much more quickly."

"The End?" I asked. "The end of what? I thought *we* were the ones coming to an end."

"The Xenominds do not see it that way. They can only see the grand picture, and the *Radaskim* in particular see opposing life forms – aliens, in their eyes – as insects that must be brushed aside, or made useful, to pursue their goals."

"You said the Xenominds were in a race against time. Are they coming to an end? You said they've existed for three hundred million years."

The Wanderer gazed at me, so piercingly that I knew what he was about to say was the crux of everything. Why we were being invaded. And, maybe, how we could stop it.

"The *Radaskim* are trying to stop the End of All Things."

I stared at the Wanderer, dumbly, not sure if I had heard him right. What he had just told me was so unreal, so unfathomable, that I couldn't wrap my mind around it.

"All things? You mean...the death of the universe?"

The Wanderer didn't respond, and his lack of response was my answer.

"I'm sorry, but the end of the *universe?* That's not supposed to happen for, what, billions of years? Trillions?"

"An eternity for humans," the Wanderer said. "A lifetime for the Xenominds. You see, in the grand scope of things, they still see themselves in their infancy. They still believe they have a chance to stop the End, before the stars expand so far apart that they will never have that chance again. 'Catching the stars,' they call it. They intend to catch them all, if possible, but it may be an exercise in futility. The cosmos is so vast that even with all the time the universe has to offer, it won't be enough. This does not stop them from trying, however. They are even seeking ways to invade other galaxies, with technology so advanced that it will surely seem as magic to you..."

The Wanderer paused, giving me time to process what I had heard. I didn't even know if I could process it. He was speaking of things I had never thought of before.

"The *Elekai* believe this race against time is futile, not to mention evil. Regardless, the *Radaskim* are interested in discovering what they call the Secrets of Creation – secrets that will allow the *Radaskim* to reset the universe, before it fades to cold, eternal death. The Xenominds have time – billions of years, in fact – and the knowledge of a thousand advanced races, now dead, locked in their networks. Whether this knowledge is of any use in attaining their goals – no one, least of all me, can say."

"Who are the *Elekai,* then?"

"The *Elekai* seek to end the violence and wanton destruction of the *Radaskim*. And this is not without its own sense of irony. The *Radaskim* seek to stop the disintegration of the universe, but in order to do that, they must destroy it. The *Elekai* seek to save the diversity of life throughout the cosmos, but by saving life, they doom the universe itself to die, in the end – thereby ending the Universal Cycle."

I frowned, my brow furrowing. This information about Xenominds, the end of the universe, and the Secrets of Creation was breaking my mind, if only just a little bit. I wished Samuel were here, because he would understand this better than I did. If I ever saw him again, I was going to have a hell of a time trying to explain this.

I was about to ask what this Universal Cycle was, but the Wanderer resumed by answering this question before I could even ask it.

"The Universal Cycle is *Radaskim* prophecy. They believe the universe died, and was reborn, an infinite number of times, both ahead and behind, or alongside, or however you want to envision it. They believe it is their victory, their immortality, to discover the Secrets of Creation, before it is too late. Using this knowledge, they are able to reprogram the universe to obey their will – to 'reset' it to the state it was in before it expanded – only to repeat the same thing over and over again. They claim to remember this happening an infinite number of times already, through their most ancient Xenomind, who endures even the infinite deaths and rebirths of the universe. They claim this Xenomind is God. They believe, given these premises, that their winning the Eternal War is inevitable."

"Is any of that real, though?" I asked. "It just seems so remote."

"The *Elekai* believe as you do. As far as we know, this is the only universe ever to have existed. The Universal Cycle could just be the *Radaskim* Xenominds' religion that fuels their expansion – an expansion that serves no end but to kill."

"Tell me more about the *Elekai* Xenominds, then," I said.

"The *Elekai* Xenominds are older even than the *Radaskim* Xenominds. We do not conquer or kill other creatures, as the *Radaskim* do, and we do not utilize the genes of other races unless they are volunteered." The Wanderer smiled. "I am an example of that. Or, rather, the one I used to be is."

It made sense. This was why I was not a Howler. I had the *Elekai* version of the xenovirus inside of me, not the violent *Radaskim* version.

"Wait..."

The Wanderer raised his eyebrows. It was a curious expression, when coupled with his eyes.

"You said the *Elekai* don't take genes, unless they are volunteered." I looked at him pointedly. *"I* didn't volunteer for this."

"You didn't," the Wanderer agreed. "Not yet, anyway. It is a little against protocol, but you still have your chance to refuse the call, and you can return to normal. Before you do that, listen to what I have to say."

I frowned, a sudden fear clenching my heart. "What do you mean, refuse the call?"

"You can ask the virus to leave you, right now, at this very moment. And it will. And you can walk out of here untouched."

Doing that at this moment was far from my mind. I still needed to learn more.

The Wanderer smiled. "I'm glad you are willing to listen. Because there is more you need to hear about the *Elekai* before you make your final decision."

"My final decision?"

"The *Elekai* are fighting a losing war. On a thousand worlds before this one, the *Elekai* were all but eradicated, by various causes. The longer the war goes on, the more powerful the *Radaskim* become. They are willing to kill to achieve their aims, to use their power to destroy – that is why they are the Destroyers. The *Elekai* will not compromise on this point. We seek to stop the *Radaskim*, but we are, at heart, Gardeners. We wish to grow and flourish without the need to destroy. We wish to preserve all forms of life, seeing them as the gifts of the universe. To kill is a travesty beyond words."

"No wonder you guys have been losing."

"Indeed. Still, we are seen as the threat – the mutation – when really, *we* are the original Xenominds. The *Radaskim* are the mutation."

"What do you mean?"

"We *Elekai* lived on only one world, far away, uninterested in reaching for the stars. The *Radaskim* came into existence by way of a mutation within the xenovirus itself, which freed them from the constraints of morality. We *Elekai*, non-mutated, allowed the *Radaskim* to live alongside us in peace. As the eons wore on, the *Radaskim* Xenominds became all the more aware of the End of All Things. They could not make peace with the fact that death was to come for all – even the universe. This was the beginning of their religion focused on stopping the death of the universe. Unlike the *Elekai*, the *Radaskim* do not have to obey any intrinsic moral code. This belief is what led the first *Radaskim* Xenominds on their quest for the stars, to conquer the first worlds."

"Always, we *Elekai* were right there with them. After all, the xenovirus is the same, wherever you go. It all depends on a single gene – whether that gene is on, or off, determines whether whatever form of life that virus controls is *Elekai*, or *Radaskim*. Moral, or amoral."

We sat for a moment, until I allowed myself to fall backward against the soft bed of fungus I sat on. I stared upward at the glowing cave ceiling and silvery branches of the xenotree, my thoughts a jumble. My original inclination *had* been right. This went much deeper than anyone realized. We were fighting a powerful alien race that had already conquered a thousand worlds, of which Earth was one. It seemed impossible, but it also made sense, somehow.

"How do we stop them?" I asked. "There has to be a way, right?"

"There is," the Wanderer said. "It is a fool's hope, as it had been a fool's hope on a thousand worlds before ours."

"What is it?" I asked. "Do we kill this Dark Voice – the one that leads the *Radaskim* – up in Ragnarok Crater?"

I sat back up. The Wanderer was quiet for a moment, as if going on would be hard for him. I wondered why.

"You weren't always the Wanderer, were you?" I asked.

The Wanderer shook his head. "I remember little about who I was before. What I told you, in that cave several months ago, is all true. My family and I survived in a self-made bunker close to Mt. Elden since 2030, but over the years, I was the only one who survived. I wandered into the Great Blight, seeking my own death. I almost achieved that aim, when I fell into this very pool." The Wanderer gestured around the cave. "The xenovirus entered me, but it did not kill me. I became part of the Blight. And suddenly, I understood everything – learned either through the virus itself, or the dreams the *Elekai* Xenominds transmitted across space, from the home world. You see, we Xenominds have a way of listening to our songs, even across light years of space."

I closed my eyes, trying to listen for those songs. But I heard nothing falling from the sky – just the silence of the cave, the silence of my thoughts. Just days ago, anything infected with the xenovirus was to be feared. All xenolife was my enemy. Maybe it still was, for all I knew. But now, things had changed. These two tribes – *Elekai* and *Radaskim* – were in their own war, in which we humans were but pawns. A thousand pawns had already fallen, and if nothing were done, we would fall, too, to be forgotten for the rest of time.

"We need to stop them," I said.

The Wanderer looked at me, weighing my resolve.

"You told me that it all hinged on me," I said. "I'm telling you now that I'm ready. How do we stop it? What do I have to do?"

The Wanderer said nothing. He was still looking at me in that strange way. His white eyes seemed sad, if that was even possible. Why would he be sad about stopping the *Radaskim*, his mortal enemy?

"It is possible," he said. "If you infect the *Radaskim* Xenomind with the *Elekai* version of the virus, their conquest of Earth will end."

That was it. That was the answer. It was *something*. I could take that information back to Samuel, and we could figure out, together, how we would go about doing that. We could return to the Great Blight, find the *Elekai* version of the virus, and fly to Ragnarok Crater. From there, we could find the *Radaskim* Xenomind, and...

I realized I didn't know what that looked like.

"The other Xenomind," I said. "What does it look like?"

"She – if it can be so called – is like a mother to the rest of them, the agent that creates new forms of life. Askala is the one you seek, a *Radaskim* Xenomind ancient and terrible. She has conquered a hundred worlds before yours. Once done, she leaves, and begins anew. If *she* were somehow infected, then the *Elekai* version of the virus would take her over, placing the entire invasion under my thrall."

"What does Askala look like?"

"She...changes form. I have ancient memories of her as a giant dragon, a wyrm, a labyrinth of tentacles deep within the ground – it is always different, depending on the world. But you will know her when you see her."

I thought of the massive xenodragon that had been roosting in Raider Bluff. Could *that* be Askala?

"What about the big dragon? I asked. "You've seen it, right?"

"Yes, he comes with her from world to world," the Wanderer said. "He is her Guardian. He was called Chaos, on the world before this one. And he is a fearsome enemy. A commander of hellish legions."

"Is the final attack coming?"

The Wanderer smiled grimly. "It has already begun. With the death of the Xenolith, all that held them back is now gone. The

Elekai were the only ones keeping the *Radaskim* from harming people more than they already have."

"*This* is the world, given your protection?" I shook my head. "I hate to imagine what it might be like without it."

"You will soon see," the Wanderer said. "The Great Blight will spread far more quickly now. Legions of monsters will lash out in an unending tide. Even if you kill them all, more will come, birthed within the Warrens of Ragnarok Crater. We *Elekai* will attempt to grow a new Garden, to distract Askala, but it will prove difficult to convert the xenofungus to help rather than hinder us. Even I don't know how much longer we have until this position is overrun. Until then, we can be of little aid. All you can do is run."

"That is our plan, for now," I asked. "We are running west, toward L.A."

"West is your only option," the Wanderer said. "Soon, you will forget all of your wars when faced against the full might of the xenoswarm."

"How much time do we have?"

"Weeks? Months?" The Wanderer paused. "Days? I can't say. It all depends on Askala, and when she decides the time is ripe. Remember, it is not only the Wasteland she is after. The whole world is her goal. She may forget about you for a while as she focuses on the east, or on beginning new colonies across the ocean. I wouldn't count on that, though. For now, at least, almost all her armies are focused here. And for good reason. You are the only ones with the knowledge to stop her."

"Does she know about us?"

The Wanderer nodded. "Perhaps not specifically. But she knew *someone* had come into the Great Blight, to Bunker One. Yes – my own *Elekai* agents told me about that journey. She knew enough then to attack you, and what's more, to try to find you while you were in the Empire. Something tells me that her focus follows you and your friends, and her eye is now set on Vegas and its survivors.

It will be her goal to crush it, before the city has a chance to fight another day."

"I have to get back and tell the others."

"In time. I need to tell you how to stop Askala."

Yes, I guessed that was important, too. "How?"

"The *Elekai* virus is the dominant form," the Wanderer said. "Within it is the ability to reprogram the *Radaskim* version. You see, the two viruses are the same. The only difference is whether a single gene is on, or off. The *Radaskim* have this gene turned off. The *Elekai* version has it turned on. If the *Radaskim* Xenomind is infected, the morality gene will be turned on, effectively making that Xenomind *Elekai*. Doing so is nearly impossible, as Askala is heavily guarded. Why do you think every world has failed to stop the *Radaskim* invasion? But if Askala becomes *Elekai* – so does the rest of the *Radaskim* swarm. The invasion will end."

Even if I didn't understand the mechanics of it, the premise was still simple. Get Askala infected with the *Elekai* version of the virus, and the rest would take care of itself. It was probably much more complicated than that, so all I could do was hope it was that simple.

I had *a lot* of questions, but for some reason, nothing came to mind. I had to learn as much as I could before returning to the others. The feelings of betrayal were gone, replaced with the need to share this information that would change everything.

"Where did the dragons come from?" I asked.

"They came from the First World, Askalon," the Wanderer said. "The dragons were the lords of that world – intelligent, flying beasts that had their own wars, societies, and philosophies. The xenovirus and xenofungus were all native to that planet, living in balance. The dragons would eat the fungus, while the fungus depended on the dragons in order to spread. The dragons became gardeners, tending their xenofungal fields, creating homes within them. Everything existed together with a single consciousness that individual beings could access with merely a thought. This ability was given by the xenovirus, which permeated all life on Askalon. This first consciousness was the beginning of the *Elekai* – the first Xenominds – which the dragons worshipped as gods."

"Where do the *Radaskim* come in?" I asked.

"A mutation in the xenovirus gave rise to the *Radaskim*. Somehow, the *Radaskim* virus found a way to use the dragons. However it happened, the *Radaskim* used the dragons to conquer their first worlds."

"How did they get through space?"

"The *Radaskim* Xenominds heard whispers of other sentient races. They heard them fall from the sky, from the direction of the stars. For eons, the *Radaskim* dragons evolved skins and bodies that would survive the vacuum of space, using directed evolution. Soon, they resembled nothing of their former selves, and became the Vessels. The first of these were primitive, compared to what exists now – but sufficient for the first, short journey."

"So, Xenofall is real?" I asked. "When the *Radaskim* win, more are coming."

The Wanderer shook his head. "It is the opposite. If the *Radaskim* lose, more will come. The First World is far, and it will take many thousands of years for them to return. But they *will* return, again and again and again, until the end of time."

It was almost unthinkable. Even if, against all odds, we won here, the victory was only temporary. It was strange to think of a few thousand years as temporary. But if that was all we got, well...I supposed that was worth fighting for. Maybe future generations could be taught to remember and fight.

Many thousands of years was a number so small to a Xenomind, and so incomprehensible to a human. The human side of me said that many thousands of years would make no difference, in the end. But perhaps it was the *Elekai* side of me saying that thousands of years was not good enough. The entire race of the *Radaskim* had to be destroyed, before they...

Saved the universe?

The entire reason for their conquests, at least from their point of view, was so they could recreate the universe in the same way as before. In a strange, twisted way, they were *preserving* life, making it immortal. The *Elekai* did not kill, but in the end, if they won, all would die with the eventual death of the universe.

It was mind-boggling, but the one thing I did know was that *my* world would end if the *Radaskim* won. The world of my children, if I ever had any, would end. Everyone else's world would end. The universe didn't exist so an alien race could play with the Secrets of Creation – whatever those were. It existed for all. It was so weird, to think of these things, to be processing all this information. The world – the entire universe – was so much bigger than I had ever thought.

"How do I stop them?" I asked. "I know you already said that I have to infect Askala with the *Elekai* version of the virus. But how do I do that, practically?"

Again, the Wanderer looked at me, his white eyes clouded, mysterious. "To stop the *Radaskim*...you must go to Ragnarok Crater, find the Xenomind, and sacrifice yourself."

It took a moment to comprehend what the Wanderer had just told me. I looked away, my head spinning. I saw the surrounding pond frothing in agitation, steam rising. The walls of the cave quivered.

The Wanderer gazed at me intensely, awaiting my response.

"Sacrifice myself?

The Wanderer nodded. "That is all I can say, because that is all I know. I can't tell you what that will look like, practically speaking. No one has ever been successful."

"You say other people have tried. Who *were* these people?"

"They were sentient, intelligent races on other worlds – long dead – with nothing but the memories of the *Elekai* to preserve them." The Wanderer paused. "Some were not unlike you. Some were incredibly different. But the *Elekai* have always chosen one."

"Why does it have to be one of us?" I asked. "Why can't it be one of you?"

The Wanderer smiled bitterly. "You will think this strange. Very strange. But we are prevented from doing so. On the smallest levels, it occurs. An *Elekai* dragon, for example, can kill a few crawlers and not disobey his morality, especially if it's self-defense. Still, something so direct as to strike at the heart of a Xenomind itself..." The Wanderer shook his head. "We are unable to do that."

"What do you mean?"

"Remember. We cannot kill. We cannot destroy, willingly. The difference between an *Elekai* Xenomind and a *Radaskim* Xenomind is the ability to kill the other." The Wanderer shook his head. "We cannot do that."

"So, you do it indirectly?"

The Wanderer nodded. "It is the only way we've found so far that allows us to try. But remember: it is your decision. The fact that this is your free choice is critical."

"There is no way that a Xenomind could attack another one?"

"If we changed, we would become *Radaskim*. And if we do that, the *Radaskim* win."

"But...you can *choose* not to kill, right? Maybe you have the ability to do it, like people do, but you can always choose not to." I looked at the Wanderer. "Right?"

The Wanderer smiled once more. "That is also where we are different. When a Xenomind becomes as misdirected as Askala, or any other *Radaskim* Xenomind, there is no choice. Maybe free will and the ability to choose is natural to humans. Some will choose wrongly, some rightly. For Xenominds, it is not so simple. It is all, or nothing."

That was it, then. To stop this invasion, I would have to give my own life. I didn't know what that meant, but this might be my only chance to make a difference. I had to meet my fate.

I made my decision.

"I'll do it, but...I don't know how I'm going to make it to Ragnarok Crater."

The Wanderer smiled. "What about your friends?"

"They think I'm a Howler, or worse," I said. "They saw me fly away on the dragon. I wouldn't be surprised if they just shot me as soon as I landed."

"I don't think you give them enough credit. You need to tell them what I've told you. You will need their help. This cannot be done alone. Those who have tried to stop the *Radaskim* alone have failed."

I didn't bother to point out that everyone had failed, regardless of whether they were alone or not.

"But if I go back..." The thought of making that long journey across the Great Blight and through the pursuing swarm terrified me. "I'll just get killed."

"Being *Elekai* has its own benefits," the Wanderer said. "I think you will find that xenolife will respond to you in a way it never would have before. *Elekai* xenolife, anyway."

"Respond? What do you mean?"

"The *Elekai* are all one tribe, and we help each other out, when we can. I think you will grow to understand what that means, with time."

I had no idea what the Wanderer was talking about, but I hoped that it would make sense eventually. I was just wondering how everyone would react when they saw me returning. I didn't know how long I had been on the island with the Wanderer, but it had felt like a long time.

I felt myself growing tired. I leaned back into the xenofungus. It felt soft and warm beneath me, no longer threatening. As the bed touched my skin, I felt a slight tingle that faded over the next few seconds. A sense of peace overwhelmed me, and soon I was asleep.

Chapter 20

I awoke much later. Time had passed – a long time. I couldn't remember the last time I had awoken so rested and refreshed. I felt the fungus, soft around me. Maybe it nurtured as much as it killed.

I stood, stretching stiff muscles. The cavern appeared much as it did before, except that it was now missing the Wanderer. Alone with my thoughts, I found everything the Wanderer told me still made little sense. All I remembered was the conclusion: that it all depended on my being able to infect the *Radaskim* Xenomind called Askala.

Me against *that* seemed an impossible match-up. No wonder no one had ever succeeded – no one on a thousand worlds. I wondered what they must have thought, hundreds, thousands, maybe even millions of years ago. Had they stood before a pink lake like this, a lake as still as glass, wondering if they could ever be enough? Despite this thought, I felt a sense of peace, a sense of purpose.

I guessed when you had something to be afraid of, something as big as the *Radaskim,* nothing else was so scary. Everything else burned away into nothing, becoming a void through which to travel to your goal.

I walked to the shoreline, stepping into the viscous liquid. It wrapped around my boot. I waded in further, the liquid warm on my skin. I swam forward, contemplating where I would go now, whether it would be north to meet my fate, or west to my friends, who still knew nothing of what I had learned. The Wanderer said that all who tried to go alone had failed. Still, I felt strongly that I needed to go to Ragnarok Crater and see what there was to see. Maybe I would find my final answer there. Maybe I would be the first to succeed.

I climbed from the pool and walked up the spiraling tunnel that led to the surface. The liquid slid down my skin, rejoining the xenofungal floor. Pink daylight stretched down the walls, the floor, and the ceiling from ahead. The light grew in intensity, until I was at the cavern's entrance. I stepped outside, finding the crimson clouds boiling across the sky. The air was thick with an alien spice I couldn't quite describe – like cinnamon so strong that it felt like a punch in the nose. I should have been knocked out from it, but if these were spores, they had no effect on me.

It took a moment for my eyes to adjust. The pink surface of the Great Blight stretched before me, alien and ethereal. The sunlight made it glitter like billions of gems, orange, red, and pink. I could not have named the color that spread before me, but it covered hills, rocks, and mountains. Gnarled trees grew from the fungus, along with thin, tube-like reeds in massive fields, swaying in the breeze. There was not a sound of life – only the wind, and a strange sighing not natural to Earth.

Behind, the Xenolith lay twisted and dead. I wondered what the *Elekai* would do now that it was destroyed. The Wanderer had said they would plant a new garden. I was just sorry that their old one had been uprooted. It wouldn't be long now, I imagined, until this small part of the Great Blight reverted to the *Radaskim*.

I was startled from my thoughts when a massive creature swooped over my head from behind, landing with extended claws right in front of me. A gust of wind buffeted me back, sending me sprawling to the ground. The soft fungus broke my fall.

When I stood again, I saw that it was the same dragon that had transported me here. It let out a mighty roar, and with one foot gently pawing the ground, it stretched its six long claws into the xenofungal bed. The dragon lowered its head, shutting its eyes for a moment before reopening them. Those white orbs stared into me, almost pleadingly. As strange as it may sound, I saw something almost human in them. The Wanderer had said these dragons were intelligent. Now I believed him.

"I guess you're here to take me back, huh?"

The dragon gave no reaction. It folded its gigantic wings to its sides, a deep rumble emanating from its throat. I suddenly became awed by the magnificence of this noble creature. It was probably about forty feet long, its long tail increasing its length even further. Its scales were a pink so light that it might have been mistaken for white at first glance. Low ridges trailed its back, sharpening as they neared its tail. By the time the ridges got to the tail, they transformed into wicked spikes. The largest spike was mounted at the end of the tail – a curved, organic blade that could easily rend men asunder.

"What's wrong?" I asked.

The dragon remained silent. I closed my eyes, trying to think of what to do. Maybe I had to tell it where to go.

"Take me to the army," I said. "Where you picked me up before."

Still the dragon did not move. I was starting to grow frustrated. Apparently, I was doing something wrong. I stood there for a moment, feeling like an idiot. I wondered if I was mistaken in my assumption. Maybe the dragon had just landed beside me for some other reason.

The dragon stared at me with neutral white eyes, each eye about the size of my hand. I noticed the details of its face. Unlike the dragons I had seen in the Empire, this one was not blind. It had eyes that I suspected could see in much greater detail than my own. Crimson spots speckled the face. The face was smooth, and appeared soft to the touch. I wasn't going to reach out and touch it, though, even if a part of me wanted to. I was not that stupid. This thing could bite off my hand, or even my entire head, if it wanted.

I didn't know where the thought came from, but for some reason, I felt that this dragon was young. That it was like me.

"I'm Alex," I said.

The dragon gave a strange, chortling sound that was very jarring to hear from a creature so large.

The dragon closed its eyes, and kept them closed. It lowered its head again – I didn't know why. For some reason, I reached out and touched it. The skin was warm and soft. Below my hand, the dragon's skin vibrated, and then a flood of thoughts entered my mind in a chaotic stream. I saw the dragon flying around the spire, being chased by other dragons – younglings at play. I saw the pool beneath the Xenolith, from which the dragon had come into the world. Then I felt emotions – sadness, anger, confusion, shock – as the Xenolith exploded and fell in brilliant, fiery hues. The memories suddenly stopped when I lifted my hand.

I realized that these were memories – the dragon's memories. Somehow, the dragon was transmitting its thoughts directly to me. When I took my hand off the dragon, the stream of thoughts ceased. So: I had to be touching the dragon for the thoughts to enter me.

I wondered *why* these thoughts were coming. Then I realized; the dragon was showing me who he was. It was no longer an *it*. Somehow, I knew this dragon was male. This meant that they had both males and females. That gave them at least one thing in common with humans. What the pool beneath the Xenolith had to do with that, I had no idea. Maybe the pool was important to their mating or giving birth. Which would mean this dragon youngling would have a mother somewhere, and, I supposed, a father.

The emotions I had felt from the dragon were shocking, just as great and full and colorful as any human being's. This was a creature of intelligence – a creature that was, perhaps, smarter than humans. Maybe the *Radaskim* dragons were different, but at least the *Elekai* dragons had thoughts, feelings, intents, sorrows, and joys.

"Do you have a name?" I asked.

The dragon, not understanding, closed his eyes and lowered his head once more. I couldn't just talk to it. I had to touch it. I placed my hand on its head once more, thinking my question.

Askal.

The word returned clear, so clear that it startled me. I wasn't sure if this was what his name would actually sound like, or if it was my brain's way of turning Askal's thought into something I would understand. Then again, if my brain was trying to do that, it probably would have picked a name less weird than Askal. Like Dave.

"Askal?" I asked.

The name was very similar to what the Wanderer had called the *Radaskim* Xenomind – Askala. I wondered what the connection was. Perhaps Askala was just the name for their entire species. Maybe they had no *need* for names. After all, the Askala did not communicate with language, but with direct thoughts and images. There it was – I was now beginning to think of them with that name. Even if Askala was what they were called, why shouldn't I be able to name my own species? The only confusing part about it was the other Askala – the *Radaskim* Xenomind. But this could be easily differentiated by saying "the Askala," or "an Askala;" then people would know I was talking about one of the dragons. But, if I just said, "Askala," then they would know I was talking about the Xenomind.

I noticed that the dragon was looking at me while my mind rambled on. My hand was placed on his head. I wondered what *he* thought of that jumble of thoughts circulating around in my mind, or if he even understood it.

I realized at that moment that I still had to tell Askal my name.

Alex, I thought.

Alex. The Askala repeated the word in my mind, as if it were unfamiliar.

I remembered how Askal had shown me his life with images. I decided to do the same thing. I gathered my thoughts, trying to think of how best to tell my story. Then, I realized, I was already telling it. Any thought that crossed my mind could be read and interpreted by the dragon instantly. So I thought my story from beginning to end, everything coming out in a whirlwind. A minute later, I had gotten the hang of it. It was like remembering – when I remembered something, it was communicated. Mixed in with my thoughts were Askal's reactions – his interest, his sadness when I talked about Khloe and my father, his fear any time I thought of Howlers. For some reason, it made me feel better that this giant, powerful creature was just as spooked by those ghouls as I was.

Once finished, I took my hand off Askal's head. The creature gave a long sigh, pained by what he had heard. Was my story really so painful? Well, I guess it was. When my story would end with my death, I guess it couldn't be any other way.

Askal nodded, as if telling me to put my hand back on his head. When I did, Askal transferred a thought to me.

We need to go back.

"Go back? Go back where?"

To your friends.

"They'll shoot you."

The image of guns spewing toward the sky left my mind, entering Askal's.

Your puny weapons will not harm me. If all of what you said is true, then we do not have time.

"You can only take me if you drop me off somewhere in the distance. I don't want them hurting you. They won't understand." I sighed. "Hell, they might even shoot *me*, for all I know."

Askal paused, considering.

"I think maybe we should just...go."

I didn't have to explain where I meant. Askal knew immediately. Ragnarok Crater. It was time to end this – and waiting wasn't going to help anything.

No, Askal answered. *One day, we will go, brother. But not now. They are too strong.*

I just wanted this to be over with. All the same, I realized Askal was right. The others needed to know about everything I had learned. Everything, in case I failed. After they knew, *then* I could go.

I nodded. "I don't know how my friends will feel about a dragon walking around their camp..."

During the next transfer of thought, I imagined a sharp, toothy smile, although Askal's face remained expressionless.

Perhaps they will change their minds when they see me fighting for them.

"Fighting for us?"

Yes. The Elekai and the humans are on the same side. We both hate the Radaskim with all of our souls. The sooner we realize that, the sooner we can stand against them.

This was all growing much larger than I could have ever imagined. It wasn't just the humans we were trying to bring together. It was a whole tribe of aliens. I wondered what the aftereffects would be. Would the *Elekai* and humanity live together in peace, if they ever won?

I could sense that Askal thought this was a strange question. One, because no one had ever beaten the *Radaskim* before, not on a thousand worlds. And two, the *Elekai* were at their core peacemakers, and would never attack humans.

"We are different, then," I said.

Askal still did not understand, but he saw my thoughts when I realized that it was not the *Elekai* who would attack us. It was *we* who would attack *them*.

Askal was shocked at this, and for a moment, no thought crossed over from him. Finally, he responded.

There are always second chances. There are always new beginnings.

Then I knew it was time. "I'm glad to have met you, Askal."

The Askala nodded, closing his white eyes. Upon opening them, he readied his legs to cast off.

I circled around the dragon's back, hopped on, and settled between the two ridges. Immediately, Askal took off for the west. The fungus fell away before me. The warmth of the Great Blight was left behind, and the cold air whipped at my face and body, shocking my senses.

I leaned forward, both to get a steady grip and to keep warm from Askal's body. We were flying west, and soon crossed the border of the Great Blight. For hours, we flew across the Wasteland, past the smoking ruin of Vegas, past tall mesas and cracked mountains. It was hard to believe, looking down at the city, that it had been brought down so quickly. We flew on, past flat deserts and ridges of mountains capped in red cloud and snow.

Things had changed, so much so that I wondered how it would all ever work out. The hard part, the immediate problem, was going to be making the others understand everything – for them not only to accept me back, but to believe what I had to tell them. I had seen the *Elekai*, had spoken to the Wanderer. I was the messenger. I had the revelation.

Would any of them believe? It was hard to imagine Samuel or Ashton buying it. I realized then what I would have to do. I would have to agree to go back to Skyhome, so that Ashton could test me. He could see for himself, beyond the shadow of a doubt, that the virus that infected me was different from any other kind. Maybe when he saw that, he would understand.

Maybe they all would.

Chapter 21

Askal landed a good distance away from where the army was camped. The Askala settled behind a tall, wide mesa that would completely block him from view. I told him to wait there, and that I'd be back in an hour or two.

As I jogged away, I saw ripples in my vision once more. My eyes were reverting to their normal state. So I had to be touching something with the xenovirus, somehow, for my eyes to turn white. When I walked into camp, I wouldn't be mistaken for a Howler. Maybe the whitened eyes were an effect that only happened while communicating with xenolife. That would make sense. It made me wonder why my eyes had been white back on *Odin,* after I had first woken up. Then again, hadn't I been communicating then, too? The Wanderer had sent me that vision, so maybe the vision had something to do with it. It was good news, because it meant I could have some control over when my eyes were white, and when they were normal. Or at least, that's what my hope was. I would have to test that theory later. Maybe it was something Ashton could test. Hopefully, going back to Skyhome wouldn't be necessary to figure that out.

After hiking a mile or so, *Odin* came into view on top of the same bare hill where I had departed from it. It was mid-afternoon – the warmest part of the day, which meant the frigid air was barely tolerable. *Gilgamesh* was gone; *Odin* was the only ship left. The hill was surrounded by crude tents, shanties, and blazing fires to keep back the cold. Off the back of the dragon, out of the Great Blight, I was hit in full force by the reality of the frigid air.

I rushed ahead to get to the ship. My mind raced with everything I would tell everyone. I didn't even know where to start.

As I passed the outer ring of tents, I started to feel nervous. I passed under the gaze of fearful men, who stared to the east from where they had fled, huddling in groups around fires for warmth. I hurried past them, averting my eyes. I passed women and children, wrapped in blankets inside tents. The army had remained camped on the hill rather than moving on, which meant that Makara and the gang lords had come to some kind of impasse. With both the cold and the xenoswarm, any lack of movement was death.

I wished I had a mirror, so I could make absolutely sure my eyes were not white. Just in case, I had my hood drawn up, and kept my face down. Getting mistaken for a Howler would be the worst thing possible right now. I'd be dead before I even had the chance to do my job.

I climbed the hill, the sharp wind blasting against me. I started to run, the cold air like ice in my lungs. I crested the hill, and *Odin* hulked above me. I couldn't see inside the tinted windshield, but if anyone was in the cockpit, they would now see me. I just stood there, in the cold, waiting for someone to come out and meet me. I didn't want them to think I was being aggressive. I also didn't want them to somehow capture me before I had a chance to explain what had happened. I grew colder the longer I stood there. It looked like I was going to have to go into *Odin* myself. Maybe they were all away, for some reason. If luck was with me, Samuel or Michael would be the first one out that door. Both of them had been the calmest at my change.

I grew impatient, and started walking forward toward *Odin*. It was then that the blast door slid open. Makara walked out, alone, wearing a thick black parka with the hood pulled up. She stood on the boarding ramp a moment, arms folded, staring in my direction. Her expression was inscrutable.

Finally, she sighed and walked the rest of the way down the boarding ramp, and came forward. The fact that she was approaching me rather than calling for backup was a good sign, I guess. Maybe she had changed her mind. Still, I felt nervous, even though it was only Makara and I had known her longer than any of the others. I thought of all we had been through, and how much had changed. We had experienced a lot in the last three months, and our journey to Bunker One had changed everything – had given us new purpose in our lives.

The thought didn't have more time to develop, because Makara now stood before me. Even though she was playing it cool, I could tell that she was glad to see me. I could see it in her eyes.

"You're back," she said.

"It was inevitable."

She arched an eyebrow. "Quit being cryptic. Where did you go? Thought you would have been inside a dragon's stomach by now."

"That dragon is actually pretty nice," I said. "His name is Askal."

Makara stared at me. "Askal?"

"Turns out all of you guys are right," I said. "I'm infected, but it's something different. There are two different kinds of the xenovirus." I forced a smile. "Turns out I have the good kind."

"Alex..." Makara said. "We have a *lot* to talk about."

"Where's everyone else? Anna? Samuel?"

Makara looked away, shaking her head. "Ashton and Michael left in *Gilgamesh* yesterday, not too long after you left. They're going to New America, trying to find recruits."

So I had been gone *two* days rather than one. I was starting to lose my hold on time.

Something in Makara's face told me that there was something else. Something she didn't look forward to telling me.

"Where's Anna?"

I knew the news was not good.

"Samuel and Marcus are off looking for her," Makara said. "An hour after that dragon took you, she ran off, that way."

Makara pointed to the east. The direction of the xenoswarm. The direction of the Great Blight.

"And you let her go?"

"Of course I didn't," Makara said. "You think my opinion would have stopped her? It was an hour before anyone realized she was gone. Marcus found one of his bikes missing." Makara looked at me. "Not hard to figure out what happened. He and Samuel went after her, but they haven't found anything yet."

"It's been two days," I said. "You should have found her by now."

Makara nodded. "I know. Either she doesn't want to be found, or..."

Makara didn't finish, but she didn't have to.

"What about Ashton? Michael?" My voice was becoming more emotional. "They could find her with their ship."

"They're on their way back, and I just got off the comm with them," Makara said. "They're bringing Julian and some new recruits from New America; that'll add more to the search. As for me and Char, we need to stay here and keep an eye on things."

My next question was why Anna had run off. I didn't want to believe that she had done it because of me. That was a bit difficult to comprehend. I didn't see why anyone would want to do that.

"I'm going after her," I said, turning around.

"I guess there's nothing I can say to convince you otherwise."

"No. I'll find her before the day is out. I promise you that."

"You sound very confident of that."

"I have every reason to be. I've got something no one else has."

I ran from the camp, and Makara stood there on the hill, watching me go. I didn't truly believe I had every reason to be confident. I just wanted to prove to Makara that I was right.

And hopefully, I was.

***

I ran down the hill, past tents and startled people, past the fires and into the cold afternoon. My boots churned the bare, rocky ground as I set out across the Wasteland. The mile pretty much ran itself, and within minutes I was circling the mesa, only to find Askal was not where I had left him.

I slid to a stop, throwing up a cloud of dust. I was crestfallen that he had flown off. I hadn't counted on that.

It was then that I heard a mighty roar that shook my bones. I stared upward at the mesa's side. The dragon was roosting on a thin ledge, his long neck snaking around to the mesa's side, where he sniffed at a small patch of xenofungus. He then noticed me below, staring at him. With a flap of wings, he glided to the desert floor, his light pink body catching the sun's rays and glowing golden. He settled onto the dirt in front of me.

"About time," I said, rushing to climb on his back. I held onto the ridge in front of me, preparing for flight.

"We have to find Anna."

What happened?

He read my thoughts about Anna. My worry about finding her had now become his. Askal charged forward, nearly sending me careening rearward off his back. He flapped his wings mightily, pushing off the ground. We were once again in the air, each new beating of wings carrying us farther above the crimson desert.

Where is she? Askal asked.

"She's somewhere east of here," I said. "She left yesterday, to go after me."

I had no idea what Anna thought she was doing. She was strong, but she wasn't invincible. If she ran into the crawler army, then she wasn't going to survive. All I could do was find her before that happened. If it hadn't already.

Your mate? Askal asked.

"Yeah," I said. "Sort of."

Askal was confused by my answer, but did not respond directly. Clearly, relationships among the Askala were far less complex. Instead, I focused on scanning the ground for signs of motion.

An hour passed in this way. We took the same route as we had on our way to the Great Blight. If Anna was heading there, then we should find her on that path. Neither Samuel nor Marcus knew exactly where she had been going, so they might have gotten off-course.

We had been flying an hour when Askal veered for the ground.

"You found something?" I asked, teeth chattering.

I believe that is her.

I gazed in the direction we were descending. I saw a solitary female figure, katana in hand. She had long black hair, blown by the wind, and held a blade in her right hand. It was definitely Anna. She turned, gazing up into the sky at us. I wondered what she would be thinking, seeing a dragon flying down at her. She placed herself in a ready stance, her katana held in both hands in front.

Askal swooped down, landing a good distance away. He landed face out, I guess to let Anna know that he wasn't a threat.

I hopped down and ran toward her, keeping my face turned until I felt my eyes return to normal. When I turned to face Anna, her eyes were wide with disbelief. She sheathed her katana, and started walking my direction.

Suddenly, she was in my arms. I held her tight.

"Don't do that again," I said.

"I could say the same for you."

"It doesn't matter," I said. "I found you and that's what counts."

She looked at me with tearful eyes. "I should have trusted you. I thought, if I hurried…I might be able to find you. To say I'm sorry."

"It's alright," I said. "None of that matters now. You were doing what you thought was right. I would have done the same."

She pulled back, looking me in the face. It was hard to read those green eyes.

"You really just took off after me?" I asked.

She gave a small smile. "I knew you were in the Great Blight, somewhere. An hour after you left, I tried to get Makara go fly the ship there. She wouldn't budge. Said her place was with the army. So that morning, I left, with nothing but my pack and my katana."

"What about your bike?" I asked.

She shrugged. "That old thing broke down. Tried for hours to fix it, and just ended up leaving it there." She stopped, looking up at me. "I knew, even at the time, that going east after you was stupid. But I figured if *you* could be stupid about something you believed in, why couldn't I be, also?"

I didn't have an answer for that. Her logic was flawless.

"I don't know," I said. "I flew back on that Askala there, and..."

"Askala?"

"Yeah. His name is Askal, and he is an Askala." I smiled. "It's what their entire species is called."

Anna laughed.

"What's so funny?"

"*Told* you they weren't dragons."

I laughed as well. I remembered our conversation from earlier, of how Anna hated for them to be called dragons. I wasn't even thinking of that when I decided on the name.

"I guess we all got what we wanted, in the end."

Anna gazed over my shoulder, at the Askala. "You just got on that thing and flew away, like you owned it. There was no hesitation." She paused. "I couldn't have done that."

"I don't know," I said. "You might have, if you knew what I knew."

Anna stared off doubtfully. I brushed a strand of hair out of her face.

"You'll never believe what happened to me," I said.

She looked at me. "You went to the Great Blight."

"How did you know that? You mentioned it a second ago, but..."

"It really wasn't that hard to figure out. With the way your eyes were, I thought you were one of *them*. I thought you went to go join them. I planned on doing the same thing."

"What?"

"Well, I don't know what I planned, really. The thought did cross my mind, though. I thought it would all make sense, when I got there."

She took a few steps toward Askal. She didn't seem afraid of him. Admittedly, for an Askala, he was on the cute side. The dragon, in turn, gazed at Anna silently with his white eyes. Anna smiled.

"Funny name," she said. "Askal."

"Don't let him hear you say that."

"He can talk?"

"To me, at least. It's a side effect of..."

I didn't finish my sentence, but Anna pieced together the rest on her own.

"You *are* infected, then."

"Yes. But it's not what you think. I will actually be okay. At least, for a while."

"What do you mean by that?"

As she looked at me with worry, I explained everything I had gone through, leaving nothing out. I told Anna about my dreams of the Wanderer while the rest of them had been fighting for their lives. I told her about how Askal had taken me to the broken Xenolith, and about the pool beneath its roots. I told her what the Wanderer had related to me on the island – about the *Elekai* and the *Radaskim*. Finally, I got to the part where I had agreed to try and fight the *Radaskim* Xenomind, by infecting it with the *Elekai* version of the xenovirus. She was a little confused when I said that

that Wanderer had called the *Radaskim* Xenomind Askala, so maybe I could have chosen my name for *the* Askala better. The Wanderer had also called Askala the Dark Voice. That, at least, was enough to differentiate that Xenomind from the Wanderer, who was the *Elekai* Voice.

Anna said nothing once I was finished telling her my story. I wanted to give her time, so I waited for her to break the silence. Such things took time to process.

The first thing she said, however, was unexpected.

"The prophecy is true, then. I thought when I saw you here, safe, that perhaps I would have more time." She sighed. "The old man was right, in the end."

"What are you talking about?"

"The Wanderer told me that I would lose someone I loved. So, I stopped trying...to love, I mean."

Anna said nothing more, and I felt myself tearing up. What she was saying I couldn't believe. She *loved* me? She hadn't said it directly, but...

"I had no idea," I said. "And..."

I didn't know how to go on. Instead, I held her as her eyes watered up. Her tears fell to the cold dust. Finally, she looked up at me, her eyes haunted.

"You can't go dying," she said. "We need you still."

She broke down in tears. I could do nothing but hold her.

"It's alright," I said. "It will all work out, somehow."

"No, it won't! You're going to die, you know? You've just told me that much."

"Maybe there's a chance I won't die." I knew it was a long shot, but I just didn't want Anna to be sad anymore. "He just said 'sacrifice.' He didn't say that sacrifice was me dying."

"Everyone else's prophecy came true, didn't it? Why wouldn't mine? Why wouldn't yours? They are one and the same."

I didn't have an answer for that. Instead, I kissed her. She stilled, settling into me, her muscles going slack.

"It is the only way," I said, when we parted. "If this is my path, and if it saves everyone, I have to do it. He told me, in that cave, that it all hinged on me. I know what I have to do."

From far in the past, a thought came to me. Something my father always told me. I said it now.

"A man does not do what he wants. He does what he must."

She pulled back, wiping her eyes. "There *has* to be another way. We'll find it. We'll talk to the Wanderer, together, and we'll make him tell us."

I felt only sadness. Though the Wanderer was an *Elekai* Xenomind with millions of years of memory and knowledge, he did not know everything. All he knew was what it would take to win. And that meant infecting the *Radaskim* Xenomind, and bringing about the end of the invasion.

"We have to find Askala," I said. "The Wanderer said that she is like the mother of all the *Radaskim*. She is the source of the Great Blight's power. She directs it, and without her, they would be powerless. If she is infected, then it all reverts to the *Elekai's* control. The invasion will be stopped in its tracks."

"You don't know that," Anna said, stubbornly. "If we can just kill her, somehow..."

"Another Xenomind would rise up and fill her place," I said. "All the memories are preserved in the xenofungus. All it would take is a new body to manifest them. Askala cannot be killed. She can only be converted."

"Maybe you're right," Anna said. "Still – I'm not giving up."

I loved her for saying that. And looking into her eyes, I believed her. I hoped, foolishly perhaps, that she would find a way. If only it were that easy.

Askal snorted from behind – probably impatient to be off. I turned, seeing him watch us with his alien, white eyes.

"Now that I can see one up close," Anna said, walking toward Askal, "they are kind of endearing, aren't they?"

Askal cooed in answer to Anna's statement. This Askala knew how to play his cards. It was a strange sound to be coming from a creature so large and so dangerous.

We went to stand before the dragon together. Askal regarded Anna with his white, intelligent eyes.

"Can I touch him?" she asked.

"Go ahead."

Slowly, Anna placed a hand on him, rubbing Askal's neck.

"He's warm," she said, surprised.

Askal nodded his head toward me. He wanted to say something. I placed my hand alongside Anna's.

Your mate?

I felt my face go red. *I'm working on it.*

You should mate with her.

My face burned even hotter at the suggestion. Askal didn't understand that we humans worked a little differently from the Askala.

"What is he saying?" Anna asked, with a smile.

I was too flustered to answer immediately. I felt my vision swim, and Anna's form wobbled before me.

She paused a moment. "Your eyes..."

"They turned just now, didn't they?"

She nodded.

"So, it *is* when I'm interacting with xenolife. Otherwise, they are normal."

"That's it, then?"

"They were white while I was in the Great Blight. They are white here, touching Askal. And when I awoke on *Odin,* after having my dream, they were white..." I paused. "I think the connection is clear."

"Well, what is he saying? You still haven't answered me."

I hesitated, wondering how to respond. Clearly, the Askala liked to cut to the chase. Askal felt insistent that I should tell her *exactly* what he had said.

I decided to compromise a bit.

"He says..." I paused. "He says that you and I make a good pair."

She smiled, and blushed slightly.

I hopped onto Askal's back, reaching out a hand for Anna. She hesitated at first. After a moment, she took it, and I helped her onto Askal's back. She sat behind me, wrapped her arms around me, settling her head on my shoulder.

With a thought, I gave an image of the mesa we had left behind. With a roar, Askal cast off, leaving the ground below.

It was time to meet with the others.

Chapter 22

When Askal flew near the mesa, I decided on impulse to fly directly into the camp. These people would have to get the idea that at least some of the Askala were on our side. What better way to do that than flying one and landing it in the middle of all of them?

It seemed like a great idea at the time.

"Um..." Anna said. "Are you sure we shouldn't be landing this thing farther away?"

"A little shock might do everyone good," I said.

"I think they've had enough shock..."

Just when I realized that Anna was probably right, it was too late. The camp came alive, having spied the dragon from a distance. People ran into tents, grabbed rifles, and pointed them into the air.

They reacted far more quickly than I would have thought. They must have trained or something.

"Pull back," I said.

Askal obeyed, and I could feel his gratefulness. Several shots fired, but they were so distant that they missed by a wide margin. Askal wheeled around, turning to the direction we had come from.

Only to find *Gilgamesh* approaching at lightning speed.

"Down!" I yelled.

The ship's turrets opened fire, bullets whizzing through the air. Anna began to slide off the Askala's back. She screamed, but Askal jerked to the side, throwing her back on before she could fall. Her fingers dug into my torso, and I gritted my teeth in pain.

"You alright?" I asked.

Anna didn't answer as the ship swooped overhead, the turret disengaging.

Tell your girl to hold on.

What?

There was a lull for a moment.

"Anna, hold on!"

She complied, and immediately after, Askal made a nosedive, letting out a mighty bellow. We both cried out as we zoomed toward the nearby mesa. *Gilgamesh* was turning around, chasing Askal away. They meant to shoot us down, right here, right now.

I can't outrun that metal Askala, Askal said.

I knew he couldn't. *Gilgamesh* was *way* too fast. Instead, Askal circled round the mesa, then roosted on a ledge. His long neck craned to the left, the right, searching for somewhere to hide.

But it was too late. Slowly, *Gilgamesh* glided round the mesa sideways, its front facing toward us. Its twin turrets spun, aiming directly at us all. Anna and I threw up our hands, waving at the ship's crew to stop.

Gilgamesh paused. One second. Two. Three.

They knew it was us.

"We're safe!" I said.

Gilgamesh turned sideways, facing the blast door toward us. As it slid closer through the air, the door opened, revealing a familiar face I hadn't seen now in over a week. He wore an unbelieving smile.

"Alex!" he yelled.

"Julian! Thanks for almost killing us."

He shrugged. "I see you found a new ride, huh?"

Michael was next to appear in the doorway. He cupped his hands around his mouth. "Ashton says to follow him back to camp. Fly in sync so that they know we are together."

I gave a salute of acknowledgement. Both Michael and Julian disappeared from the doorway, and the blast door closed. *Gilgamesh* veered away in the direction of the camp.

"You get all that, Askal?"

Askal snorted, and cast off from the ledge. Anna gripped me more tightly.

"That was *too* close."

"We got lucky."

Askal eased in beside *Gilgamesh,* flying at the same slow speed. I could feel the Askala's nervousness. I didn't blame the poor guy.

"You'll be fine," I said, patting the creature's back.

Gilgamesh circled and alighted atop the hill next to *Odin*. When Askal flew right along next to it, people that had once fired now lowered their weapons. They could clearly see Anna and me on the Askala's back.

The worst of everything was over – at least, for now. Askal flapped his wings a couple times, slowing his descent. He gingerly landed next to *Gilgamesh*. He kept his head down. I could feel his body shaking beneath me. I could feel his fear in my mind, emanating in waves.

"It's alright, buddy," I said. "Nothing's going to happen to you."

While I tried to calm the Askala, Anna tapped my shoulder.

"Look," she said.

A large crowd had gathered before us. At the front were Makara, Char, Ashton, Julian, and Michael, all staring up at me.

Makara was the first to speak.

"Alright. You have a *lot* of explaining to do."

I nodded. "I know."

"I'll let Samuel know they're back," Michael said. "Hopefully, they won't be out too far."

While Michael raised his radio to his mouth, Ashton took a step forward. His expression was more curious than afraid. Was he already beginning to piece together what the rest had yet to figure out?

"We can talk about this," Char said, "but first, let us step inside the ship." He gazed in the direction of two of the gang lords, who had been drawn to the commotion. There was Rey, and Cain beside him. Their eyes stared, hollow and cold. I suppressed a shudder.

It had been a while since I had seen any of these men – Rey, Cain, Jade, Grudge – even Boss Dragon. They were here with us, too, but I had not had the burden of dealing with them, fortunately. That had been Makara's and Char's prerogative, and I had no idea what their plans were regarding the gangs. I guessed I would find out as soon as I went inside *Gilgamesh*.

***

We sat around the conference table. It was quiet, and no one spoke for a while. It was me, Anna beside me, and on my other side, Michael. Across the table were Makara, Char, and Ashton. On either end of the table were Boss Dragon and Rey. They were both here to represent the Vegas gangs. The others had balked at not being included, but with a word from both the Dragon and the King, they had backed down quietly.

First, everyone wanted to know what I had learned. So I told my story. It was a lot of catching up, so I tried to keep it brief – I would elaborate in greater detail later, with Makara and others of the inner crew. For now, I just stuck to the main points. I didn't want to take up too much time with a play-by-play. This is what I *did* say: I told them that I was infected, but that there were two different versions of viruses – *Elekai* and *Radaskim*. I told them that I had the first one, and that each virus corresponded to a different alien faction. The *Elekai* were trying to stop the *Radaskim* from taking over Earth. Next, I told them about the war between the *Elekai* and *Radaskim* that had been waging for millions of years. I told them how we were just one world out of a thousand that had been attacked, and that it was my job to stop the *Radaskim* Xenomind, Askala – that as both a human and an *Elekai*, I was the only one who could infect Askala – that this was the only way to stop the Blights and the invasion.

After I finished, everyone sat in silence. Julian's eyes appeared dazed from the information overload. Everyone had a question or two, and I did my best to answer. It was a *lot* of information, and I wasn't even sure I understood it all.

"That's quite the report, Alex," Ashton said. "And yet, the pieces fit. As soon as I saw that dragon – that Askala, I should say – I thought you were controlling him. But the fact that you are connected to that Askala through the *Elekai* xenovirus makes more sense."

Everyone looked at the doctor, surprised at hearing this.

"There is still so much to be discovered about the xenovirus," Ashton said. "But I think the greatest piece of evidence supporting the existence of the *Elekai* and the *Radaskim* is that second Voice. The one we silenced when we killed the Xenolith."

"I had no idea that..." Makara began.

"None of us did," Ashton said. "We were right to consider it a threat. Still, it would not make sense for there to be *two* Voices – *two* Xenominds – controlling the same side. The entire time, the second Voice was in direct opposition to the first." Ashton paused. "As Makara said, we had no idea."

"The Wanderer called it 'the Dark Voice,'" I said. "Maybe we can say the same thing to differentiate between the two."

"How do we know these *Elekai* aren't the bad ones?" Rey asked.

"They would have killed me a long time ago," I said. "Why would they bother to show me all this information if they were just going to kill me?"

Rey shrugged, apparently satisfied at that answer.

"Then, the Blighters came," Boss Dragon said, resigned. "You guys had no idea what you were messing with."

"No, we didn't," Ashton said. "But now, we have our answer. Perhaps too late."

"It's not too late yet," I said. "We have our newest ally now – the *Elekai*. Together, we can push back against the *Radaskim*. We can stop the invasion if you guys can get me to Ragnarok Crater. I have to find Askala, the *Radaskim* Xenomind, the Dark Voice. It's the only way to stop them."

"No," Anna said. "You are not going to kamikaze yourself on Askala. We're *going* to find another way." She looked around at everyone at the table. "Right?"

No one answered Anna. It wasn't a good sign.

"We have more important priorities for the moment," Rey said. "We need food. Water. Shelter. We've been camped here for two days. My eastern patrols are finding more and more crawlers breaking away from the xenoswarm." He looked at Makara, hard. "This cannot go on. Soon, they will grow bored of that feast that used to be our home. They'll come after *us.*"

Rey gestured at everyone at the table. No one denied the truth of his words.

"What do we do, then?" Boss Dragon asked. For a moment, the former enmity of the two gang lords was forgotten. They were on the same side now.

"Pyrite is another day out," Makara said. "Now that everyone is here, we can set off in the morning. We can pick up whatever people want to come with us there, and they can join the Exodus."

The Exodus. That was new. So that was what they were calling this now. Maybe they had been this entire time, ever since we'd left the ruins of Vegas behind.

"We have other problems," Michael said. "The Reds are still out there. When we left by the western gates, that entire side of town was vacated."

"Where do you think they went?" Char asked.

"My guess?" Michael asked. "They probably went south to throw in their lot with Augustus."

I glanced at Rey, to see his reaction. It was not a move I would put past him or his gang, either, if it came to that. His face, however, remained blank.

"That is something the Reds would do," Boss Dragon said. "We picked up some of their slaves on our way here. They said as much. The Reds took their bikes and rode off, even while we were fighting for our lives inside the walls."

"There's still so much to do," Makara said. "And no time to do it in." She sighed. "But Rey is right. We have to take care of our own, first. We can reconvene when we make sure our people aren't starving and freezing."

"That will be difficult," Char said. "It is cold. And getting colder."

"Anything that affects us will affect Augustus's army as well," I said. "Unlike us, they are not used to this cold. The attrition might send his army back before we have the chance to."

"I wouldn't count on such luck, kid," Ashton said. "Augustus is a planner, and would have accounted for this. I checked on his position while in the air, and they are still marching up the Mexican coast. If it's too cold by the time they get here, which should be in February or so, they'll probably hole up in Colossus, their farthest-north colony. That's at the mouth of the Colorado, so it's just a stone's throw from us. However long they end up taking, there's still not much time to work with."

"The best plan would be to find a place to shelter," I said. "Somewhere large enough to fit two thousand people until the weather warms."

"There is no such place," Makara said.

"There is one," Michael said.

At first, I was the only one who knew what he was talking about. And it was a place I never in a million years wanted to return to.

"It's on the way to Los Angeles," he said. "It is still far – about two hundred miles – but it is our closest, most realistic option."

Makara's face blanched when she realized what Michael was talking about.

"Even Bunker 108 isn't perfect," I said. "It was only designed for five hundred people. We have two thousand."

"Who says that two thousand are even going to make it *that* far?" Rey asked.

"That's a fair point," Ashton said. "But we can speed things up by using the spaceships. The main Exodus can head southwest, going as fast as it can. Meanwhile, *Gilgamesh* and *Odin* can start ferrying people over. The first group will contain the best fighters, who will have the job of going in and clearing out the Bunker, making it safe to use. Anyone else who comes along can start doing cleanup. I say it's a week before we have everyone over there."

"A week?" Boss Dragon asked. "That's not so bad."

"But how will we fit everyone in there?" I asked. "It's way too small."

"People don't have to stay in the dorms," Ashton said. "There is plenty of floor space, such as the commons and the cafeteria, which can both be used. And it's only temporary – to wait out the weather until we can start fresh in late spring."

"*Spring?*" Makara asked.

It seemed so far away. But with winter coming on and two thousand people to care for, many of them already weak, what other choice did we have? And a lot depended on Augustus. If he charged into the Wasteland in winter, we would have no choice but to face him.

But sheltering in Bunker 108 was a bad idea, for many reasons.

"There should still be plenty of food and supplies in the Bunker. My main fear is the xenovirus. Even *if* we clean everything up, all it takes is one person to get sick for all to come crashing down."

Ashton looked at me. "I didn't realize how bad it was. Did the attack happen in every part of the Bunker, or just certain parts? We could avoid the infected areas."

"It was pretty much everywhere. If everyone there is infected or dead, who knows how many Howlers we'll have to deal with?"

"It's too dangerous, then," Makara said. She looked frustrated. "Are there any other Bunkers we can use? Ones that did not fall from the xenovirus?"

"That would be much safer," Ashton said. "Since 108 is off the table, and 114 for the same reasons, we have to look at other Bunkers. Our options will be very limited, both by location and other reasons. Most Bunkers aren't as large as 108; that closes off most even from consideration."

"Any Bunkers you know of that are nearby?" I asked.

"Then there are others that haven't been heard from in years – even decades. I can't remember all of them off the top of my head, but 111, 112, and 106 are all nearby. I'd have to go through my files to refresh my mind on the details of each."

"You have access to that information?" Makara asked.

Ashton nodded. "I was able to save some important documents – digitally of course – during my escape from Bunker One. One of these was a Bunker manifest, which gives names, descriptions, coordinates, and the reasons each Bunker fell – at least for the ones we have information on. The manifest stopped being updated with the fall of Bunker One, but I've my own notations whenever I discovered something new."

"And you've been sitting on this for how long?" I asked.

"I haven't really been sitting on it," Ashton said. "I've told Samuel most of it already. I only thought to mention Bunker 108, because in theory, it would be the perfect place to shelter, if not for the xenovirus."

"You said 111, 112, and 106," I said. "I don't even know where those are."

"When the U.S. started the Bunker Program in 2020, they created twelve Sectors," Ashton said. "The Sectors are of varying size and are designated as letters A through L. Each Sector has its own twelve Bunkers: 1-12 are in Sector A, 13-24 are in Sector B, and so on. Bunker 108 is in Sector I. Often, the Sectors are called by their rough location – in the case of Sector I, it's the Mojave Sector. The last in each sequence, such as 12, 24, and 108, were designated as Command Bunkers – ones that were to manage the rest within their Sector. The only exception to this was Bunker One, which controlled all the Bunkers."

"This is all interesting," Makara said, "but what's the point?"

"I'm just trying to illustrate that there are lots of Bunkers," Ashton said. "None will be as large as 108, unless we find the last in each sequence – which were all Command Bunkers."

"So, to fit in everyone, we would have to find Bunker 12, 24, and so on," I said.

"Precisely. And none of these Bunkers are close to each other. A great many are covered in Blight. Others are prohibitively far away, such as on the East Coast, or too far north." Ashton sighed. "I'll do some more research, but after all is said and done, it might *still* turn out that Bunker 108 is our best option."

I hoped that wasn't true, because Bunker 108 would be a horrible option.

"Well, we have to find something," Rey said. "And it can't be far. We don't have time for that."

Everyone was silent as they thought.

"We'll talk it over with Samuel when he gets back," Makara said. "I'm sure he'll have his own opinion. For now, the plan remains the same. We keep going west, away from the Great Blight. We'll stock up once we hit Pyrite. Hopefully, by then, we'll have more information to go on."

"I'll start researching possible options," Ashton said.

I was glad Ashton was giving himself another project. It meant he would probably forget about me, for the meantime.

As if reading that thought, he looked in my direction. "We'll have to put that *Elekai* research on hold for a few days." He gave a thin smile. "I'm sure you don't mind."

"Not at all," I said.

At that moment, Michael's radio crackled to life.

"Michael? Michael, you there?"

It was Marcus. His voice was panicked.

"Yeah, come in," Michael said, his eyes nervous. "What's going on?"

There was a long, dreadful pause. Instantly, I knew something terrible had happened. Something we could never come back from.

"It's Samuel," Marcus said. "I think...I think he's dead."

Chapter 23

Immediately, Makara snatched the radio from Michael's hand.

"What do you mean, you think he's dead?" she yelled. "Answer me!"

The radio sizzled with static for a moment. From the other end, Marcus cursed, as we all sat in shock.

"We got ambushed by a crawler. We were speeding away on our bikes, back for the ship, but it was too fast. It tackled Sam, and he went crashing down. I stopped and fought the thing off. But now, Sam isn't moving."

"When did this happen?" Makara asked.

"Just now – I called you first thing."

"Did you check for a pulse?"

"Of course I did! I got nothing. If he's still alive, he doesn't have long."

"What's your location?"

"We're two miles out from the mesa. I can hear more of them coming..."

"We're on our way," Makara said.

Makara ran out of the conference room, followed quickly by Anna. Within minutes, the ship was in the air, flying east.

And all I could think was – Samuel was not dead. He couldn't be. A single crawler couldn't do this to him. It had to be another false alarm, like what had happened to Makara in the *Coleseo*.

A couple minutes later, we found Marcus far below, standing above a figure sprawled on his back. The twisted corpse of a crawler lay nearby on its side, facing the east. Sam's bike lay sideways in the sand where it had crashed. All was just as Marcus had described.

When we landed, we all ran outside. The cold wind blew, stinging me with dust. In the distance, I could hear high-pitched screams. Marcus had been right on that count as well. More crawlers were coming.

Makara ran to her brother, grabbing his shoulders. His forehead was bleeding, and a giant black welt was forming there, even as Makara held him.

Char knelt beside Makara, feeling for a pulse. For a few, terrible seconds, he said nothing. Finally, he nodded.

"He's not dead. Not...yet, anyway. He has a head injury, so it could be very bad. It's hard to say now, but it looks like he hit his head on a rock or something during the impact."

Makara did not react. She didn't have the strength to. "Let's just get him on the ship. Do what we can for him."

Char, Julian, Michael, and I lifted Samuel, doing our best to keep his body even. He did not stir the entire time. We carried him to the ship. Once inside, we carried him to the clinic, laying him on the bed. Still, he did not move.

Char and Makara came in. "Give him some space. Everyone besides me, Makara, Marcus, and Ashton, clear out."

"Take us back to the army, Anna," Makara said, her voice thick.

Anna nodded, turning to me. "Come on."

Before leaving, I took one last glance at Samuel. His eyes remained closed, and he had not moved a muscle, other than in the almost imperceptibly small breaths he took.

Michael, Anna, Julian, and I walked to the bridge in silence. It was not looking good. Boss Dragon and Rey stood in the galley, watching us, their faces unreadable. They said nothing as we passed through the galley, into the main corridor, and to the fore of the ship.

"Will he be alright?" Julian asked, after Anna had settled down in the captain's chair – a place I had never seen her sit before.

Anna shook her head. "I don't know. Maybe he gets better. Maybe he doesn't."

Slowly, Anna took off for the hill we had left behind. It wasn't until we were gone that I remembered we had left both bikes, including Marcus's, in the dust. It was too late. As the ship spun away, the last view I had was of crawlers overwhelming the position. They were just a few miles out from the army's camp.

"Julian, go tell Makara that we've got contact with crawlers," Anna said.

Julian nodded, and turned down the corridor.

Samuel was hurt, and maybe dead, and an army of crawlers lurked just miles away from two thousand people. And even if we survived those two things, it was only the beginning.

***

Anna landed in the camp. As we rushed off the ship, Makara met us in the galley.

"Char and Ashton are going to stay with Samuel," she said. "There's nothing I can do there besides worry. We have to get everyone on the hill immediately and set up whatever sort of defense we can. There's no time to run."

We ran out into the cold. Evening was coming on, and in the oncoming dusk, hundreds of people were already fleeing toward the hill and the safety of the ships, many of them women and children. Any who could took up arms, pointing them in the direction of the east, where already I could see the teeming mass of the Blighters swarming. There were so *many* of them – hundreds – maybe even thousands. If they surrounded this hill, there was little chance of any of us living to see the dawn. We didn't have any sort of perimeter set up. We hadn't thought we'd be staying here this long.

Both ships sat pointing toward the east, meaning the turrets could be aimed at any oncoming threats. That had been intentional. But even with hundreds of men and women armed with rifles, it wasn't going to be enough.

We were all going to die, right here on this hill.

The first of the crawlers broke into the camp, ripping through tents and shoddy shelters, canvas and rubble flying through the air, in their mad search for something living to rip into. Still, the people flooded up the hill, screaming in terror. Those who were not armed ran up the boarding ramps and into the ships for shelter. It wouldn't be enough space for everyone – not by a long shot.

In the madness, we all just tried to get anyone with a gun to the front – in a protective ring around those who couldn't fight.

Anna drew her katana, facing the oncoming horde. I stood nearby, raising my AR-15 to my shoulder. I took my first shot into the mass of creatures. I had no idea if I was hitting anything – it was so chaotic, so loud, with both screams and gunfire and alien screeches.

Then, *Odin's* turret opened up, followed by *Gilgamesh's*. Someone was in those ships, firing – perhaps Ashton, perhaps Char or someone else. The spewing bullets made a dusty line at the base of the hill, where the crawlers charged up.

The frontrunner of the crawlers, a nasty, sizeable beast, shot straight for me. Its white eyes glowed with hatred, and I *knew* I was the one he was coming after. Maybe these creatures could somehow sense that I was *Elekai*. I aimed my rifle, shooting at the creature multiple times. My bullets did nothing against its thick exoskeleton.

The crawler was just a few dozen feet away, now. I thought for sure I was going to die. Anna readied her blade for the inevitable impact.

That was when something swooped right in front of me with a beastly roar. Talons extended outward, pummeling the crawler in the side. The crawler screamed in pain, its wide-open mouth revealing twin, forked tongues and long, yellowed teeth. It flew through the air, landing with a sickening crunch far away from the action.

The crawlers hesitated for a moment at the sight of Askal, who was now wheeling around for round two. As Askal entered another dive, the crawlers spread, trying to avoid his sharp talons. One particularly unlucky crawler got the full brunt of the attack, spiraling several times when Askal slammed into its neck. The crawler squealed, its long, spiked tail twitching in a feeble attempt to protect itself.

It was the distraction all of us needed. Although the number of crawlers running up the hill swelled, they all hesitated upon seeing Askal. This gave us the chance to push back. With a yell, I ran forward, taking shots into some of the frontrunners. Others followed my example.

"Aim for the gut!" I yelled.

Hopefully the message would be passed along. Any time one of the crawlers exposed itself, I aimed carefully and shot. Some of the hideous monsters were starting to fall. But for every one we killed, more replaced it in the ranks.

Soon, several of the creatures had broken off, watching Askal's movements carefully, marking when and where he would next fall. When Askal made his next dive, these crawlers ran forward to that location, readying their long tails to swipe. Noticing this, Askal ducked away at the last moment, before he could be struck.

The battle was in full force now. Red and purple blood hit the ground. Before my eyes I saw a Raider get rent in two from the swipe of a crawler blade, a flood of red pulsing from his torso. Anna, beside me, skewered a small crawler through the side, expertly pulling her blade from the creature's insect-like form. From around me, gunshots rang out, deafening. The cold air stank with the smell of human blood and the fetid stench of the crawlers.

As time passed, I noticed fewer and fewer human forms among the crawlers. We had retreated to the base of *Gilgamesh's* ramp, and the crawlers were forcing themselves on us. We were outnumbered at least three to one.

And, as a further sign of our doom, I could see in the distance at least twelve Askala coming to join the fray.

"It's over," I said.

Anna hacked at another crawler, fighting for her next breath. She looked at the dark sky, her blade falling to her side.

The Askala swooped down toward the ship with primal, reptilian screams. The remnants of the Exodus braced themselves for impact.

But the Askala ignored us, and instead started attacking the crawlers.

"They're on our side!" I said.

Once again, our ships' turrets opened up, letting out the last of our volleys. What people were left let out their own war cries, waving guns in the air. In the mix I saw Cain and Grudge, both of their faces bloodied, charging forward with what men they had.

The crawlers had been halted in their tracks, unable to fight the dozen or so Askala now in their midst. Just a few feet in front of me, an Askala with crimson scales swooped down, picking up a crawler with its talons. It beat its wings, rising into the air, dropping its payload into another group of crawlers that had ganged up on a grounded Askala bleeding purple blood. The crawlers screamed as their comrade crashed into them from above.

Blood and bits of crawler flesh sailed through the air as the *Elekai* dragons ripped into the *Radaskim* horde. Even though this was more crawlers than we had ever fought, I knew this was just the beginning. This was but a small fraction of the entire horde – and if it weren't for these *Elekai*, we would be dead right now.

Finally, we had the edge. Between the aerial attacks of the dragons and our comeback on the ground, the crawlers were routed.

They scuttled away down the hill, fleeing to the east.

I stood, dazed, as I watched the hundred or so crawlers that were left disappearing into the darkness. In a mere minute, they had vacated the entire battlefield. They had, as one, been called back. Had the Dark Voice summoned them home?

While it was good that they were gone, they had dealt a mortal blow. Dozens, maybe even hundreds, lay dead on the hill around us. Severed limbs and heads lay in gory piles. While we had won the battle with the help of the *Elekai,* we were now much weaker for it.

And, in the distance to the east, I could still hear the screeches of the crawlers. I couldn't help but feel it was them having the last laugh.

Chapter 24

The *Elekai* Askala landed among the survivors, the dead, and the dying. The Askala had suffered no losses, but the one that had been grounded had several lacerations and puncture wounds on its side. It said a lot for the power of a crawler that the dragon's thick skin could be breached like that.

I found Askal among his Askala brethren. Rushing up to him, with Anna at my side, I placed a hand on his neck.

Are you alright?

We are fine, brother. It is you that I am worried about.

I didn't answer for a moment. No, I wasn't fine. None of us were.

Did you call for these Elekai to come fight?

This is all of the Elekai dragons. They did not want to come, because they still remember losing the Xenolith. But our Father told them to come help. So like good children, they listened.

Father? You mean, the Wanderer?

Yes, Askal answered.

The Wanderer was their father. Askala in the north was called the mother. I wondered what connection, if any, there was between the two.

It is a difficult thing to understand, Askal said, sensing my thoughts. *It is hard to put human terms to it. But both are needed, if the dragons are to exist – both Askala, and Askalon.*

Askalon, I thought. *Is that the Wanderer?*

It is our name for him, yes, Askal said.

The way these creatures thought was very confusing. How could the two Xenominds on Earth, Askala and Askalon, be both mother and father to them all, and yet be on different sides? I felt that anything I could learn about them might help our cause, but maybe now wasn't the time for that.

My brothers are ready to leave, Askal thought. *I am going with them.*

When are you coming back? I asked.

When we are needed. Which may be soon. There was a pause in Askal's thoughts. *Find a place to hide, little human. I sense a great tempest in the north, sweeping in this direction. You will not want to be caught in it.*

Suddenly, Askal stepped backward, taking me by surprise. With that, our communication was severed. As the dragon backed further away, I became all the more aware of how large he was. A creature like him could not be kept as a pet. He was an equal.

I realized I hadn't even said thank you.

Askal looked me in the eyes a moment before turning to his brethren. Together, without so much as a sound, they cast off into the night. With a flapping of wings, they left us behind, watching in amazement.

"They saved us," Anna said.

I nodded. "Now there can be no doubt. They are on our side."

Anna turned to me. "We need to check on Samuel. Maybe he woke up while all that was happening."

Her voice told me that she didn't believe much in that possibility, but it was worth finding out. We started back to *Gilgamesh*, where refugees were already exiting, entering the battlefield with expressions of shock and horror. How many had lost loved ones? How could we go on after something like this?

Michael was forcing himself up the boarding ramp to *Gilgamesh* against a tide of people, trying to find his wife and daughter. I had been so out of the loop lately that I had never even had a chance to meet them. Michael finally found his way inside the ship as the last of the survivors exited. Lauren and his daughter, Callie, hadn't been among them.

Anna and I walked up the boarding ramp, fearing the worst. But when we entered the galley, we saw Michael embracing his family, crying tears of joy that they were alive. I saw his wife's face over his shoulder, her eyes closed with tears streaming down, her blonde hair falling in waves. Their daughter, Callie, couldn't have been more than seven or eight. She hugged her father fiercely.

They both opened their eyes, watching me and Anna. The eyes were blue, and with a start, I realized I had seen Lauren before. Seeing a familiar person, even a person I didn't talk to all that often, was hard to describe. I definitely recognized her from my time at Bunker 108.

"You must be Alex," Lauren said, parting from Michael. "I'm glad to see you've made it."

From the way she said that, I knew she wasn't just referring to the battle. She was referring to everything I had been through in the past three months.

"It's a miracle I'm still here," I said.

"Isn't it a miracle that any of us are?" she asked.

Michael turned to face me, keeping an arm each wrapped around his wife and daughter.

"I'm sorry it took so long," he said. "But this is Lauren, my wife, and my daughter, Callie."

Lauren forced a smile, while Callie just looked afraid. I didn't blame her. I was covered with blood.

"I wish it could have been in better circumstances," I said. "I'm just glad everyone here is okay." I sighed. "A lot of people out there are not."

"Did everyone else make it?" Anna asked.

"Char and Ashton were on the ship the entire time," Michael said. "I saw Makara outside still, giving orders, trying to organize all the gang lords. I imagine they'll be taking stock of who is hurt and who isn't, trying to find time to help everyone they can."

With so many wounded, so many to bury, finding shelter would become all the harder. We were not far out of reach of the *Radaskim* horde. It was a question of when, not if, they would attack again.

"We have to find a Bunker," I said. "We can't stay out here in the open any longer."

The blast door opened, letting in both Makara and Julian. It was a relief to see them both standing when so many had died.

"Good, everyone's here," Makara said. "Bring both Char and Ashton here. I need to lay out the plan."

Before anyone could move to get the doctor and the Alpha, both appeared in the hallway from the direction of the clinic.

"Is it bad?" Char asked.

Makara nodded. "It's horrible. At least two hundred dead, and more dying. I've ordered that the wounded be divided between the two ships. The rest are to strike immediately west, and on the double. We're not stopping until we reach Pyrite, where at least we'll have the safety of the walls. From there, we can hunker down until Ashton can find out which Bunker will be our best bet."

"The wounded..." Ashton began. "I assume you want me and Char to take care of that. How am I supposed to find time to research?"

Makara sighed. "You will somehow have to find time for both, Ashton. We all have too much to do, and not enough time to do it in. I want you to first get the wounded in the galleys of both ships. Should be several dozen; treat them in order of severity. The worst cases we can shuttle to Skyhome. As long as they don't stay there too long, they shouldn't be such a drain on its resources." Ashton was about to counter that, but Makara continued on. "We don't have time to argue. We only have time for action. Train anyone who is able, or try to find anyone with any experience with working with the wounded. Work in shifts. Whatever the case, let's get this done."

"What about Samuel?" I asked.

Char looked at me. "Samuel is still out, but stable, hopefully. We have more people to take care of than him, now."

"He's right," Makara said. "For now, let's do what I've already said. Move the wounded on board the ships. Once that's done, Rey and the rest will lead what's left of the Exodus to Pyrite. Char, you can take *Odin*. Ashton, you're assigned to *Gilgamesh*. I assume that Bunker manifest can be accessed from the ship's computers?"

He nodded. "It can be accessed from either, but yes, I can man *Gilgamesh*."

"Good. Get to work. Find anyone who can help out. I want to clear this hill within the hour. Pyrite is still twenty miles out. If we push ourselves, we can make it by evening tomorrow."

I doubted that. With the wounded and the weak, we'd be lucky to make the town in double that time. I kept my mouth shut, however.

"I can help with nursing," Lauren said. "I have some experience, though I was never registered with the Bunker."

"Anything we can get helps," Makara said. "You can help Char here."

With that, we broke up. Anna and I headed outside, leaving the bodies of the dead but moving the wounded on board the ships. With everyone in the Exodus working with a single purpose, it was all done in thirty minutes. From there, anyone with any sort of medical experience was assigned to either Ashton's or Char's team. Admittedly, that wasn't much. With Lauren, we had about a dozen people spread across both ships tending the wounded. There was not much we could do for any of them – not with the ships' limited resources. Painkillers ran out very quickly, along with bandages. It was an impossible ordeal, but it was the best we could do. It was decided that the priority was getting to Pyrite before the swarm closed in on us again.

It was a long, hard journey. The first of that tempest Askal had warned us of closed in just as dawn broke. Of crawlers, there were no sign, but the bleak, cold wind from the north did a sort of work that crawlers could never do. Dozens died from exposure, and where they did, they were left behind, stripped of anything useful. We had become like the monsters we were supposed to be fighting. The only thing that kept people going was the promise of warmth, the promise of safety.

In the end, it might have turned out to be an empty promise. *Gilgamesh* reached Pyrite first, leaving *Odin* to guard the Exodus's rear. The people there were hostile, according to Ashton – unwilling to take in either *Gilgamesh's* wounded or *Odin's*. We weren't going to get in there with anything short of battle. Not that Pyrite was the strongest town, but the thought of having to fight any more, much less fighting people instead of the monsters behind us, was simply exhausting.

All the same, Makara ordered that fighting men be loaded into both ships along with the wounded, and landed in the city. If there was resistance, then we had orders to take it out. It was desperate, it was amoral, but we didn't have time for morality. Not with so much on the line. Thankfully, it turned out the leaders of Pyrite had been bluffing. They begrudgingly accepted our takeover, and tents and a large fire were allowed to be set up in the town's center. The town, at least, was surrounded by a tall wooden fence. Not great, but better than nothing.

While the Raiders, Exiles, and gang members stood guard in the town center, Anna and Makara ferried the ships back and forth, picking up the weakest members of the Exodus before the cold could get to them. Anna had to learn a great deal in order to pilot the ship on her own. However, necessity had been her teacher, and she was able to get the job done. More and more of the Exodus was unloaded in the town until finally, after two days and several ferrying trips, the last of the Exodus was inside the walls of Pyrite.

With everyone inside, we had escaped the xenoswarm, but at great cost. A few days later, a head count revealed that we were now down four hundred and twelve people – about half from the battle, half from the extreme cold. This left us with about sixteen hundred souls. In a single night, we had lost twenty percent of our total force. And if it hadn't been for the *Elekai*, it would have been one hundred percent.

An inventory of Pyrite's granaries revealed that, for everyone, there was probably enough food for two weeks. Though angered, the leaders of the small settlement could do nothing about it. In the end, they were forced to join us on our mad journey to escape the growing power of the Great Blight and reach Los Angeles, before it was too late. They soon saw, once they heard our stories, that they would not escape the coming storm. Our numbers had taken a huge hit, but recovered somewhat with the addition of the town.

It was small condolence when so much had happened, and so many additional threats faced us. And with Samuel still out and apparently in a coma, it was only going to get worse. We had to find a shelter large enough for two thousand people, and we had very little time to find it in.

It was this desperation that led to us to commit our gravest error.

***

Ashton's research concluded our best option for shelter was Bunker 84. Bunker 84 was in Northern California, buried in the mountains near the border of what used to be Oregon. It would be far colder there than here, especially given the season – however, as long as we could find a way to get everyone underground, I supposed that wouldn't matter.

According to Ashton, Bunker 84 had been designed to house one thousand people, making it twice as big as Bunker 108. It had fallen in 2045, three years before even Bunker One had. It had been one link in a chain of consecutive Bunker falls, barely a blip on the radar. Most Bunkers began going offline in the early 2040s, and the huge string of falls hadn't ceased until the mid-2050s.

The last transmission received from Bunker 84 had come on May 6, 2045, though the Bunker Manifest's information didn't give specifics. The Bunker had been offline for more than fifteen years, so it was anyone's guess as to what happened.

It was eerie, but the fact that Bunker 84 had gone offline so long ago, even before Bunker One, cast doubt that its demise was caused by the xenovirus. The failure of a critical part may have forced its shutdown.

If that was the case, we might be able to fix it and get the Bunker online again.

Whether, after the last fifteen years, there was any food, water, or supplies left, remained to be seen. It didn't seem too likely. All the same, Makara immediately ordered a recon team to check the Bunker out. We were getting desperate for any option, and for now, Bunker 84 was our *only* option.

Selected for that team were Anna, Michael, Julian, and I. We were selected to fly up there with *Odin*, find Bunker 84, recon its interior, and return to Pyrite with our findings. Supplies in the town were low, and with the xenoswarm so near, time was of the essence. Makara wanted us there and back in two days.

Nothing, however, could have prepared us for what we found in Bunker 84. It was something so terrible, so horrifying, that I probably would have preferred Blighters.

About the Author

Kyle West is a science fiction author living in Oklahoma City. He is currently working on *The Wasteland Chronicles* series, of which there will be seven installments. Find out immediately when his next book is released by signing up for The Wasteland Chronicles Mailing List.

Contact

Facebook
Twitter
Goodreads
Blog
kylewestwriter[at]gmail[dot]com

Glossary

10,000, The: This refers to the 10,000 citizens who were selected in 2029 to enter Bunker One. This group included the best America had to offer, people who were masters in the fields of science, engineering, medicine, and security. President Garland and all the U.S. Congress, as well as essential staff and their families, were chosen.

Alpha: "Alpha" is the title given to the recognized head of the Raiders. In the beginning, it was merely a titular role that only had as much power as the Alpha was able to enforce. But as Raider Bluff grew in size and complexity, the Alpha took on a more meaningful role. Typically, Alphas do not remain so for long – they are assassinated by rivals who rise to take their place. In some years, there can be as many as four Alphas – though powerful Alphas, like Char, can reign for many years.

Batts: Batts, or batteries, are the currency of the Wasteland and the Empire. They are accepted anywhere that the Empire's caravans reach. It is unknown *how* batteries were first seen as currency, but it is rumored that Augustus himself instigated the policy. Using them as currency makes sense: batteries are small, portable, and durable, and have the intrinsic quality of being useful. Rechargeable batteries (called "chargers") are even more prized, and solar batteries (called "solars," or "sols") are the most useful and prized of all.

Behemoth: The Behemoth is a great monstrosity in the Wasteland – a giant creature, either humanoid or reptilian, or sometimes a mixture of the two, that can reach heights of ten feet or greater. They are bipedal, powerful, and can keep pace with a moving vehicle. All but the most powerful of guns are useless against the Behemoth's armored hide.

Black Reapers, The: The Black Reapers are a powerful, violent gang, based in Los Angeles. They are led by Warlord Carin Black. They keep thousands of slaves, using them to serve their post-apocalyptic empire. They usurped the Lost Angels in 2055, and have been ruling there ever since.

Black Files, The: The Black Files are the mysterious collected research on the xenovirus, located in Bunker One. They were authored principally by Dr. Cornelius Ashton, Chief Scientist of Bunker One.

Blights: Blights are infestations of xenofungus and the xenolife they support. They are typically small, but the bigger ones can cover large tracts of land. As a general rule of thumb, the larger the Blight, the more complicated and dangerous the ecosystem it maintains. The largest known Blight is the Great Blight – which covers a large portion of the central United States. Its center is Ragnarok Crater.

Boundless, The: The Boundless is an incredibly dry part of the Wasteland, ravaged by canyons and dust storms, situated in what used to be Arizona and New Mexico. Very little can survive in the Boundless, and no one is known to have ever crossed it.

Bunker 40: Bunker 40 is located on the outer fringes of the Great Blight in Arizona. It is hidden beneath a top secret research facility, a vestige of the Old World. Many aircraft were stationed at Bunker 40 before it fell, sometime in the late 2050s.

Bunker 108: Bunker 108 is located in the San Bernardino Mountains about one hundred miles east of Los Angeles. It is the birthplace of Alex Keener.

Bunker 114: Bunker 114 is a medical research installation built about fifty miles northwest of Bunker 108. Built beneath Cold Mountain, Bunker 114 is small. After the fall of Bunker One, Bunker 114, like Bunker 108 to the southeast, became a main center of xenoviral research. An outbreak of the human strain of the xenovirus caused the Bunker to fall in 2060. Bunker 108's fall followed soon thereafter.

Bunker One: Bunker One was the main headquarters of the Post-Ragnarok United States government. It fell in 2048 to a swarm of crawlers that overran its defenses. Bunker One had berths for ten thousand people, making it many times over the most populous Bunker. Its inhabitants included President Garland, the U.S. Senate and House of Representatives, essential government staff, and security forces, along with the skilled people needed to maintain it. Also, dozens of brilliant scientists and specialists lived and worked there, including engineers, doctors, and technicians. The very wealthy were also allowed berths for helping to finance the Bunker Program. Bunker One is the location of the Black Files, authored by Dr. Cornelius Ashton.

Bunker Six: Bunker Six is a large installation located north of Bunker One, within driving distance. It houses the S-Class spaceships constructed during the Dark Decade – including *Gilgamesh,* the capital ship, and three smaller cruisers – *Odin, Perseus,* and *Orion*. While *Gilgamesh* and *Odin* are under Cornelius Ashton's care, *Perseus* and *Orion* are still locked inside the fallen Bunker.

Bunker Program, The: The United States and Canadian governments pooled resources to establish 144 Bunkers in Twelve Sectors throughout their territory. The Bunkers were the backup in case the Guardian Missions failed. When the Guardian Missions *did* fail, the Bunker Program kicked into full gear. The Bunkers were designed to save all critical government personnel and citizenry, along with anyone who could provide the finances to construct them. The Bunkers were designed to last indefinitely, using hydroponics to grow food. The Bunkers ran on fusion power, which had been made efficient by the early 2020s. The plan was that, when the dust settled, Bunker residents could reemerge and rebuild. Most Bunkers fell, however, for various reasons – including critical systems failures, mutinies, and attacks by outsiders (see **Wastelanders**). By the year 2060, only four Bunkers were left.

Chaos Years, The: The Chaos Years refer to the ten years following the impact of Ragnarok. These dark years signified the great die-off of most forms of life, including humans. Most deaths occurred due to starvation. With mass global cooling, crops could not grow in climates too far from the tropics. What crops *would* grow produced a yield far too paltry to feed the population that existed. This led to a period of violence unknown in all of human history. The Chaos Years signify the complete breakdown of the Old World's remaining infrastructures – including food production, economies, power grids, and the industrial complex – all of which led to the deaths of billions of people.

Coleseo Imperio: *El Coleseo Imperio*, translated as the Imperial Coliseum, is a circular, three-tiered stone arena rising from the center of the city of Nova Roma, the capital of the Nova Roman Empire. It is used to host gladiatorial games in the tradition of ancient Rome, and serves as the chief sport of the Empire. Slaves and convicts are forced to fight in death matches, which serves the dual purpose of entertaining the masses while getting rid of prisoners and slaves who would otherwise be, in the Empire's eyes, liabilities. Many festivals, and even ritual sacrifices, take place on the arena floor.

Crawlers: Crawlers are dangerous, highly mobile monsters spawned by Ragnarok. Their origin is unclear, but they share many characteristics of Earth animals – mostly those reptilian in nature. Crawlers are sleek and fast, and can leap through the air at very high speeds. Typically, crawlers attack in groups, and behave as if of one mind. One crawler will, without hesitation, sacrifice itself in order to reach its prey. Crawlers are especially dangerous when gathered in high numbers – at which point there is not much one can do but run. Crawlers can be killed, their weak points being their belly and their three eyes.

Dark Decade, The: The Dark Decade lasted from 2020-2030, from the time of the first discovery of Ragnarok, to the time of its impact. It is not called the Dark Decade because the world descended into madness immediately upon the discovery of Ragnarok by astronomer Neil Weinstein – that only happened in 2028, with the failure of *Messiah,* the third and last of the Guardian Missions. In the United States and other industrialized nations, life proceeded in an almost normal fashion. There were plenty of good reasons to believe that Ragnarok could be stopped, especially when given ten years. But as the Guardian Missions failed, one by one, the order of the world quickly disintegrated.

With the failure of the Guardian Mission *Archangel* in 2024, a series of wars engulfed the world. As what some were calling World War III embroiled the planet, the U.S. and several of its European allies, and Canada, continued to work on stopping Ragnarok. When the second Guardian Mission, *Reckoning,* failed, an economic depression swept the world. But none of this compared to the madness that followed upon the failure of the third and final Guardian, *Messiah,* in 2028. As societies broke down, martial law was enforced. President Garland was appointed dictator of the United States with absolute authority. By 2029, several states had broken off from the Union.

In the last quarter of 2030, an odd silence hung over the world, as if it had grown weary of living. The President, all essential governmental staff and military, the Senate and House of Representatives, along with scientists, engineers, and the talented and the wealthy, entered the 144 Bunkers established by the Bunker Program. Outraged, the tens of millions of people who did not get an invitation found the Bunker locations, demanding to be let in. The military took action when necessary.

Then, on December 3, 2030, Ragnarok fell, crashing into the border of Wyoming and Nebraska, forming a crater one hundred miles wide. The world left the Dark Decade, and entered the Chaos Years.

Exiles, The: The Exiles are led by a man named Marcus, brother of Alpha Char. The Exiles were once raiders, but were exiled from Raider Bluff in 2048. Raider Bluff faced a rival city, known as Rivertown, on the Colorado River. A faction led by Char wanted to destroy Rivertown by blowing up Hoover Dam far to the north. Marcus and his faction opposed this. The two brothers fought, and in his rage, Marcus threw Char into a nearby fireplace, giving him the severe burns on his face that Char would live with for the rest of his life. For this attack, the Alpha at the time exiled Marcus – but in solidarity, many Raiders left to join him. For the next twelve years, the exiled Raiders wandered the Boundless, barred from ever returning farther west than Raider Bluff. The Exiles at first sought to found a new city somewhere in the eastern United States, but the Great Blight barred their path. Over the next several years, they hired themselves as mercenaries to the growing Nova Roman Empire. Now, they wander the Wastes, Marcus awaiting the day when his brother calls upon him for help – which he is sure Char will do.

Flyers: Flyers are birds infected with the xenovirus. They fly in large swarms of a hundred or more. They are only common around large Blights, or within the Great Blight itself. The high metabolism of flyers means they cannot venture far from xenofungus, their main source of food. They are highly dangerous, and cannot be fought easily, because they fly in such large numbers.

Gilgamesh: *Gilgamesh* is an S-Class Capital Spaceship constructed by the United States during the Dark Decade. It holds room for twelve crewmen, thirteen counting the captain. Its fuselage is mostly made of carbon nanotubes – incredibly lightweight, and many, many times stronger than steel. It is powered by a prototypical miniature fusion reactor, using deuterium and tritium as fuel. Its design is described as insect-like in appearance, for invisibility to radar. The ship contains a bridge, armory, conference room, kitchen, galley, two lavatories, a clinic, and twelve bunks for crew in two separate dorms. A modest captain's quarters can be reached from the galley, complete with its own lavatory. Within the galley is access to a spacious cargo bay, where supplies, and even a vehicle as large as a Recon, can be stored. The Recon can be driven off the ship's wide boarding ramp when grounded (this capability is the main difference between *Odin* and *Gilgamesh*...in addition to the cargo bay boarding ramp, *Gilgamesh* also contains a passenger's boarding ramp on the side, that also leads into the galley). The porthole has a retractable rope ladder that is good for up to five hundred feet. *Gilgamesh* has a short wingspan, but receives most of its lift from the four thrusters mounted in back, thrusters that have a wide arc of rotation that allows the ship to fly in almost any direction. The ship can go weeks without needing to refuel. As far as combat capabilities, *Gilgamesh* was primarily constructed as a reconnaissance and transport vessel. That said, it has twin machine gun turrets that open from beneath the ship. When grounded, it is supported by three struts, one in front, two in back.

Great Blight, The: The Great Blight is the largest xenofungal infestation in the world, its point of origin being Ragnarok Crater on the Great Plains in eastern Wyoming and western Nebraska. Unlike other Blights, the Great Blight is massive. From 2040-2060, it began to rapidly expand outside Ragnarok Crater at an alarming rate, moving as much as a quarter mile each day (meaning the stretching of the xenofungus could actually be discerned with the naked eye). Any and all life was conquered, killed, or acquired into the Great Blight's xenoparasitic network. Here, the first monsters were created. Animals would become ensnared in sticky pools of purple goo, and their DNA absorbed and preserved. The Great Blights, obeying some sort of consciousness, would then mix and match the DNA of varying species, tweaking and mutating the genes until, from the same pools it had acquired the DNA, it would give birth to new life forms, designed only to spread the Blight and kill whoever, or whatever, opposed that spreading. As time went on and the Xeno invasion became more sophisticated, the Great Blight's capabilities became advanced enough to direct the evolution of xenolife itself, leading to the creation of the xenovirus, meaning it could infect species far outside of the Blight – including, eventually, humans.

Guardian Missions: The Guardian Missions were humanity's attempts to intercept and alter the course of Ragnarok during the Dark Decade. There were three, and in the order they were launched, they were called *Archangel, Reckoning,* and *Messiah* (all three of which were also the names of the ships launched). Each mission had a reason for failing. *Archangel* is reported to have crashed into Ragnarok, in 2024. In 2026, *Reckoning* somehow got off-course, losing contact with Earth in the process. In 2028 *Messiah* successfully landed and attached its payload of rockets to the surface of Ragnarok in order to alter its course from Earth. However, the rockets failed before they had time to do their work. The failure of the Guardian Missions kicked the Bunker Program into overdrive.

Howlers: Howlers are the newest known threat posed by the xenovirus. They are human xenolife, and they behave very much like zombies. They attack with sheer numbers, using their bodies as weapons. A bite from a Howler is enough to infect the victim with the human strain of the xenovirus. Post-infection, it takes anywhere from a few minutes to a few hours for a corpse to reanimate into the dreaded howler. Worse, upon death, Howlers somehow explode, raining purple goo on anyone within range. Even if a little bit of goo enters the victim's bloodstream, he or she is as good as dead, cursed to become a Howler within a matter of minutes or hours. How the explosion occurs, no one knows – it is surmised that the xenovirus itself creates some sort of agent that reacts violently with water or some other fluid present within the Howlers. There is also reason to believe that certain Howlers become Behemoths, as was the case with Kari in Bunker 114.

Hydra: A powerful spawning of the xenovirus, the Hydra has only been seen deep in the heart of Bunker One. It contains three heads mounted on three stalk-like necks. It is covered in thick scales that serve as armor. It has a powerful tail that it can swing, from the end of which juts a long, cruel spike. It is likely an evolved, more deadly form of the crawler.

Ice Lands, The: Frozen in a perpetual blanket of ice and snow, the northern and southern latitudes of the planet are completely unlivable. In the Wasteland, at least, they are referred to as the Ice Lands. Under a blanket of meteor fallout, extreme global cooling was instigated in 2030. While the glaciers are only now experiencing rapid regrowth, they will advance for centuries to come until the fallout has dissipated enough to produce a warmer climate. In the Wasteland, 45 degrees north marks the beginning of what is considered the Ice Lands.

L.A. Gangland: L.A. Gangland means a much different thing than it did Pre-Ragnarok. In the ruins of Los Angeles, there are dozens of gangs vying for control, but by 2060, the most powerful is the Black Reapers, who usurped that title from the Lost Angels.

Lost Angels, The: The Lost Angels were post-apocalyptic L.A.'s first super gang. From the year 2050 until 2055, they reigned supreme in the city, led by a charismatic figure named Dark Raine. The Angels were different from other gangs – they valued individual freedom and abhorred slavery. Under the Angels' rule, Los Angeles prospered. The Angels were eventually usurped in 2056 by a gang called the Black Reapers, led by a man named Carin Black.

Nova Roma: Nova Roma is the capital of the Nova Roman Empire. It existed Pre-Ragnarok as a small town situated in an idyllic valley, flanked on three sides by green mountains. This town was also home to Augustus's palatial mansion – and it was around this mansion that the city that would one day rule the Empire had its beginnings. Over thirty years, as the Empire gained wealth and power under Augustus's rule, Nova Roma grew from a small village into a mighty city with a population numbering in the tens of thousands. Using knowledge of ancient construction techniques found in American Bunkers, Augustus employed talented engineers and thousands of slaves to build the city from the ground up. Inspired by the architecture of ancient Rome, some of the most notable construction projects in Nova Roma include the *Coleseo Imperio,* the Senate House, the Grand Forum, and Central Square. An aqueduct carries water over the city walls from the Sierra Madre Mountains north of the city. The city grows larger each passing year, so much so that shantytowns have overflowed its walls, attracted by the city's vast wealth.

Nova Roman Empire, The: The Nova Roman Empire (also known as the "Empire") is a collection of allied city-states that are ruled from Nova Roma, its capital in what was formerly the Mexican state of Guerrero. The Empire began as the territory of a Mexican drug cartel named the Legion. Through the use of brutal force, they kept security within their borders even as other governments fell.

Following the impact of Ragnarok, many millions of Americans fled south to escape the cold, dry climate that permeated northern latitudes. Mexico still remained warm, especially southern Mexico, and new global wind currents caused by Ragnarok kept Mexico clearer of meteor fallout than other areas of the world. At the close of the Chaos Years, Mexico was far more populous than the United States. Many city-states formed in the former republic, but most developed west of the Sierra Madre Mountains. Language clashes between native Mexicans and migrant Americans produced new dialects of both Spanish and English. Though racial tensions exist in the Empire, as Americans' descendants are the minority within it, Americans and their descendants are protected under law and are entitled to the same rights – at least in theory. The reality is, most refugees that entered Imperial territory were American – and most refugees ended up as slaves.

Of the hundreds of city-states that formed in Mexico, one was called Nova Roma, located inland in a temperate valley not too far east of Acapulco. Under the direction of the man styling himself as Augustus Imperator, formerly known as Miguel Santos, lord of the Legion drug cartel, the city of Nova Roma allied with neighboring city-states. Incorporating both Ancient Roman governmental values and Aztec mythology, the Empire expanded through either the conquest or annexation of rival city-states. By 2060, the Empire had hundreds of cities in its thrall, stretching from Oaxaca in the southeast all the way to Jalisco in the northwest. The Empire had also formed colonies as far north as Sonora, even founding a city called Colossus at the mouth of the Colorado River, intended to be the provincial capital from which the Empire hoped to rule California and the Mojave.

Because of its size and power, the Empire is difficult to control. Except for its center, ruled out of Nova Roma, most of the city-states are autonomous and are only required to pay tribute and soldiers when called for during the Empire's wars. In the wake of the Empire's rapid conquests, Augustus developed the Imperial Road System in order to facilitate trade and communication, mostly done by horse. In an effort to create a unifying culture for the Empire, Emperor Augustus instigated a representative government, where all of Nova Roma's provinces have representation in the Imperial Senate. Augustus encouraged a universal religion based on Aztec mythology, whose gods are placed alongside the saints of Catholicism in the Imperial Pantheon. Augustus also instigated gladiatorial games, ordering that arenas be built in every major settlement of his Empire. This included the construction of dozens of arenas, including *El Coleseo Imperio* in

Nova Roma itself, a large arena which, while not as splendid as the original Coliseum in Old Rome, is still quite impressive. The *Coleseo* can seat ten thousand people. By 2060, Augustus had accomplished what might have taken a century to establish otherwise.

Oasis: Oasis is a settlement located in the Wasteland, about halfway between Los Angeles and Raider Bluff. It has a population of one thousand, and is built around the banks of the oasis for which it is named. The oasis did not exist Pre-Ragnarok, but was formed by tapping an underground aquifer. Elder Ohlan rules Oasis with a strong hand. He is the brother of Dark Raine, and it is whispered that he might have had a hand in his death.

Odin: *Odin* is an S-Class Cruiser Spaceship built by the U.S. during the Dark Decade. It is one of four, the other being *Gilgamesh,* the capital ship, and the other two being *Perseus* and *Orion,* cruisers with the same specs as *Odin*. Though *Odin's* capabilities are not as impressive as *Gilgamesh's, Odin* is still very functional. It contains berths for eight crew, nine counting the captain. It has a cockpit, armory, kitchen, galley, two dorms, one lavatory, and the fusion drive in the aft. A cargo bay can be reached from either outside the ship or within the galley. Unlike *Gilgamesh,* it is not spacious enough to store a Recon. It contains a single machine gun turret that can open up from the ship's bottom. *Odin,* in addition to being faster than *Gilgamesh,* also gets better fuel efficiency. It can go months without needing to refuel.

Praetorians, The: The Praetorians are the most elite of the Empire's soldiers. There are one hundred total, and they are the personal bodyguard of Emperor Augustus. They carry a long spear, tower shield, and gladius. They wear a long, purple cape, steel armor, and a white jaguar headdress, complete with purple plume. They are also trained in the use of guns.

Raider Bluff: Raider Bluff is the only known settlement of the raiders. It is built northeast of what used to be Needles, California, on top of a three-tiered mesa. Though the raiders are a mobile group, even they need a place to rest during the harsh Wasteland winter. Merchants, women, and servants followed the Raider men, setting up shop on the mesa, giving birth to Raider Bluff sometime in the early 2040s. From the top of the Bluff rules the Alpha, the strongest recognized leader of the Raiders. A new Alpha rises only when he is able to wrest control from the old one.

Ragnarok: Ragnarok was the name given the meteor that crashed into Earth on December 3, 2030. It was about three miles long, and two miles wide. It was discovered by astronomer Neil Weinstein, in 2019. It is not known *what* caused Ragnarok to come hurtling toward Earth, or how it eluded detection for so long – but that answer was revealed when the Black Files came to light. Ragnarok was the first phase of the invasion planned by the Xenos, the race of aliens attempting to conquer Earth. Implanted within Ragnarok was the xenovirus – the seed for all alien genetic life that was to destroy, acquire, and replace Earth life. The day the Xenos arrive, according to the Black Files, is called "Xenofall." The time of their eventual arrival is completely unknown.

Ragnarok Crater: Ragnarok Crater is the site of impact of the meteor Ragnarok. It is located on the border of Wyoming and Nebraska, and is about one hundred miles wide with walls eight miles tall. It's the center of the Great Blight, and it is also the origin of the Voice, the consciousness that directs the behavior of all xenolife.

Recon: A Recon is an all-terrain rover that is powered by hydrogen. It is designed for speedy recon missions across the Wastes, and was developed by the United States military during the Dark Decade. It is composed of a cab in front, and a large cargo bay in the back. Mounted on top of the cargo bay is a turret with 360-degree rotation, accessible by a ladder and a porthole. The turret can be manned and fired while the Recon is on the go.

Skyhome: Skyhome is a three-ringed, self-sufficient space station constructed by the United States during the Dark Decade, designed to house two hundred and fifty people. Like the Bunkers, it contains its own power, hydroponics, and water reclamation system designed to keep the station going as long as possible. Skyhome was never actually occupied until 2048, after the falls of both Bunker One and Bunker Six. Cornelius Ashton assumed control of the station, along with survivors from both Bunkers, in order to continue his research on the xenovirus which had destroyed his entire life.

Voice, The: The Voice is the name given to the collective consciousness of all xenolife. It exists in Ragnarok Crater – whether or not it has a corporeal form is unknown. However, it is agreed by Dr. Ashton and Samuel that the Voice controls xenolife using sound waves and vibrations within xenofungus. The Voice also sends sound waves that can be detected by xenolife while off the xenofungus. The Voice gives the entire Xeno invasion sentience, and is a piece of evidence pointing to an advanced alien race that is trying to conquer Earth.

Wanderer, The: A blind prophet who wanders the Wasteland.

Wastelanders: Wastelanders are surface dwellers, specifically ones that live in the southwestern United States. The term is broad – it can be as specific as to mean only someone who is forced to wander, scavenge, or raid for sustenance, or Wastelander can mean anyone who lives on the surface Post-Ragnarok, regardless of location or circumstances. Wastelanders are feared by Bunker dwellers, as they have been the number one reason for Bunkers failing.

Wasteland, The: The Wasteland is a large tract of land comprised of Southern California and the adjacent areas of the Western United States. It extends from the San Bernardino Mountains in the west, to the Rockies in the east (and in later years, the Great Blight), and from the northern border of Nova Roma on the south, to the Ice Lands to the north (which is about the same latitude as Sacramento, California). The Wasteland is characterized by a cold, extremely dry climate. Rainfall each year is little to none, two to four inches being about average. Little can survive the Wasteland, meaning that all life has clung to limited water supplies. Major population centers include Raider Bluff, along the Colorado River; Oasis, supplied by a body of water of the same name; and Last Town, a trading post that sprung up along I-10 between Los Angeles and the Mojave. Whenever the Wasteland is referred to, it is generally not referred to in its entire scope. It is mainly used to reference what was once the Mojave Desert.

Xenodragon: The xenodragon is the newest manifestation of the xenovirus. It is very much like a dragon – reptilian, lightweight, with colossal wings that provide it with both lift and speed. There are different kinds of xenodragons, but the differences are little known, other than whether they are large or small. A particularly large xenodragon makes its roost on Raider Bluff.

Xenofall: Xenofall is the day of reckoning – when the Xenos finally arrive on Earth to claim it as their own. No one knows when that day is – whether it is in one year, ten years, or a thousand. It is feared that, when Xenofall *does* come, humans and all resistance will have been long gone.

Xenofungus: Xenofungus is a slimy, sticky fungus that is colored pink, orange, or purple (and sometimes all three), that infests large tracts of land and serves as the chief food source of all xenolife. It forms the basis of the Blights, and without xenofungus, xenolife could not exist. The fungus, while hostile to Earth life, facilitates the growth, development, and expansion of xenolife. It is nutrient-rich, and contains complicated compounds and proteins that are poison to Earth life, but ambrosia for xenolife. It is tough, resilient, resistant to fire, dryness, and cold – and if it isn't somehow stopped, one day xenofungus will cover the entire world.

Xenolife: Any form of life that is infected with the xenovirus.

Xenovirus: The xenovirus is an agent that acquires genes, adding them to its vast collection. It then mixes and matches the genes under its control to create something completely new, whether a plant, animal, bacteria, etc. There are thousands of strains of the xenovirus, maybe even millions, but most are completely undocumented. While the underlying core of each strain is the same, the strains are specific to each species it infects. Failed strains completely drop out of existence, but the successful ones live on. The xenovirus was first noted by Dr. Cornelius Ashton of Bunker One. His collected research on the xenovirus was compiled in the Black Files, which were lost in the fall of Bunker One in 2048.

Also by Kyle West

The Wasteland Chronicles
Apocalypse
Origins
Evolution
Revelation
Darkness

Watch for more at kylewestwriter.wordpress.com.

29214640R00156

Printed in Great Britain
by Amazon